To Sue
Enjoy

# A B C

# GILL OLIVER

ahBut
BOOKS

Copyright © 2016 Gill Oliver
All rights reserved.
ISBN-10: -0-9935976-0-2
ISBN-13: 978-0-9935976-0-2
eBook: 978-0-9935976-1-9

Ah But Books
ahbutbooks@gilloliver.info

## ACKNOWLEDGEMENTS

It's a pleasure to thank all those who have helped along the way with this book. Susan Elderkin has challenged and encouraged in equal measure over the long haul; thanks, Suse, for your shrewd observations and practical advice. Thank you to William Davidson, who read with such care and good sense; and to Eloise Bartholomew, Sarah Pickard, and Jules Adair, who have also pulled me back from the brink of greater folly. Thanks to the enthusiasts, without whom the world is flat: Roey Paige, Jenny Dwyer, Rachel Allen, and many others. To Tom Payne for translating the epigraph – a passage which, it turns out, left a mark on both of us in our teenage years. To Terry Oliver not just for expanding his skill set in ways he'd never expected, but for more than I can say. And thanks to every teenager who ever taught me.

*Illa, Quis et me, inquit, miseram et te perdidit, Orpheu,*
*quis tantus furor? En iterum crudelia retro*
*fata vocant, conditque natantia lumina somnus.*
*Iamque vale: feror ingenti circumdata nocte*
*invalidasque tibi tendens, heu non tua, palmas!*


She said, 'What mighty rage is ruining me,
Poor me, Orpheus, and you? They call us back,
Again, the cruel fates; sleep drowns our swimming eyes.
Goodbye – I'm ringed and taken by huge night,
Not yours any more, but stretching frail hands to you…'

—Vergil, *Georgics IV. 494–498*, tr Tom Payne

# Part One

*ESSEX*

# 1

*Wednesday October 13*

MARTIN'S OFFICE DOOR was supposed to be shut, because it was a fire door. It was also supposed to be open, because he was a man. That was what the Head and her Deputy were telling him, having finally made it up the stairs on their walkabout; they were checking for inspection risks, they said. When he asked which stick they wanted to beat him with, Gareth Whittaker looked almost hurt.

'Martin, it's not about you, it's about the door.'

They all turned to stare at it, Gareth, the Head, and Amy Hammer, Martin's colleague, who'd only popped in for a moment to ask a question, and now found herself trapped by the visitors. It was a pretty ugly door when you came to look at it, heavy, old-fashioned, glossed in white which the years had soured to cream, with a light of greenish safety glass threaded with fine wires to look like wobbly graph paper, but set at such a height that only an adult could see through. Or crack their skull on it. The doorknob had a dent which must have been there for years, but which he'd never noticed before today. Gareth was making an effort to be sensitive, as befitted one of the chief doctors in this asylum where Martin Harper was just a lunatic. Martin mistrusted this sympathy, he knew where it led. Next thing, Gareth would be rushing him again with that bloody hypodermic full of concern and action plans and *there's a way through this Martin* bollocks.

'Well, rationally the best thing to do is to take the door off its hinges. Let's go open plan. Let's stop calling it a door.'

Gareth was not going to rise to the bait. 'If there's a fire door it must be there for a reason.'

The Head added, 'It's there for your protection in case there's a fire.'

'The only other way out of this office is the window, so it rather depends which side of the door the fire's on, and where you happen to be at the time.' They exchanged glances, because they knew he had a point. Ha. Now everyone stared at the window, except Martin, who sat at his desk in front of it, where he could benefit from the brightness up here on the second floor without having to see the grimed frosted glass muting the dull red of a wall opposite. Gareth Whittaker eyed the flimsy, frankly domestic window stay, which was half-latched, then muttered to the Head, 'That needs seeing to, it opens,' and made a note on his tablet.

Martin hadn't finished. 'Look at the library. There's an archway there where there used to be a door. Now, say fire breaks out in European Philosophy, and the main exit is over by Physics, is anybody going to miss the fire doors? I think not. I think they will intuit the need for speedy egress.' Ha.

Then Amy said, "Are we sure this is a fire door?' So then there was a ten minute discussion on when was a door not a fire door. In all seriousness. They'd got there before him, of course; they'd already written another policy. Their Policy on Wedges. No laughing matter. All Martin had to do was read it and comply. So they could all sleep soundly at their desks. Whittaker tried on a word-to-the-wise look – obviously impossible with those piggy blond-bristled eyes – and emphasised that Martin must take all this seriously, especially during an Inspection. Everyone knew he didn't trust Harper. Which proved there was one tiny tiny bit of his tiny tiny brain that still worked.

And guess what? Every institution had a Policy on Wedges. Every school, every care home, every remand centre. Every lunatic asylum would, if they still existed. Here at Hanningford Grammar everything was polite and professional and there was total patient confidentiality, or there would have been if Martin hadn't had that bad habit of sharing everything with the group. He would surely entertain the staff room with this one later. And thank God for the group. When evening came he would return to an empty house, and the red wine in his right hand would be a much, much better listener than his wife could now ever be. It wouldn't stop him from addressing her photograph. He would lie on the sofa waving his glass in her direction, because she used to understand all this; she used to get all the jokes, she used to find the funny things to say. She would have found a good riposte for the yes-man of all yes-men, Deputy Head Mr Gareth let's-turn-a-problem-into-an-opportunity Whittaker. He of the MA in Educational Management, Mastermind special subject The Life and Times of the Tick Box. That stupid stupid cretin who truly truly believed that every problem had a solution and that every solution came from Management. Julia could only stare back at him with that eternal expression of surprise. Her sweet, sweet face, fixed in shock. No more could he watch daydreams dance across her face, in these dark days.

When the Inspection Risk walkabout was over, and Amy had scuttled away, he went into his emails and learned that pious Mrs Jeffreys had contacted Mr Whittaker again with one of her helpful observations. She hadn't copied

Martin in, but Whittaker forwarded it to him all the same, with some guff along the lines of, see below, I'm sure this is an overstatement and I know you're going through a difficult time in your personal life, but I think you ought to be aware that this parent has raised a concern... Mrs Jeffreys didn't want to lodge a complaint but what assurances could we give? To be fair to the bloke, it looked like a complaint to Martin. Charlotte got a B for her last essay and she didn't know why it wasn't an A and this was her best subject last year so what had happened? What had happened? What indeed, Mrs Jeffreys, what indeed. *Dies irae, dies illa*, the end of Mr Harper's world. That was what had happened. But he was not insensible. The thought that fumes of sulphur might be working their way up to the kids' nostrils did trouble him. Charlotte seemed to be losing confidence in her teacher. Her mother did not feel that she should be forced to arrange extra tuition at significant cost simply to make up for the school's deficiency. Martin sighed. If he was at fault, he was man enough to put it right. He would gladly give poor hapless Charlotte a little individual consultation. A lunchtime, or one day after school. Julia would remember Charlotte from year 10, gormless blue goggle eyes, liked to be called Char. His wife was a hard act to follow.

Then he realised he'd forgotten to enter the assessment marks for year 11. Then he realised he'd left the whole bloody lot at home since Friday, in direct contravention of policy. So he looked at the clock and thought, there was time now, if he just nipped back, there'd just be time, ten minutes there, ten minutes back, ten minutes to get it on the system before his 2 o'clock lesson. Which seemed reasonable enough. Mistake number one, didn't pass GO. Missed out the School Office completely. Didn't think to tell them he was off site. When he got home, Julia's photograph seemed to ask what was he doing back home in the middle of the day, which made him feel oddly guilty. He picked up the scripts and a banana. He thought he'd be back to school in ten minutes, if that. Except that he was half way round the roundabout at Green Lane when some idiot ran into him. He hadn't looked, he just came on. The driver got out of the car. Martin thought he recognised him. His face was pasty. Like a swollen maggot. Neither of them was hurt. Asked for his insurance details, the lad refused. Martin lost control for a moment, and pushed him, not hard, he just poked him in the chest, rather pathetic really, and he may have said some stuff, well he must have, but he didn't remember what. He had written the registration number here, on the back of some kid's exercise book. The youth looked maybe nineteen, twenty, but he could've been a minor and if anyone had seen the assault, Martin knew he'd never hear the end of it.

Faye in reception clocked Mr Harper's late return, of course, nosing out of the office window, on the lookout for the hunk from Parcelforce. This in turn facilitated another supportive chat from Gareth. Then Amy turned up in Martin's office, once the kids had gone home, saying she heard he'd had an accident and was he sure he was alright. Faye probably tipped her off – he'd driven past her window prang-side on. Amy was in aunty mode.

'Mart,' she said, 'You're worn out. You're volunteering for everything, every duty, every working party, every cover…' He said the cover was making him very popular and surely it was beneficial to have mates and feel good about himself? As for the committees, they both knew that Management knew that it was better to have him inside the tent pissing out than outside pissing in. Amy accused him of haunting the staff room and always being the last one home. She said it was beginning to look like a coping strategy. He reminded her that strategy involved conscious consideration of the means to achieve an aim. And you couldn't call his half-life coping. But she was right: he was keeping himself far too busy sucking the pointless little boiled sweets of life – doing people favours, a lift to the garage, a hospital visit to a sick tutee – instead of eating his meat. He'd even been an Extra Adult with the silver band on the coach to Birmingham. All that pompous stick-waving. The thing was, he loved to see what they could do, these kids, the way they concentrated, the way they kicked the nerves to one side and forced themselves to perform. That was inspiring. It was just that he was so relieved when the tasteless bloody racket was over and the clockwork maestro sat down.

THERE WAS STILL half an hour before Pastoral Committee so he told Amy all about going back home for the scripts, and the bump in the car. He felt a bit better for watching Amy's comic wince. The little mouth puckered, the little nose wrinkled, and it sent her oval glasses up and down, and she somehow looked more than ever like a cartoon cat. Some ten years younger than him, Amy dressed older, and wasn't his type; Mrs Sensible in every way, starting with the crude short hair. But a good, daytime, friend to him. He told her he still needed to get his marks in and she said, 'Look Mart,' – she was calling him by name a lot just lately – 'just stop hiding and do a bit less. Do less and do it properly. It doesn't all have to unravel. You need this job, you know.' Which was unsettling because notwithstanding the Head's letter and the sabre-rattling from Gareth Whittaker, he hadn't thought his job was really ever in question. Then she said something about needing people like him in a place like this, people who cut through the crap. Amy never said crap so it sounded fake. She said he only annoyed them when they knew they'd got it wrong, and asked did he realise they'd started talking about ideas being 'Martin-proof'. He said there you are then, the critical friend. Every organisation needed one. But if Whittaker told him one more time he was on his side there might be a second case of assault. And she said it wasn't about sides and couldn't we transcend the adversarial politics here. And anyway what did he mean, a second case of assault? She gave Martin that knowing look of hers, and solemnly told him that he still had a contribution to make.

'You've got brains and imagination. And a heart,' was what she said. He bookmarked all that for later: how would it compare with Julia's account of him over the years?

He put his grades in like a good boy, which only took ten minutes. He peeked into his inbox then looked away again. Nothing about the accident, but how could there be? If there were going to be repercussions, they would come in the form of a knock on the door or a brown envelope. Or a white envelope, these days, such is our desire to camouflage bad news. They couldn't possibly know his school email.

*Stop it, stop it, slow down...* Suddenly he saw the day as one of those squat little roundabouts they have in play parks, where he was a child passenger, only half on, but straining to grip the tubular metal handrail, and spinning round too fast, and he knew if he didn't shift his weight and find his balance it was going to throw him off and he'd end up on his arse in the dirt. He thought over what Amy had said. She had a point, it was about time he applied his imagination to something constructive. So he imagined for a moment there was a knock on the door, and outside stood Martin Harper. Himself, like some year 12, referred by Mr Whittaker for a dose of pastoral care because he was behind with his work, his grades were down, he was spreading himself too thin, and he was, in their locution, losing it, sir. What would he say to himself?

'What do you want to happen now, Martin?'

The answer refused to be safely taped up in his head. He felt the tight fist of a voice in the throat that hammered out loud, 'I want you back.' Not her. You. Every articulated thought, every narration, every account of his miserable life was told to Julia; she was the only listener who counted, and could no longer answer or argue or console. And that evening he would end up waving at her picture, panting, and pausing, and recounting all this in a rush, because he needed her to know. Without her mirror he had no breath.


THE PASTORAL COMMITTEE met as usual in the Food Technology Suite. It was home ground for the Head of Key Stage 4, Mary Parry; there was a king-size table and you could make tea or coffee. Sometimes there was cake, but mostly there was just a smell where cake had been. That day the Head was there, and there were chocolate brownies, such was the gravitas of the agenda. Preparing for Inspection. She looked taller than ever sitting there on the high stool; her elbows rested on the table, and the long skinny forearms tilted and crossed as she clasped and unclasped her hands, and stroked the backs of her fingers. The little round head turned this way and that on her long neck, while the narrow shoulders somehow remained immobile. Someone once told. Martin she used to be a dancer. One of the discipline-loving, pain-denying sort, no doubt. The way her limbs folded and unfolded, together with the bin-lid spectacles and pointed chin, put one in mind of a praying mantis. And prayer was indeed on the agenda.

There was an urgent need to review the school's SCMS targets. Some members of the committee fumbled to remember exactly what that stood for. A catch-all confusion of stuff you couldn't really measure and might be able to lie about, thought Martin, the unbeliever, who nevertheless reminded them: pupils' spiritual, cultural, moral and social development. There. They all stared at Mary's SWOT analysis. The head's dry mandibles snapped: 'We're not spiritual enough.' Followed by, 'They're going to pan us on the spiritual.' It seemed that they were doomed, unless they came up with a plan for salvation; but fortunately they as a school were very good at that, so they whacked in themed assemblies, created a space for reflection under the trees outside the library, set up a series of faith talks. Bish-bash-bosh, job done. Martin suggested maybe they should encourage the kids to take up something useful for Lent, which was a genuine proposal, but earned him a lot of sideways looks and sighs because today's kids didn't know what Lent was so, depending on how you looked at it, they shouldn't be ramming any one religion down their throats (that was Queen Mary of GCSE) or they shouldn't superimpose an assumed set of faith values (that was Dr Tobias, Archbishop of RE). Martin said he was just a sinner and at least he knew it, and John Tobias came out with more bollocks about respect for those of faith. He thought Martin was joking. Ha.

They went back to the bottom-heavy SWOT analysis and Martin drew some beautiful arrows resolutely promoting several of the Weaknesses to Strengths, then coloured them in. They got on to culture. An International Club. An Art Appreciation Society. Another series of themed assemblies. It beggared belief, honestly, to the point that Martin asked himself what they all thought they were doing there? He could feel something inside him threatening to erupt. He made an effort of restraint, because he wasn't in the best of humours, and if he were to steer into one of his set pieces it would not end in applause. Amy's good advice about transcending adversarial politics was a spiritual target if ever he'd been given one. A worthy aim. So he toned it down and listened and then made his observation quietly, deliberately, sincerely. He said they had their work cut out broadening the pupils' horizons when the chief reason parents had for choosing this school was its embodiment, and indeed its propagation, of the white middle class monoculture to which 90 per cent of them belonged.

OK, it was an exaggeration, but no more. He had often poured this particular rant into Julia's lovely ear, God forgive him, and there he went again. There remained a handful of isolated Education Authorities which had held on to their grammar schools and still shook their children through the riddle of the eleven-plus. Hanningford belonged to that elite. Wherever a primary school was skilled at getting their year 6 through the test, house prices had soared. They were flooded by migrants from the London Boroughs who couldn't afford to go private, but were willing to pay the heavy price of daily commuting to the city in order to give their kids a better chance in life. Their motivation was impeccable. Hear them talk for a moment about the reality of negotiating your child through school in London, and you were outraged on their behalf; but you also realised that since moving out, they had built a mental Hadrian's Wall about the capital, on the other side of which lived a lot of bad people, poor people, and foreigners. (At that point in the rant Julia always used to say, well you can talk. And Martin used to admit it suited him to live there and be able to teach classics to people who wanted to learn. He was no missionary.)

Anyway, he said what he said, and Mary huffed and the Head's insect head rotated to see who was going to speak next. Nobody did. So he suggested – and he didn't know why, but it just came out – 'We should do an exchange with Manchester, or Birmingham, or Bradford. And we should send the parents with them.'

Mary tutted. The Head said, 'Maybe not the north. But foreign travel always goes down well. If we invited the parents on our trips, we'd score on Parental Involvement as well.'

And everyone bounced along happily, until the meeting was over and the Head came across and told Martin he should have more faith in his own insights. Convert analysis to action, she said. Afterwards he meant to pick up his things and go, but somehow sat for twenty minutes behind his desk saying shit shit shit and shaking the mouse to see whether there was anything ominous in his inbox. Which of course there couldn't be.

*Thursday October 14*

WHEN ARIADNE CLAY hung back at the end of the lesson, Martin was wary. Julia had first encountered her in year 7, at an age when she drew attention to herself by an extreme anxiety about the correct width of margins and how to write the date. Then a couple of years ago – was it really that long? – she was the one whose mother had complained about his wife's absences. Mrs Clay was relentless: what were the arrangements for covering her classes? They simply weren't adequate, these were her GCSEs and the supply teacher was too little too late and a poor substitute for Mrs Harper. No substitute at all, as far as Martin was concerned. She had a fat arse, for a start. Martin had spent hours coaching the teacher, and coaching the kids, and going back and forth to the deputy head and Mrs Clay with email after email. In the end he told this woman – who had never once asked how Mrs Harper was, mind, not once in all that time – that his wife was in intensive care now, so could she please get off his back and just fuck off. It was worth the verbal warning from the Head. Martin wore that as a badge of honour.

Ariadne, known to the pupils as Ari now, was in her final year, and had grown into an immaculately groomed, petite and tidy young woman. She wore tiny pearl studs in her ears, not school uniform, but definitely not the conventional anti-uniform either. Mummy's, probably. She used to be quite a cute-looking kid, but now her face had become spookily symmetrical. Her nose had grown longer since last year, straight and thin, and it worked like the fold in an ink-blot test. The eyes were dead level too, with no discernable expression of any sort any more. Martin could not look at her without wondering what had happened there. The hair was confident: big, whipped-up, glossy hair, the colour of sticky toffee pudding. So: most politely, she said she had *a concern* about Class Civ, because they were all getting low marks and they had no notes. Perhaps they were getting low marks because they had no notes? Yes, she said, that's it, so if you could give us some, that would be great. Oh dear. Was she not taking notes in the lesson? There was plenty to write down. And she annotated her Tragedy, didn't she? Oh yes, sir, we do annotate our Tragedy. Well, all she had to do, in the Architecture lessons, was to write down all the things they said, in much the same way. But how did she know it was right? Maybe if he gave them headings... So he advised her to leave a line space between every couple of sentences, and stupidly suggested she would learn better if she processed the information for herself. Those words drew forth a frown. She had a friend in another school who was getting proper notes, ones the teacher gave them, so you knew they were right. Look, Ariadne, he said, you are welcome to use your friend's notes provided they make sense to you. But please make notes in lessons too. I can check them for you, if you wish, and your file, just to be sure you're organising everything properly. Oh yes, says she, she's very organised, she puts everything useful in a plastic cover. Only there's nothing much there, whereas her file for Geography is *this* thick. The little hand described a house brick.

Martin wondered if that verbal warning had an expiry date. He didn't recall. Either way, he supposed he had better make a gesture. Or at least remember not to swear at anyone this time. He promised to see what he could find. And look, he could send her some links right now. He opened a few tabs and pasted them into a personal email, before her eyes, which went down very well. He showed her the school's Classics pages and she cooed approval, but could he send her the link because she might not find it for herself? One click and she had gone off happy.

Martin sat for a while, asking himself whether the girl might have a point, and staring at the horseshoe of empty plastic chairs and the blank blue sky which filled the window of this first-floor classroom. Every poster on this wall, every display of student work, had been put there either by Amy, or his wife. What had been his contribution all this time? An irritatingly perky little two-note tune tapped him on the shoulder as an email notification flew in: *Reminder: self-assessments due.* He realised that the classics page he had last navigated to was still open and projected onto the whiteboard behind him, so that an eyeless marble bust of Socrates peered over his shoulder. 'Thank you for your support,' he said, and logged off.

*Ah Mrs Harper, see how you are missed by us all. School is so much worse off without you. You always had the knack of making the kids think for themselves, but feeding them just enough to keep them safe from realising that they ever had.* She must have left some notes on the Parthenon somewhere. He went over to the pair of grey filing cabinets in the corner of the classroom, and knew exactly where to start. There. Look. *A, Architecture. P, Parthenon: structured notes.* This would be useful. There must be other things in there. *You don't mind, do you? You don't mind me pillaging your hoard.*

In the drawer below, there was a whole folder on Pompeii. That could be useful for the trip. *Pompeian plumbing* or lack of. *Herculaneum.* If they let him go. Gareth Whittaker was still umming and ahing about it being too soon, and Martin had learnt from Amy that they wanted a member of the Management Team to go instead of him. Although if Amy was organising it, the paperwork would be immaculate, the risk assessments, the medical stuff and contacts lists, and all the bollocks. He silently addressed his wife: *But as we both know, there's the official risk assessment – which is the one typed out in tripping fucklicate – and there's the unofficial risk assessment, locked in the cold grey filing cabinet which is the collective brain of the Management Team, and which consists of One Big Risk, the Risk of Risks, i.e., Martin Harper. He has blown before, he will blow again. Lose it. Go off on one, as the kids say. Which is why they keep taking the auspices every time I walk into a room or say something in a meeting. Can they trust me? That's the question. Is he on board? Is he on message? Will he swear? Will he lose his temper? If we let him do the Pompeii trip again, will he weep in front of the children?*

*I don't know. I might. Amy said it would be strange to do this trip without you. I told her I wasn't intending to. Her eyes popped out of her head; this look of surprise and then relief swept over them... She thought I'd decided not to go after all. I put her right. I don't go anywhere without you. I come home to you each night. I cling to the places where you've been. I open your cupboards and your drawers, mop up my dripped Shiraz with towels frayed by your use... I'm not one of those who sell up and move away and tell you they can't live with the memories, as if memory was a threat to life and health, to be suppressed, avoided, or supplanted. This is the age of analgesia. But pain tells us we are alive. And anyway, if I deny you, I deny myself. Let others attach themselves to their beloved by a preposition, cum, per, pro; let these sellers-up of marital homes define their spouses as having a reality external to them. You are my inflection, my ablative, my instrument, my mode of being. You were, you are, a change in me. Nothing is over. Why would I not want to walk where you have walked?*

His eyes were already smarting and his throat tightening, well before he came across some photographs of the last school trip. A dozen pupils, Julia, himself, and everybody smiling. And here in Oplontis, and here in Sorrento... Julia smiling again, eyes screwed up against the sun. There were figs in that shopping bag. The view to Capri. Best seen from afar. The group waiting for a train at Ercolano station. Out of shot, but central to his memory of the surprisingly shabby, graffiti-splattered platforms, was the message *I love Julia* sprayed in yellow on a wall. Only last week he had told Amy, when you do this trip, you have to remember, there are three types of ruin in Campania. The ancient ruins, the recent ruins, and the ruins they're still building.

*Friday October 15*

THE PARENTS' BRIEFING for the Pompeii trip. Amy was to make the main presentation. Mary in attendance because of the year 11s, unnecessarily in Martin's view. She did fuss. He was invited to be there, whether as nominal Head of Classics or as Head of Sixth nobody quite wanted to say; probably they were still hoping that he wouldn't actually be accompanying them next April. He was given the task of drawing down the blinds ready for the powerpoint presentation, and lingered at every window. The small lecture hall looked onto a wide expanse of green grass, made luminous at the insistence of the descending sun; the playing field was bisected by a long flat drive where cars were approaching now. They were in the oldest part of the school, built in the fifties in red brick with concrete icing, in a room which ran parallel to tree-lined dual carriageway. It had been one of those warm, radiant October days; now, after school, the sun was protesting at being dragged down to the bed of the trees, and although its warmth had gone, the light it threw out made the object world glow magically hot, as if cooling from some supernatural forge; those little apple trees, and even the ugliest things – the tall brick gate posts at the bottom of the drive, the squat pavilion – were beautiful, seemingly molten, still tractable.

Half way through his task, and sorry to be blocking out so extraordinary a sight, he called to his colleagues, 'Just look at this.' They turned their attention from the laptop; Amy took it in and smiled, while Mary, predictably really, asked, 'What?' and had no clue. Heart of stone, that woman.

Parents, sons and daughters filtered in and were asked to sit near the front; such a small group would nowhere near fill the room. Mrs Clay came in, wearing an unnecessarily smart winter coat for the event – maybe she was on her way to church? – and they exchanged quite civil greetings. At the last minute Whittaker pitched up to represent the Management Team, in other words, to keep an eye on Martin Harper. He kicked the whole thing off. Came out with some tosh. 'We do hear in the media that some schools are cutting back on trips because of the perceived liability, but here at Hanningford Grammar we don't see it that way.' At which a big bloke on the front row – grinning from ear to ear, mind – asked, 'So if my daughter's raped, whose fault will that be?'

Loathsome ass. But Whittaker went straight for the bait, explained that they had *protocols*. Christ, thought Martin, that man's language. Why not just call them rules? Was he paid by the bloody syllable? Whittaker went on to explain that the pupils, male and female, were expected to go around in twos on all school trips. Fortunately the other parents shouted the idiot father down. *That's more than I'd ask mine to do that at home... You wouldn't want to, would you? Why d'you buy them a mobile phone?*

Then a woman sitting on her own asked whether this had been negotiated with the students. She was striking, with heavy features in an oval, made-up face, but handsome in a way, tall, sleek, in pale grey and beige, with big fluffed-out hair the same colours as her outfit. From his seat in front of her and to her side, by the window wall, Martin strained to read her makeshift sticky-label name badge, and saw she'd written in huge letters that filled it a 4 letter word. Barb. He scanned the list of attendees on Amy's briefing sheet, distributed to all of them. *Mrs B Blake.* It must be Whisper Blake's mum. Whisper was sitting with Ariadne Clay and her mother, on the opposite side of the aisle, showing no reaction whatsoever to her own mother's intervention. Little blond Whisper, who got suspended when she was in year 8 for fighting. Julia would remember, she'd been her form tutor. There were all those suspicions about bullying, but she claimed to be the victim, and they could never quite nail it. The kids believed it though. Then after she was caught cheating in her GCSE mocks last year, she got glandular fever, and Mary said, good call. Threw a spectacular wobbly on the first day of term in the middle of baseline testing. Since then, she had been in Martin's Classics group and on the whole she'd kept her head down  He hadn't met her mum before.

Mrs Blake gave a short talk on the need for adolescents to develop independence within a supportive framework, and explained the importance of mediation in introducing what might be seen as restrictive measures. Now, had the school considered this? When she got on to *trust issues,* Shannon Matthews' parents, a cheery looking couple in the row behind, exchanged glances and chuckled: kids were kids, weren't they?

The subject was changed by Mrs Clay, who asked why the school had organised this so close to the exam term. They needed their Easter holiday for revision. That sent them all rustling.

'The fact is,' Martin broke in, 'this is England, there's no time of year that doesn't clash with assessments, is there?' Of course he should have kept his mouth shut. He could see Gareth Whittaker getting his masterful expression ready.

Mrs Clay eyed Martin Harper as if he were wickedness personified and in a hurt voice said, 'My daughter has a lot of catching up to do in Classics, and I have to say it isn't through any fault of hers. And she needs two As and a B for Durham.'

Amy was so much more astute than Martin, especially these days. More nimble. She jumped in and reminded the parents that they would be visiting monuments directly relevant to the examination specifications. Smiles all round, even from the Clays. Safe pair of hands, Amy.

But the grinning dad was back. They were going to a volcanic zone, weren't they? So what would be the arrangements if the volcano were to erupt? Amy was ready for him.

'Seismic activity is constantly monitored, so there would be plenty of warning of any eruption.'

One of the mothers chipped in: 'That's right, volcanos don't just erupt overnight, there are all sorts of chemical and seismic indicators.' She checked herself and reddened. 'You know, gases, little movements in the earth, that sort of thing.' Martin recognised that habit of saying everything a second time more simply, so as not to sound too clever. She must be a teacher.

Amy positively beamed at her from under her almond-shaped spectacles, glad of the support, and picked up: 'And don't forget, the school has travel insurance, which would cover us if we needed to be repatriated.'

They were happy enough with that. Martin, however, was stung. They'd never been there, had they? Never seen the traffic on the peninsular road. Never waited for an ambulance on a road where nothing moved.

After Gareth and the parents had gone home and the teachers were packing up, Mary shared her opinion that Whisper Blake was a right nutter and nobody should have to take a kid like that on a trip of any sort, never mind a residential. Total liability. Couldn't they have found a way to put her off? Mary claimed that Whisper had bitten her when she broke up the famous fight. Martin snorted: you could understand anybody wanting to bite Mary. He kept that reflection to himself, simply pointing out that maybe Whisper had grown up a bit in the last four years, and they had to take her motivation at face value.

'You mark my words,' said Mary, 'she's an out-and-out attention-seeker.' There she went again, making a diagnosis out of a symptom. Obsessed with clean surfaces, that woman.

They disagreed their way into a full-blown argument. It was the same old one as usual, the classic sheep and goats thing where there are Good kids and Bad kids and once they've been sorted that's it, they live in that pen for ever. And yes, Martin went too far. He said he didn't understand why Mary only seemed to want to work for the people who needed her least, which she found deeply offensive because of course they all needed her. Martin asked her tartly, did she find her prophesies came true? Well yes, actually, they did, she said. Priceless. She might as well have said, I, Mary Parry, am a complete cretin. And Martin thought, Mary, you are not intelligent enough to be the devil incarnate but you are pernicious enough to qualify as one of his lesser little helpers.

'And another thing about Whisper,' she said. 'Give her what she wants, and you watch, she won't want it any more.'

'Well there you are Mary, she'll change her mind, stay at home, and it'll never happen, so let's not play games with our blood pressure, eh?'


THAT WAS A POSED PHOTOGRAPH if ever there was one. Martin and Julia had always had it on display in the hall, in the cabinet she christened the *lararium* because it held the outward show of piety and honoured the family gods: pottery gifts from other people's holidays, photographs of gatherings taken by various relatives. He had never recognised the version of Julia offered here as genuine; white was never her colour. There mightn't have been any photographs at all if it hadn't been for her mum, Dorothy, who had insisted. Julia had said, after an argument about the wedding cars: 'The thing I've come to realise about your wedding day, Martin, is that it isn't your wedding day at all. It belongs to other people. If we don't satisfy the Gods of the Hearth, we've messed up.' And it was true. So now he had discovered for himself that the same went for your funeral. *It turns out it isn't yours, it's theirs. It's taken over in much the same way by much the same people...* Julia's father, in this case. Martin had been too numb to disagree, too fixed on the truth that no parent should ever have to bury a child. In Geoffrey's case, weddings and funerals were what he did for a living, so how could Martin tell him, *no, not like that...?* Meek with grief, he had handed it all over to the professional, and now he could only beg his wife to forgive him.

*Your parents insisted on the car. You the dark red flowers. They the photographer. You vetoed cine photos. But it would have been unkind to be married anywhere other than your father's church. In private, I'd been scathing enough about ritual and tribalism. I saw marriage as a formality. We both did. An outward show. Until the day it happened. I can still feel that moment, when the priest said, you may kiss the bride, and I kissed you full and deep not as your parents would have wanted, and not to shock them, not to spite them, or offend the congregation, but because I understood that all the sands of my life so far had been rushing to that moment, and I was there at the waist of the hourglass and my existence had become infinitely dense, and in this tiny moment the stilled universe was pausing only to explode, and the energy released would last a lifetime. Or two. The gawping congregation knew nothing, nothing of that. The essential witnesses were not able to witness that, which was in fact the essence. No photograph could ever show it. Nobody but you and I would ever know.*

*From that slowed second on, it didn't matter what the weather did or what the catering was like; we left the guests to make of their day what they would. I was transfigured. Before that kiss, I would have said I loved you, body and soul; but I would have been wrong, because until then, I had not known what that meant. Nothing had prepared me for the wave of joy that carried me through the rest of that long, short day, and far, far beyond.*

*The funeral was terrible. I'm so glad you weren't there.*

# 2

*Friday October 22*

THE LIBRARY at Hanningford Grammar was designed for plotting and conspiracy, or at least a good old-fashioned whispered gossip. There was 'casual seating', next to the windows which overlooked the playing field, but although this area had low armless upholstered chairs which could be shared by two pupils at a time, it was not the prime spot for socialisers. Their business was far more serious than simply thumbing through *New Scientist* and hoping to make a good impression. There were two adjacent offices, one for the Librarian, one for the Head of Sixth, although in practice the students were largely untroubled by the staff at the moment; the librarian had left in the summer holiday and hadn't been replaced, duties were begrudged, and Mr Harper would most likely be either somewhere else teaching or sitting at his desk with his headphones on. On the three windowless sides of the library were tall stacks jutting out at right angles to the walls, around a maze of bookcases, some perpendicular to them, some at right angles to each other, all of which created little rooms each with a large table in its centre, where the kids were meant to work. The smaller ones could run about with reasonable anonymity, and of course, once a table was occupied and heads were down, there was an instant cosy complicity. Add the scent of polish and warm paper, and you had the perfect den.

On the Friday morning just before the holiday, Martin happened to consult a dictionary in the Reference bay and overheard his year 12s in the middle of one of their Staff Review sessions.

'Mr Harper ought to get married again.'

Mixed reactions, giggles, groans, disgust. The speaker – unmistakably, that was Shannon Matthews – stood her ground. 'He's all right, and he's not bad looking really for his age.'

More squeals and protests. 'I'm only saying!'

'How old is he?'

'Well he must be at least 40 because he remembers Kurt Cobain.' He was 43.

'Who?'

Then Martin heard Ariadne's voice. With all the authority of an experienced year 13, she pronounced him weird.

'What kind of weird?' Whisper Blake spoke in a flat, toneless voice. Ariadne couldn't explain.

'Just weird.'

Martin didn't want to embarrass them and sidled out as quietly as he could, opting for an early break. Discretion was everything. He knew it would make little difference whether he jumped out from behind the bookcase, or whether they caught him creeping away – either would have provided proof positive of his weirdness.

So, it was official then. He'd have liked to quiz Ariadne on her definitions. Weird meaning creepy? Weird meaning eccentric? Insane? Grotesque? Cranky, perhaps? He ought to set her a multiple guess question, to help her work out what she meant. He made a coffee and sat with it in the very middle of the staff room, knowing that the space would fill and that in minutes he would be talking about something else.

There was a folded newspaper on the low table in front of him, with an advertisement for some sort of savings investment. It incorporated a printed application form with a little black scissor icon eating a dotted line. Marital Status. At least Martin had grown into his new status in the world. Nowadays he would tick a box marked *widowed* as obediently as he'd tick *male*. It helped the world to know how to treat him. Don't ask about the wife. Don't ask about the weekend. Not a couple, don't invite. Or: keep a kindly eye on him. Make allowances. Do invite, as long as there'll be crowds of people there. But whatever you do, don't touch. How many people had touched him since the funeral? Handshakes were precious now. He put the mug down and stroked his left hand with his right, tenderly, as Julia might do.

That afternoon, bang on the stroke of half term, Whisper Blake turned up in Martin's lamp-lit office, with a problem. They'd been given their A level predictions two weeks before, and hers were all too low, so what was he going to do? She'd been sitting on this grievance for some time and he wondered why it was suddenly so urgent to deal with it now. She claimed it was wrong to base her predictions on the test they had all done during the first week of term, because nobody had told her what to revise. Martin remembered how indignant she'd been, getting up from her seat at the computer, asking what the questions meant. The sort of thing you might expect from a young child. Thinking about it now, the most extraordinary thing was not the fuss she had kicked up at the time, but the fact that none of the others paid her the least attention. Anyway, out it all came again: she hadn't answered a whole section, because the school hadn't prepared her for it and she'd never seen these three-dimensional puzzles before, so she would only have got the answers wrong. Which would count against her. As if missing them out was somehow the safer option.

'Look,' said Martin, 'the whole point of these tests is that you can't revise for them. They're like taking an X-ray.' That was a stupid thing to say, and he regretted it immediately. Was he telling her she was thick? Because she wasn't. No, of course not. All she ever wanted to do was work hard and get good marks, but everybody put her down and now she had the same predictions as Ariadne Clay who'd got Bs in her AS levels and was not, *I'm sorry but just not*, on Whisper's level. As she railed, she tossed her head about, winding her paper handkerchief into a shredding ball. Martin listened and waited for her to stop. When the torrent of words finally turned into a dribble from a tortured little gargoyle face, he woke up his computer screen and saw she must have spoken without a break for a good ten minutes. That was quite a feat. After much reiteration – she didn't take in any of his explanations – she seemed to come round, and they ended up agreeing that the 4 Bs could turn out to be 4 As. There was something chilling about her, though. In spite of the verbal and physical thrashing about, there was no colour in her face; she stayed pale as her name, and the handkerchief was dry.

When Whisper Blake got up to go, she asked: 'Why is your office door open?'

'It always is.' It seemed a quite haphazard question.

'Only we were discussing *personal data*, weren't we, so it ought to be a private conversation.'

'Surely you've noticed that all male members of staff work with the door open. It's school policy.'

'Yes, I've noticed.' She looked vaguely offended. 'But why is it school policy?'

'It's to do with safeguarding. Child protection.'

And she said the strangest thing. She asked him, 'Why? Don't you trust me?'

*Saturday October 23–Sunday October 31*

FROM THE VANTAGE point of September, when the school year had begun, the October half-term holiday cast such a long low shadow that Martin thought he would neither need nor want it. But now that it had come, he found himself almost pleased to be able to take better care of Julia's memory. If the weather was kind and they had a bright day, he would go to Burnham, and cast her ashes there. And whatever the weather did, he could write down their story, or begin to. *I'm going to bring you back up to the sun, where I can see you,* he told her. Their last week together had been so bleached of colour, under those hospital lights. It was a protracted, well-intentioned torture, and towards the end she had seemed to shed herself bit by bit until one day, he turned to find she'd gone. The horror of those sounds and sights and smells had stuck in his head for far too long. He would take his time and write their history down and honour her, and bring her back as she deserved to be remembered.

*Whenever staffroom gossip turns to weddings, we hear Amy's story of how she found her husband in Yellow Pages, and how Tony and Rose got married during morning break without even missing a lesson; and I tell the story of how I met my wife at an interview, and say, 'of course, she got the job'. That's the short, public version, the well-worn counter that I know just how to place upon the board.*

*The day we met – here, in Great Hanningford – I'd felt pretty confident about my chances. I knew my academic record would equal anybody's. I had experience, but no baggage. I knew the school's shortcomings, as identified in the last Inspection Report, and had memorised its stated aims. I brought experience from outside the classroom, too; after Classics at Cambridge, I'd worked in the City and trained as an accountant. A decade later, I'd grown bored with coping easily, and tired of the loneliness of working with people I disliked, so I switched career. I'd seen the ad campaign and – more heroically than I realised at the time – I thought I might be able to teach kids to think, and it seemed to me that if you could think, you had a head start in making sense of your life. So after two pretty manic, upbeat years which had included training on the job, I pitched up here for the post of Head of Classics, believing it was mine.*

*You looked pale and stiff and military, I thought, in your dark suit, with your hair tied back and no expression on your face; just like one of the city zombies that I'd fled. We'd done the round of teaching, tour, and interviews, and by mid-afternoon the candidates had all fetched up on low chairs in a chilly corner of reception, to await the Head's decision. So there we were, looking at the floor, when a little lad came up and asked if one of us could to sign his form. Somebody told him that we couldn't, and suddenly the boy was fighting back the tears and saying that it wasn't his fault and he'd been trying to find a teacher who would sign it all day, and if it wasn't in by four o'clock it wouldn't count. You held your hand out and said something like, 'Let's see this form, then,' and suddenly your face was animate, smiling and lovely. That was the moment you were born to me. You called him by his name and congratulated him on his clear handwriting. Then you took a pen from your handbag and signed it with a theatrical scribble. He went off happy. The other candidates remained po-faced, and one of them said she didn't think you should have done that. And I said, 'Oh, I think you should,' and we grinned at each other, and we joked about the things it might have been, like a nomination for Head Prefect, or permission to spend the afternoon down the dog track, and the others got pious, because there could be consequences, and you grinned from ear to ear and said that if the Chess Club turned out to be over-subscribed, it might just make some poor sad teacher's day.*

*We talked and joked and left the stooges to listen. A full hour passed in one swift rally, back and forth, you and me. When the Deputy came out and called you in, it seemed entirely proper. Of course they'd picked the right one. You were brilliant and beautiful, and my only disappointment was that we'd not meet again. When I got home – feeling giddy, because somehow I was both full and empty – I rang Alice, who was my girlfriend at the time, and told her I didn't fancy going out for the curry that we'd planned. She probably still thinks it was sour grapes about the job. It didn't matter what she thought, I never wanted to see her again. So I didn't.*

*Up to that day on which I learnt the truth about beauty, I'd always had a girlfriend, and they'd always been the ones that other men lusted after. Leggy blondes, as they say. Oval faces, big-eyed and lipsticked, and the record confirms they were what people call photogenic – they always looked as if they were posing. What you saw was all you got. I had considered myself a lucky guy, moving effortlessly, with neither guilt nor regret, from one babe to the next. But beauty, real beauty, is in movement. I re-played your many changes of expression, the way your nose and eyes wrinkled in that mood Victorians called merriment, the softness about your heavy brown eyes, the changing curve of your parted lips. I didn't remember how tall you were or what your legs were like. But I was sure that you had dark brown hair, which meant that you were not my type. Which made you magical.*

*I flat-lined for the best part of a school year and don't remember much about it. I was off women, like a sick kid might be off games. I forgot about promotion and plodded on at Dunstan School. Then right at the eleventh hour, in May, a clutch of jobs came up again at Hanningford Grammar. A part time Classics post – 0.6 full time equivalent to be precise – was one. I needed a full-time post, of course, but I was obsessed by the idea of seeing you again, of checking out your shape and legs and whether I'd been wrong about the magic. I applied and came for interview, and finally there you stood before me, and I could tell that you remembered me, by the way you avoided looking me in the eye until there was no one around to see: then you let me hold your gaze just that bit longer than was professionally necessary. Your hair was chestnut and wavy; you wore it long now, and your smile was as unspoilt as a little girl's, and you laughed companionably as you jangled the departmental keys, unlocking a cupboard as you had my heart, showing me around and giving me the run-down on the Classics curriculum. You were even lovelier than I'd remembered. Then came the formal interview with the Head and Deputy, who probed to find out why I was taking a step down, because leaving a full time post in west London for 0.6 here, a stone's throw from the bad lands of the Estuary, made no sense. Which was fair comment, and indeed now that I'd satisfied my curiosity, my only plan was to wait until they had rejected me, and then ask you out with a clear conscience. But from nowhere I blurted out, 'Maths. I'd like to teach Maths as well.' Maybe I'd sensed that they were trawling, because they'd advertised so many bin-end jobs at once; they were looking to see what they could pick up in the end-of-season sale. The offer of a shortage subject to make up my hours was tantamount to saying, you've struck gold. And that was how I got the Classics job and started teaching sums.*

*That year's summer holiday, my life was as intense as it was flat. Perhaps I was just lonely. The band I was playing with had no gigs lined up, so we hardly met at all; there was always somebody away, and besides, they all knew I was leaving. And they all thought I was mad. I bought a new guitar, the Spanish one, with nylon strings and a fast action, and I practised like a man possessed. I couldn't keep her in tune. Maybe it was the weather. I wasn't going to go abroad without a girlfriend, so I spent a couple of weeks in Dunwich with my sister and the kids, hitching a ride on family life, so different to my own. I played a lot of football with the boys. I learnt to ignore the background hum of arguments and eat three meals a day. Then I came over to Essex to find a place to live, and spent longer than I strictly needed looking round, always half hoping to find you round the next corner. I especially remember taking myself across to Burnham and walking along the Crouch, because that day summed up my state of mind. The flat grassland shivered in the heat; spinnakers clattered, but couldn't shake the low tide awake. I scrutinised the indecisive line of the horizon in much the way a hypochondriac might peer into a mirror.*

*So was my life about to start? It wasn't simple, once I began to work alongside you. Because this was work, and worse, it was a school, so everything was public, and any slip would be marked down. And we were both terribly correct because, I realise now, that was the sort of people we were. You always tried to engineer things so we were never left alone; you denied this afterwards, but even if it wasn't conscious on your part, I swear it happened. Two terms passed, throughout which I was thrilled to have you near, and wretched not to have you closer. And it never occurred to me for one minute that anyone else might know. Then Paddy invited you and a couple of other Heads of Department to join the Mathematicians in their end of term bash. We've told this story to each other a million times but it still makes me laugh out loud: how no one else turned up but you and me; and a waiter asked if we were Paddy Clancy's party, and we said yes, and he waved us to a table that was far too small. On the stroke of 8 Paddy texted me to say, "4 Chrissake Mart make your move.' And I said, 'Paddy's set us up.' And you said that you thought as much and we'd better give him a run for his money. I was astonished: why did you think as much? And was it really that obvious to everybody else? Well of course it must have been. Five minutes later, there was another text: "If J slaps yr face, we're in the Cricketers." But by then we were both committed, and in any case he knew full well you wouldn't slap my face: you'd known all along. It was another of his serious jokes, and the reason why we drank his health at every anniversary. I ran my fingers across the hand you had laid flat upon the table, and we debated: was this unprofessional conduct? You said my line manager had given me permission. I said, one of my line managers. And you turned your hand palm upwards, and replied that they both had. Then every permission followed, and so quickly, that I was bewildered by it.*

*I hadn't known the ways in which I wanted you, until you led me to them. I can't write this down. Not that we have children to worry about who may read it some day. When it's my turn to go, this love song will be indistinguishable from invoices and bills, lost under the lava flow. Or more accurately, the last fluttering gasp of our love is likely to be a flapping paper in some skip with a view of Canvey Island. It's just that I can't turn flesh into words. And yet I think about it all the time.*

*Once we were drawn together, that was it. We were like two halves of a mussel shell, not to be prised apart; no woman that I'd ever known had drawn me so close. I had thought I was experienced; you assured me you were not. I stroked the length of you, and you said I made you gleam like Aladdin's lamp; which may have been true because, when we lay still together, I seemed to feel the shine. At every subtle move, at every urgent turn, you met me; and you could outstrip me, too.*

*In those first nights, we talked the stars down from the sky. The stars we'd been born under, and the stars that now witnessed our surrender to the fates. You were naked in my arms, when I learned that you were a clergyman's only and adopted child, and so annoyed by the impostor aunts and uncles who were always buzzing round the vicarage, that now your deepest craving was for privacy; if people crowd me out, you said, I'll just flounce off. I on the other hand hated to be alone, and all my habits guaranteed company, starting with Venture Scouts, then five-a-side football, and playing in various bands. So we agreed that if ever my mates came round, you'd be entitled to stomp off. It's funny to think that somehow we exchanged places over the years, and now it's me who's ended up the recluse. We were black sheep, though, each disappointing our respective families. Your father had always encouraged you with Greek, because he hoped it would help you properly to understand the New Testament; but you had discovered Ovid, and walked the other way. My family numbered several accountants and loss adjustors and even one actuary who'd made the move from Manchester to London; they all accepted Classics as a stepping stone to banking, but I know my dad thought it was a slightly effeminate way of getting a degree. When I left the city to teach classics, my parents considered that a doubly backwards move. The more fool them: it had led me here, to you. Whereas several of my kinsfolk turn out to have spent the last decade saving up for a divorce they didn't know they wanted. (Ha.) We spent hours in the dark that Easter holiday, sharing biographies, comparing loves and hates. It's odd now to think there was a time when we knew so little of each other, whilst never doubting we were meant to be.*

*I was shaken by your coolness when the summer term started and we were back at work. You've never acknowledged this, but it was maddening and to this day I do not understand. Why were you so straight-laced? When half the common room was in on Paddy Clancy's little ruse? I couldn't reconcile it with what I knew. I was in torment, thinking something had changed your mind, wondering whether we had just lain too close to see each other, arguing with myself that it had been a physical affair – and then against myself, because surely I knew a physical affair when I saw one; and how could you have said what you said, and shown what you'd shown, without feeling what I felt? For a few days it seemed as though I'd lost all ability to read the world. I mooched round my flat muttering, what do I know, like some lovesick philosopher.*

*Then the weekend came and you let me take you up to Burnham to walk by the river, and we came back to my flat where we made love and had our first massive row. In point of fact I'm not quite sure now about the order in which those things happened. Gradually, I suppose, your public manner with me evened out. You were always reminding me, 'Martin, we work in a school.' The air was charged enough with hormones as it was, I suppose. Marriage promised to be such a relief, because it would regularise everything. It served a social purpose. But at that moment when I made my vows, I felt it as much more than that. As my destiny. Working side by side each day was easy, although it left most people incredulous. Not everybody wants the intimacy which we cultivated, do they? Many's the wife who'll buy her husband a shed, as it were, and all around me I see men who seem perfectly happy to be supplanted by their children. Men can be eclipsed by the desire for children, too, and that was the acid test, that you clung to me, when I could so easily have been sacrificed. But I run on.*

*I said that I was going to bring you back to the light, but reading this over, I see it's all me, me, me. The main effect you had was to reveal me to myself. But even when you were beaming down and circling round me, there was always a dark side to your moon.*

*The clocks go back this weekend. From here on it will all be down, down, down, and the dark will be official. You liked that turning point when it was black by four and we could be cosy indoors together, making tea and toast. Will you be there to meet me at the pivot of the year? Will I follow you? Will we descend together? This time last year, it drained me more than ever to live by artificial light, that awful yellow-grey that makes us all look like cancer sufferers, and which I know is going to claim me soon. Everything is going to sink to earth. I don't remember much about this time last year, beyond the weight of tasks I dragged behind me; except that one day I deleted the entire contents of my inbox. Which did create some problems here and there, but surely solved a few.*

ON THE FRIDAY, the sun shone, and he decided that would be the day. He had received the ashes from the funeral directors in a polythene bag placed in a plain grey cube of cardboard. It did not contain the whole of her remains, they had told him, only a token, but he could be assured that it was her. The box had sat in a drawer in the bedroom, alongside Julia's handkerchiefs, her makeup and a few items of jewellery, unexamined, ever since; that was ten months ago. Now, it seemed to have nothing to do with her, and looked alien amidst her belongings, things he'd seen her wear and use and handle. It was utterly disconnected from the almond-scented body he remembered cradling, and also from the constant presence that was with him now, a voice which trembled on the very threshold of actual sound, and which no-one but he could hear. He opened the flimsy lid and loosened the bag, to touch the dull, uneven powder. Nothing was less like his Julia.

Ash. On their first trip to Italy together, they had stood on the top of the volcano; it was a clear day after rain, you could see for many miles around, and the horizon had seemed to span not only place but time, the future as well as the past, and she had told him, *this is the most extraordinarily beautiful place I've ever been. You must promise never to come here without me.* He had promised. It was the sort of easy promise lovers made, never dreaming that they would be separated. She had been immortal in his arms. Remembering this conversation, as he stared into the open drawer, an impulse overtook him. He would go up to the riverside at Burnham today as he had planned, and cast most of the ashes there. But he could also keep a little of her back. *If I get there – if they let me go – I'll take you to Vesuvius. In fact, from now on, I'll carry you with me everywhere.*

He needed a receptacle in which to place this last of her. His eye fell instantly upon a small make-up bag; more like a purse with its metal jaws and clasp, big enough to hold lipstick, eyeliner, mascara but not much more, and made of a very fine, tight-grained red brocade. She had spent ages choosing it in a little shop in Florence. The dense weave created a miniature Persian carpet, but fell in silky mounds which caught the light and multiplied its shades of vermilion, with specks of black and gold. It had a life to it. He picked it up and found it warm and soft in his hand, with a perfect, gratifying weight. It sat comfortably in his palm, a pretty thing, just right.

*Wednesday November 3*

IT HAD BEEN less than a week back after half term, and there he was, called again to Gareth Whittaker's office like a naughty child, to discuss the ongoing saga of Ariadne Clay's Class Civ notes. It was a soulless place, bled of all colour. Statutory notices, lists, tables and charts, all printed in black on white paper, shivered down at you from the walls; with one fluent swivel of his ergonomically designed, sci-fi black leather chair, the Deputy Head could tell you who was where, and what their cousin would be doing Tuesday week.

No fire notice, mind you. But this was maybe not the best time to point that out. The strip light hummed overhead.

Gareth at least had the decency to look embarrassed, poor sad bastard; you could always tell when he was anxious by the way his usual pork-chop pallor flushed to veal, and today he must be feeling particularly stressed, to judge by the perfusion of bloody pink around his ears. He motioned to the comfy chairs (bad sign), offered tea and biscuits (another bad omen), then went back to his desk to dial the beverage hotline, i.e. Faye in reception. Whittaker had the biggest handset of any of the academic staff, with his favourites programmed in and labelled in someone else's handwriting: Head, Office, Home, Ho6 (Martin was Head of Sixth), HoKS4, HoKS3, IT. All posts or places, no names. People move on, names change, thought Martin.

So. Mrs Clay had sent her daughter to a private tutor over the holiday. *Just to help build up her confidence, you understand.* And this was *the sensitive issue*, said Gareth: the chap had contacted the school with, um, some concerns. Gareth freely admitted that this was all new territory for him. And rather awkward. Mrs Clay, you see, seemed to have a very high opinion of the author. Gareth was at pains to say that he was in no position to judge; she could be right, she could be wrong. Martin asked who this paragon was. Gareth fidgeted in his seat, crossed and uncrossed his legs, and gave that open eyed look which meant, I don't want to tell you but it's a reasonable question and I'm a crap liar. The private tutor's name was Tim Slipman.

'I know him. He used to teach at Inchester Sixth Form College, but he isn't there now.'

There was a knock on the door and they both sat motionless, their conversation checked, whilst Faye brought in the tea. Timothy Slipman. Martin and Julia had both known him through JACT, the Association of Classics Teachers. Not someone you'd forget, he was so odd. Glasses with heavy black frames, neat collar and tie, long hair in a ponytail. They first met at a talk that Julia had given, and at the time his conversation was much taken up by something he was in the middle of writing... a big project... yes, a concordance of Greek and Roman myth. It was cross-referenced tighter than an Edwardian corset by the sound of things, and all on a database. It was, according to him, incomparably better than anything previously produced, and he was wanting to put it out on the internet, but afraid someone would steal his intellectual property. So he was looking into other ways of marketing it. The sort of marketing where you don't tell anybody.

Immediately the tray was set down, Gareth began to pour, and Faye disappeared. The door clicked shut.

'The man's an idiot. I know that for a fact.'

Gareth picked up a shortbread biscuit, smiled at it good-naturedly, and gobbled it in two bites. Martin listened. It turned out that far from just being a specky Greek-geek, Timothy was a wonderful tutor and a generous human being, according to Mrs Clay. Timothy Slipman had the highest opinion of Ariadne's potential, but the contents of her file simply didn't correspond to the way that he would expect to prepare a candidate for AS, and this had made him so very worried that obviously the Clays had to alert Mr Whittaker. Only it wasn't just the Clays – Slipman had also emailed the school direct. Copying Mrs Clay in, of course. Gareth read out a couple of choice sentences from his appraisal of Mr Harper. Something about gaps, and the lack of an explicit framework. Martin appealed.

'Surely you can see it's ludicrously imaginative. All he had to base his judgment on was a few notes from, let's be honest, a nice enough girl but a limited scholar.' He suspected, though, that Ariadne would have made great play of Mr Harper's callous neglect. Gaps? What had he withheld, he asked himself? Perhaps the obvious, which she hadn't recognised without the flashing bloody lights.

'I have to admit, in fairness to you, Martin, this chap Slipman comes across a bit odd, a bit obsessive. He sent us the same email three times in as many minutes.' Gareth sat back and placed his hands on his knees; he was looking magisterial now. 'Mrs Clay won't see it that way, though; she thinks the sun shines; so I'm wondering, Martin, can we find a way of dealing with this that doesn't make things worse?'

'You can back me up and tell Mrs Clay not to worry.' But Gareth looked askance, and twitched his piggy snout, and said, 'Of course the school wants to support you, Martin.'

This wasn't the same thing, was it? The S word again. As if Martin was the one with special needs.

'Look,' said Gareth and leaned back to his desk for a stapled set of papers, which he handed over. 'Mr Slipman provides his own revision notes. This is a sample of the sort of thing. It's not my academic area. I'd value your comments.'

'Wouldn't it be better to ask Amy's opinion, since my judgment is in question?' The patronising sod smiled as if Martin had paid him a compliment, and admitted he already had. He'd known Martin wouldn't mind. But he personally valued Martin's perspective. *He personally*, of course, in case Martin had forgotten that the Head didn't value his perspective one bit.

He thumbed through the document. It wasn't anything special. It could have been another chart on Gareth's wall. The document linked the set texts, topic by topic, to the assessment criteria – *this is what you have to do; do it, and it is done.* The exam board provided something similar. Well that was all fine and dandy but it was killing a living thing stone dead.

'It's the academic equivalent of selling indulgences.' Gareth blinked; Martin sighed. He'd have to explain.

'The kids are victims. They know they're feckless and dim and didn't really work as hard as they should. You tell them, if you are in possession of this' – he waved the notes in the air – 'you will be spared the torments of purgatory. Or getting an E.' Martin filled his lungs now. 'You convince them that they need you, and they go round terrifying their friends. End result, repeat business.' Excited by his own vocal crescendo, he knew, even as the next dramatically quiet words came out, that he had gone too far in poking fun at an economist: 'You'd understand that, Gareth. Instead of worrying about me, you ought to be studying that man's business plan.'

Gareth Whittaker stared at him for a minute, piggy-blinking, then he smiled the sort of conciliatory smile a little man might use to say, *don't hit me*. 'Right,' said Gareth, 'I think we can find a compromise. We'll post these on the Classics page. Leave it with me.'

Martin left his office thinking, *He's got an arse full of splinters, that man, from sitting on the fence. I hope they fester painfully.*

He needed to tell Julia about all this. Before he had even exited the car park that afternoon, and protected by the thickening November gloom, he sang out his justification to her. *There has to be more to this than teaching kids to pass exams. We're talking about Greek tragedy here. It has to do with life. It has to do with our experience. It has to do with dilemma and fear and desire and torment – all the things that capture the kids' imagination in a soap opera, and rightly too, we should never knock the soaps, because they have the highest moral purpose, because human beings need this, as a fish needs water, we need somebody else's imagination to help us process all the things that make no sense in our own lives. And right now Timothy sodding Slipman is eating my bloody liver and I'm not best pleased about it.*

He heard his Julia whisper, *you're too clever for your own good, Martin.*

Oddly enough, he reflected, he didn't wish Timothy Slipman ill, because he was clearly a fellow maniac. He must have been unmanageable at the Sixth Form College. *Maybe they sacked him.*

Oh, what did he just say? Listen to yourself, Martin. *You're right, Julia. There's a lesson to be drawn here. I ought to listen to myself. I must learn to step over the crap, instead of always kicking it aside and thereby spreading it about. I must stop ranting and start doing, go back to the basis of it all, to the love of it. Stop posturing. Find my mojo. Last seen buried somewhere underneath a pile of targets. Help me, love. You can help me. I've let things slip, but you would not have wished this... what...? this... decadence on me, and I can feel your sadness and your disapproval at my back, and I can't live with that.*

Home was almost far enough away to reach some sort of perspective, or at least to realise that he needed to treat all this less flippantly. Slamming the car door, he said aloud,

'Oh Julia, that was just another bloody day at the house of fun. I'll straighten things tomorrow.'

He made himself a promise. He was going to mark these homeworks, and then he might order some new strings for his Spanish guitar. She was a beautiful girl and he had neglected her too long.

THE NEXT DAY, though, things got worse. He found Gareth Whittaker sitting at the back of his year 12 lesson, beaming encouragement and interest, as if he'd know an Attic vase from a plastic beaker. He informed Martin discreetly, afterwards, that he was being monitored. The Head had been concerned by Mr Slipman's findings – *findings?* – and she thought there might be competency issues. They were going for him. They were out to get him.

The accusation against him was set down in writing. Charge number 1, inadequate lesson planning. He disputed this. But it was true that he didn't follow the recipe – viz., tell them what they're going to do, do it, tell them what they had just done – because that was the intellectual equivalent of eating at McDonalds. Number 2: failure to cover the specification. Complete bollocks. The whining had started when he strayed beyond it, as a matter of fact. Number 3: failure to return marked work. Guilty as charged. His dog ate their homework. Which saved them the embarrassment of getting it back.

If they thought he was going to drink hemlock over that little lot, they had another think coming. Of course, management was in a complete muddle. They had switched horses from disciplinary, last year, to competency now. Underpinning his scorn, however, was the sickening realisation that this was getting far more serious. In the lunch break, Martin singled out his allies and showed each of them the letter. Brian, the union man, clicked smoothly into protocol, noting with approval that proper targets had been included in the letter - a show of objectivity which Martin took as mildly treacherous, although Brian promised he would phone the regional rep that evening for advice.   Paddy Clancy shrugged; God knew what they were up to, *all Greek to me, mate*. Amy was the most upset. She said they'd got him all wrong. Also that they were thrashing about. But she thought the reason for all this was that they were looking to axe the whole Classics department. Which was a great comfort, wasn't it? Martin told her she *would* think that, because all classics teachers were a bit paranoid, because how could you not be, when your subject was based on two great empires lost? But anyway, he consoled himself, what about the Maths? They couldn't cut Maths, could they? And nobody had ever had a bad word to say about his Maths teaching. Paddy readily concurred.   A bell rang and they all dispersed.

His year 11 Maths class had a block test on vectors scheduled next, which was just as well, because his thoughts were flying out in all directions. He watched them work quietly, heads bowed, in straight rows of tables. They were more or less contented; however much they grumbled, they liked the regime of tests that Paddy had imposed in maths. He wondered whether he'd still be sitting there come next September. Sums were the tax he had paid to teach Classics there with Julia. Would it be worth limiting himself to that? Why did it matter, now that he was on his own? He didn't want to have to leave, of that much he was sure.

But for the rest of that day and well into the night, Julia didn't seem to be listening. He pleaded with her, to no avail.

All I can hear is me. Maybe, surely, what if; and it echoed, echoed, echoed round, until the racket of his own inner voice was deafening. No sign of an answer. Nothing to soothe him tonight, no possibility of resolution over this weekend, or next week for that matter, just the prospect of fighting and feinting stretching way ahead. His fate in the balance all over again.

# 3

*Julia Chamberlain    My Family History*
*10 September*

The title is underlined, the date straightforward; in fact, she might as well add the year, 1981, so she does, as a token of good faith. Julia Chamberlain takes her preps seriously; she likes to use a fountain pen when everybody else writes in biro, and favours a dark blue ink, not black, which looks better on cream paper, not royal blue, which is for kids. She has no idea what to write, but she can look at the little white alarm clock and promise herself that in forty minutes' time – the time prescribed in the prep diary, and never to be exceeded, says the school – she will have finished. She knows her family is not her family, also that telling lies is wrong. She's just learnt the word chronological, and whilst she can't think of a way to use it in the opening, she decides to begin at the beginning, and writes, "When the Romans came to Britain my ancestors had a few cattle and some sheep." The rest is easy, they did the Romans at primary school. Julia settles her ancestors on top of an Iron Age hill fort, and writes for forty minutes. It ends, "In the Middle Ages, many records were destroyed. 40 mins."

She can smell pastry cooking, and hear bubbling voices downstairs, then the front door closing as the committee leaves (that's still her word for any group of visitors to the vicarage). Her vicar's wife mum and vicar dad are having a conversation in the hall. They sound pleased with something.

Next, it's their first parents' meeting at this new school. Instead of standing by her desk and waiting for them both to come over and admire its contents, as they did at the village school, she has to follow her parents from teacher to teacher and listen to everyone's report. It's evening, a long time after school, and so dark that all the globe-shaped lights are on in the enormous hall, and you know how formal it is by the scented slipperiness of floor polish. And now, to her horror, the History teacher wants to talk about the Family History essay. Suddenly the school tie is impossibly tight, the collar scratches, and the girl realises that if you hear the story with her parents' ears, it will sound awful; it was a bad thing to have done, and mum will end up crying in the car. She hadn't meant to offend anyone, indeed, or even considered they would ever know. The adults glance at her from time to time but she is not required to speak. Her mum has a stupid habit of watching a teacher's face too closely and mirroring their expression, and she's doing it now: first she looks anxious, then surprised... and now she's delighted. Positively delighted! The teacher has told her it was such an unusual perspective to take. So original. So different. Julia shows tremendous promise. Her head begins to ache. Those flannel blazers are far too hot to wear over a pullover indoors.

LIGHT STREAMS IN from high windows opened to the scent of mown grass. It's summer in the second year, and exams are over. No more declensions, no more tenses for a while: they are doing project work, which means they have been put in groups to make a set of posters on aspects of Roman life. You have to begin by deciding who does what. Which means wasting ages for everybody else to figure it out. Their group is doing Women, and Nicola has immediately bagged Dress, which was no surprise because her main thing is drawing outfits and colouring them in. Nicola can't really draw, though, so when it comes to hairstyles she'll trace them from the book, but the teacher has fixed it so that each group has one clueless person in it, and Nicola is theirs. Julia doesn't mind. Nicola can't help it. It's being put with Ruth that has whetted Julia's appetite for an argument; Ruth's so annoying, you can't tell her anything; she's immature and hasn't got her periods yet. Julia and Ruth both want to do Marriage, so they agree to split it: Ruth will do the Weddings bit, and Julia will do Married Life.

'Don't call it Weddings, though. Call it Marriage Rites and Rituals. It sounds more Roman.'

Ruth says, 'But they were weddings. And they wore white.' This rouses Nicola who says she'll do a wedding dress then.

Julia tells them: 'But then it's too much about weddings. It's meant to be about women.'

'I'm doing the weddings,' says Ruth. 'You can do something else. And anyway, rituals sounds like sacrifices and all that.'

'That's what they did.'

Ruth says she's not drawing a sacrifice, and her mouth makes a letter M.

'Draw the feast then, or the torches.'

'I'll draw what I like thank you. I'll do my bit, you do yours.'

'Only the dresses are my bit,' says Nicola, and gives a reasonable shrug. 'I'm only saying.'

Julia reminds them that anyway it isn't all pictures. 'There has to be some writing as well. It has to be informative. And you can have opinions. Like for example, in rich Roman families, the women were not allowed to work, which was bad for their human rights. Also, it must have meant their lives were quite narrow and selfish.'

'Oh God, back to the vicarage,' says Ruth. 'I feel a sermon coming on.'

Julia is going to hold her own. 'It's true though, all the rich ones did was bear children, so they were pregnant all the time.'

'OK, you can do the writing then,' says Ruth, who's getting cross at being bossed about. Julia tells them that she doesn't really care who does what, so long as their posters aren't complete and total rubbish. They should all stop arguing, and be a bit more grown up about it. Ruth tells her, 'You sound like my mum.' She gets a lot of that. She says: 'If you were Romans, you'd probably be married by now.'

Ruth snaps back: 'If you were a Roman you would have been exposed at birth.'

'What do you mean?'

'Like where the Romans put the baby on the ground at the father's feet. Only your father didn't pick you up, did he? He didn't acknowledge you. Can't have. Otherwise you'd know who he was.'

Nicola gasps, 'Ruth!' At least Nicola knows to be shocked.

The sting of it makes Julia's eyes glaze over, but she's not going to cry. It was a cheap trick of Ruth, to turn a confidence into a weapon; but all it will take to stand firm will be to hold up a long, stiff shield, and set herself square behind it.

So she says, 'Actually, the Romans didn't really expose babies. Miss Finch said it was just a tradition, to pretend they might. Maybe you were away that day.'

## 4

*Tuesday November 9*

'I'VE NEVER BEEN in this room before. S'nice. What day's the cleaner come?'

'I've no idea.'

'Thing about a cleaner, makes you tidy up? Because cleaners, they're not allowed to move stuff really, are they, sir, they just go round it. But if you know they might do your carpet say Tuesday, you know to get those things off the floor Monday night?'

She nodded to three loosely stacked piles of paperwork placed against the skirting board, one marking, one target setting, one random circulars which weren't considered worthy of a space on the desk. He'd thought they weren't so noticeable in the gloom. Martin could generally put his hand on anything he needed, even though the desktop had the construction of one of those many-layered pastries, with flakes of A4 paper prone to littering the carpet. Now that it was dark in the mornings and again by mid-afternoon, the Head of Sixth Form's office, tucked cosily just off the library, was lit only by a black cantilevered desk lamp which bleached whatever he was working on and threw the rest of the paperwork in shade. Contrasting with the hard flat lighting of the rest of school, Mr Harper's office had something of the grotto about it as winter approached. The girls in particular seemed to appreciate the mix of pictures, posters of Italy and Greece – ruins, yes, but bleached by such a sun – and framed prints, statues, vases, a simple Greek painting of a young man diving into a pool. A bookcase held textbooks and ring binders, in no real order, yellow box files, and more piles of paper, some in plastic trays. A tiny photograph of Julia was perched in a corner where Martin could see her but his visitors could not; she smiled down in a straw hat from behind the chair where Wendy Mundy sat so comfortably now. 'But if you don't even know what day the cleaner comes you don't plan. And if you fail to plan' – mischief arched Wendy Mundy's thin orange eyebrows, and revealed her soap slab teeth – 'you plan to fail. Like Mr Whittaker says.'

'You may be right.'

'No point having a cleaner if you don't tidy up.'

'How can I help you, Wendy?'

'Sir... what was Mr Whittaker doing in our lesson?'

'Identifying Attic vases, just like you.'

'He isn't interested in that sort of thing, though, is he?'

'Course he is Wendy.' Course he wasn't.

'He doesn't like me. I mean back in induction week, right, he was like, yeah, you guys're in the Sixth Form now, and all about leadership, and he said – right – he said, you guys can take the initiative now, anything you want to improve in the school, you just tell us. Something you wanna change, you just change it? And it was student voice this, student voice that, and *we're listening* to *you*. So next day I tried to tell him and he said ooh, you gotta go through proper channels, write it down and put it to the School Council. So like two months later it's up for School Council and there he is and I ask for what we want and everyone says yeah, good idea, only he's like *ooh I don't know* and *well that could be tricky* and how it would affect a lot of people. And I said that was the point, to affect a lot of people.'

Wendy leant back in her chair opposite him with her head tilted slightly as she gazed around the walls.

'What was your proposal?'

'Flexi-time.'

Martin was starting to enjoy this. He smiled at the kid and thought, *oranges and lemons*. Matte, yellowish skin, and these coppery bits – real marmalade – in her hair and her shiny bald eyebrows. That must be orange eyebrow pencil. Perhaps it was meant to draw your eye away from the cartoon nose, which was long, masculine, wide at the bridge, and oblong in shape when seen from the front. It really was a face made for the end of the pier. He asked her exactly what she meant.

'Well, what it is, is,' – she swung easily into storyteller's sing-song – 'We have to be in school for 8.40. Then some days we don't really do anything till 9. Or later, if you've got a study period.' He noted that she didn't call it a "free," which showed she was quite savvy when it came to approaching teachers. 'Like me for example, on Tuesdays I don't start till 11 o'clock, but I've got to be in for registration at 8.40. And if you live, say, in Feldon, and you gotta get two buses, it takes an hour to get here. And if you come up from Catsea like me, you gotta get the special bus and it stops like everywhere – I mean really, there's this one stop and it's just a *field* – they should have an express service, they really should, 'cause most of us get on at the beginning anyway ?'

'Saves the council money if you all travel on one bus.'

'What's the council got to do with it? You have to pay anyway. Anyway, that's like they say a secondary consideration. And I haven't told you the Educational Argument yet. People our age, right, their brains don't work in the morning.

Our body clock's all different to the teachers, right? It's a scientific fact. So I saw on the telly there's this one school where they don't start lessons till ten o'clock for the seniors. See, what happens here, right, nobody learns anything period one and the teachers are all, come on, wake up, sit up straight, and like on our case, but it's OK for them 'cause they're old and they don't need much sleep. I'm sorry sir, but you gotta be honest. But we're not really awake. So it would be more efficient to let us start later. And like we'd get better results. For the school.' A perfect cadence, and a smile.

'Now Wendy, you know what people will say: isn't that just an excuse for a lie-in?'

'Well, duh, *yeah*, because a lie-in's what we all need. That's the point. And anyway, it's hard for people who have other stuff to do, to be stuck here whether you've got a lesson or not. When I was looking after Mum, I was always being late, it was really embarrassing. And it was stupid, because it was only for the sake of registration.'

'So if I've understood you correctly, the idea is, no more registration, come in when you need to.' She grinned: 'That'd be a start.' 'And how would you pick up notices?' 'Put 'em on Facebook.' 'Look, Wendy,' he said, 'you've got a good idea there, just keep it on the agenda. As you say, link it to school performance. Everybody cares about that. Drip, drip. That's the way.'

A beam of recognition lit up her funny face.

'My Mum used to say, if you want to get your father to do something, just mention it a few times – dead casual, you know? – and let him think it was his own idea.'

'Smart lady, your Mum.'

'Yeah but he still done a runner didn't he.'

She said this without rancour, in fact with a little ironic smile. Martin looked at her and thought, what an amazing kid. *I love her. She's doing me good.* For a minute they were silent. Then she came back to her original point.

'About Mr Whittaker... in our lesson... Only... Whisper says there's someone in year 13 who's on your case?'

'Oh?' This was hardly news.

'And... I wanted to say... Well, I like Class Civ and I don't think you've got anything to worry about.'

The embarrassment he knew he ought to feel was swept away in a warm rush of amusement, but also gratitude; he told her thanks, everything was fine. Funny the way she'd taken it upon herself to seek him out and have this conversation. Wendy Mundy never quite blended with the herd. Once, he had seen her out of school uniform, in jeans and tee shirt for a field trip, and had to look twice to realise she was a girl, she was so flat-chested. He liked her voice: it was bluesy, rounded, quite soft, not the Estuary budgerigar you heard so often here. At odds with her looks.

Then she fished something out of her bag, and held it out across the desk. It was a DVD, obviously a home recording, stroked with enviable elegance by Julia Harper's clear black marker pen: *Angus Strang – Beneath Vesuvius – BBC2 2012*. Both Martin and his wife had got good mileage out of that series. He'd always suspected Julia rather fancied old Ang Strang with his boyish good looks and his archaeologist's perma-tan.

'Mrs Harper lent it to me when I was revising in year 10. Because I missed the lesson. I should have given it back ages ago. Only after the summer holiday, she was away too, a lot of the time. Sorry. And I wanted to say... I'm sorry about Mrs Harper'.

'I'm sorry you lost your Mum, Wendy.' Martin had almost forgotten that she had. She had helped nurse her mother through a long illness which had killed her in the spring, right before her GCSEs. The staff were all waiting for the kid to crack up but no, she had plodded through her exams, passed OK, and came back to start year 12, as if nothing had happened. The elder brother looked after her now.

Martin glanced at the DVD and asked, 'What did you make of it?'

Wendy's head tilted slightly.

'There's an awful lot of men's bits,' she said. This was not something he remembered about the programmes. 'I liked the computer reconstructions though. They were cool. I mean otherwise it's just a lot of stumps, isn't it?'

'Broken columns?'

'Yeah. Thanks, anyway.'

Then the funny face became quite solemn, and she continued: 'The thing is, I didn't understand about it then. When Mrs Harper... passed away. I was just a kid. And I never said anything. Like people don't. They don't know what to say, do they, and they think it won't make any difference now, 'cause dead is dead, isn't it, so like, move on. Then after Mum died I found out. It does make a difference. For sure. Saying something. It's horrible when people you thought were your friends don't even mention what happened, like you're a sad loser, and they don't wanna hang out with a loser. Or like for them it doesn't count.'

Wendy went on, steadily, slowly; she must clearly have rehearsed this, but perhaps she'd never said it out loud to anyone before.

'For me, there are like two lots of people, right? You know what I mean? There are the people who've said something, and people who haven't. It's like there's a street, and some people are on my side of the street, but other people – and I mean, it's most people – those people are like, always on the other side? And sometimes I get so mad at them, I hate them. But it's only 'cause they don't know any better... Anyway, I found this DVD from year 10 and I realised, like, at the time, I never gave it back because I was embarrassed to? Because it belonged to a dead person? And I just thought, I did a wrong thing there, didn't I. I mean, as far as you're concerned, I'm one of those mingers on the other side of the street. So I thought, take it back, say sorry, and like, cross the road.'

His eyes had started to moisten and now it threatened to be visible; this happened so easily nowadays, in fact more than when first he had lost Julia, nearly a year ago. He looked up at the ceiling, for Wendy's sake. But the fact was, the blood was coursing round his veins, in the sheer excitement and relief of recognition. A funny-looking kid had touched him more than any of his knowing colleagues. At that moment, all the stresses and strains, the complaining parents, the written warning, and Gareth Whittaker's action plans for him just fell away. He knew he was in the right place. He wasn't going anywhere: he was going to grip this job. He could have kissed her.

Driving home later, with Julia imagined in the passenger seat, he struggled to recall any men's bits in the video *Beneath Vesuvius*, or indeed in Pompeii. But then he remembered the House of the Faun: the camera did linger on that exquisitely wicked little figure, didn't it? He and Julia had different takes on the bronze statue. As Angus Strang put it so well, this faun was "a million miles away from the dwarfish, stunted satyr of the Greeks"; but while Julia thought his delicate, prancing beauty made him the worthy object of real desire, Martin felt it only served to underscore his wickedness. He re-ran Julia's argument: the faun might be wicked, but then, so what; *any Roman walking into that Tuscan atrium would have known exactly what it represented; when he greets you, he's saying, come and play with me.*

'He's beautiful because they thought it was OK to *want* to play with him. They had no hang-ups about sex,' she'd said.

*Monday November 29*

A FEW DAYS LATER, Martin was in his office trying to remember how to pivot a spread sheet when he heard a racket from the library. Whisper Blake and Wendy Mundy were having an argument. There were some other students there, year 11s watching from the other side of a bookcase, but they were just spectators. He heard Wendy shriek, 'You knew *exactly* what you were saying. You *cow*.' He'd never seen her lose her rag before. The strength of the voice was impressive enough, and then there was a headful of trembling henna curls, like so many little shaking fists. Wendy went quiet when she saw him, said, 'I'm sorry, sir,' and looked at the floor. But there was impatience in her voice; she wasn't sorry at all. Whisper on the other hand was all dry tears, her eyebrows drawn like hands in prayer, pale, innocent, misunderstood, protesting that she never meant it like that. She ignored the pupils and directed her appeal to him, whining: 'Why is it, when I try to be friendly, I always end up getting the blame?'

Martin pointed out he wasn't blaming anybody, and Whisper exclaimed, '*She* is. *She* is!' And out it all came. Wendy's brother Jack had been on the local news last night, arrested for trying to hack the local hospital's intranet, of all things. Whisper was asking how Wendy felt about it, to check she was OK, and she had bitten her head off for taking an interest.

'I mean, *so what* if your brother's been arrested? I don't have a problem with it. It doesn't say anything about *you*, does it? I was *being sympathetic*. All I was saying was, to succeed in life, you need to grow up in a stable environment.' Martin recalled the parents' briefing for the trip, and Mrs Blake, labelled Barb.

'*I* live in a stable environment.'

'OK, so, there hasn't been an adult male in the house for like, years – which is fine – but now Jack's lost his mother.'

'So have I.'

'That's my point.' She lowered her voice, in a show of quiet concern: 'You're carrying on like nothing happened, Wendy. You do know you're in denial.'

Martin told her that was quite enough, but Whisper just shook her head and went on. 'Now, what Jack's done – at least you can understand it, it's a cry for help.'

'It was hardly a suicide attempt, for Chrissake!'

'Except it was, wasn't it, from a social point of view? I mean, everybody's gonna un-friend him now, for good. 'Cause OK, you say it was a protest, but what if he'd brought the hospital systems down? All those sick people? Everybody will un-friend him, won't they, and next thing is, they'll un-friend you. Everybody's saying that. Even the teachers. That's what I heard Mrs Parry say.'

Wendy let out a gasp of outrage.

'Well Mrs Parry's wrong,' said Martin; and whilst he had to say something, of course, he realised he shouldn't have said that.

'So my point is, sir, I'm only telling Wendy, that she needs support. And I'm prepared to be here for her. I am.' Whisper looked extraordinarily angelic as she said this; her forehead calm now, her eyes the palest grey, her hair that ash blond which you usually see on the very youngest children, and her face almost alabaster.

Wendy told her this was a funny kind of support. Then Whisper accused Wendy of being over-sensitive.

'Get help,' she kept saying. 'Get help.'

Martin asked Whisper hadn't she got a lesson, because he could see she wasn't going to move on without a shove. The year 11s made up a consolatory chorus: *Hey Wend, you OK? Just forget about her – Yeah, she's a cow. You take no notice, Wend.*

Then Wendy shouted 'Get off my back why don't you?' and began to shake from head to foot. It wasn't a scream, but a full, deep-throated call, with nothing shrill about it; a focused, grown up, loud contralto. They'd hear this from downstairs, from everywhere, and the first years who had been trickling in for their library lesson were rushing up now to see what was going on.

Martin shooed them off, smiled thank you to the chorus, and said, 'Come and sit down for a minute, Wendy.' He led her away.

He knew there were some tissues stuffed in the back of the cupboard in his office. But of course the cupboard was crammed with junk, and by opening it he set off a clumsy landslide. Holding one hand to her face, to cover the snot, Wendy bent down and started picking paper clips off the carpet; she made herself stretch to reach them, rather than move from the chair. The sobbing stopped. She wiped her nose. He waited for her to speak. Oranges and lemons: she always made him think, oranges and lemons. It wasn't just her colouring, it was her sweet-sour looks.

He tried to tell her Whisper had just been clumsy, that probably she meant well.

'Yeah, like rubbing my nose in it was a sign she cares.'

'Don't let her get to you,' he said.

Wendy dismissed Whisper with a snort, but then her features lengthened and set to stone. And Martin felt he knew, as a physical fact, the weight of the water behind this dam, the mass of it. She wanted to talk, he could see, but she glanced across her shoulder at the open door. So he got up and closed it. In the corner of his eye he could see Whisper, leaning on the wall there by the library desk, watching.

AT TIMES LIKE THIS, he understood why people like Julia's father talked about taking stuff to the Lord in prayer. Martin imagined that prayer must be like a great big dumper truck where you tipped three tons of shit at the feet of the almighty and walked away. Job done.

But Martin continued to dump it at Julia's feet instead. Once home, and in the warmth of their dove grey sitting room, he recounted it to her. Wendy's brother Jack had been arrested by the police two days ago, and they were holding him on remand. They'd taken away a pile of stuff, including quite a few things that belonged to Wendy, and that she needed – her mobile and her laptop, for example. She'd watched the house empty. CDs, files, computers, brother, all out of the door in under an hour. *Can you imagine?*

Then one of her friends had told her this morning that Jack was on the local news last night, up before the magistrates on fraud charges. Cyber crime. Until then, Wendy hadn't any inkling that this earthquake in her life might be a big story to other people too. She was still in shock. In the privacy of his office, she had kept repeating, *but he's so boring*. It seemed Jack wasn't so boring any more... Wendy told Martin that Jack had been refused bail, and asked how long before he might be home, as if Martin would know; his uncertain answer threw her into a panic. Of course, Jack was technically her guardian. This had prompted the argument: Whisper had already put it into her head that social services were going to pitch up and carry her away. Because what would happen to her if Jack went to gaol? Maybe she'd end up in care.

Martin had asked her was there family she could stay with, just for the time being, and she said, no, not round here. So he'd said, *Wendy, are you sure you're OK on your own*, and she really snapped at him then. *Yes, why wouldn't I be...* It wasn't indignation on her face, though. It had been panic. Sheer panic. Martin had tried to reassure her; what had he said? That the police were not known for mental arithmetic, when it came to social services; and not to worry, because they might never add it up.

'Was that the right thing to say?' he asked Julia now, feeling around in the soft lamplight for her approval, or at least her common sense. 'Call me a cynic, but what I was thinking, although of course I didn't say it, was, *kid, you'll be the last thing on their minds.*' It was only now, at the close of the day, that he had started to wonder whether he was meant to inform someone. Julia would know what to do.

'I think I probably am. Because what do they live on? Will she have her own income, if Jack ends up behind bars? Will she need help with benefits?' He went online and composed the email which he ought to have sent immediately, up to Gareth Whittaker, across to all Wendy's teachers, raising a pastoral concern; then deleted all the detail, wary of setting in motion the girl's very fears of being taken into care, and couching it simply as a need to be aware that, following her brother's arrest, Wendy Mundy might be upset in class. He reasoned that if it had been on the telly, the chances were that all the staff had known anyway. Nobody had told him. Perhaps he should be annoyed by that. Even offended.

He found a photo on the internet. John Mundy looked younger than his 19 years, and familiar from somewhere. He had a podgy, pasty, expressionless, light-hating maggot face. It was the lad who'd run into Martin at the roundabout back in September, who wasn't insured. The lad he'd pushed. He had been charged with offences under the Computer Misuse and Criminal Law Acts, and was alleged to be part of a hacking group who went by the name of Vulcan. Martin spent a good half hour googling them. They had targeted several hospital trusts, bizarrely protesting against mismanagement and cuts; the media spewed odium.

That evening, Martin found he couldn't get Wendy out of his mind. He made pasta, ate and drank without tasting, watched TV without seeing anything. Julia would have known what to do; what would she have said? 'Julia,' he said out loud, 'We're both so bloody needy. Me and Wendy. But she has needs right now that might conceivably be met. They're concrete things in this concrete world. I worry that they won't be. Nobody's looking out for her. And she's technically a child.' Should he try to help? It made some sense to care about someone other than himself; that was what Julia always said. Quite how to help, he wasn't sure; but although it was a shock when the telephone rang, and although he didn't recognise the young woman's voice at first, it felt right that the answer came so promptly. As if the sincerity of his impulse had been heard by a prescient universe.

Wendy had found him in the phone book. 'I'm sorry, sir, only... I don't know what to do. I need advice. I think I'm in trouble.'

'What sort of trouble?'

'I've got to talk to the police. They want to interview me. At the police station. Does that mean they think I did something wrong? D'you think?'

'No, no.' Martin knew how to sound quite sure, but the truth was he hadn't the faintest idea. He explained, 'They're just doing things by the book.' Which was what he wanted to be true.

'Only, when you're like, the victim, they visit you at home, don't they? To make you feel comfortable. We got burgled once.'

'I'm sure it's just procedure.' He clutched for the commonplace as for a handrail.

'Oh. Good.'

'Yes.'

'But what do I say? I don't know what to say.'

'Just answer their questions, Wendy. I'm sure they're not out to trap you.' Now I'm making it sound like an exam, he thought. 'Just tell the truth.'

'Well I will, obviously... but... I'm scared I'm going to get him into trouble. By mistake.'

'You didn't know, though, did you?'

'No. But that's just it... I might say something... without knowing... and drop him right in it.'

'Wendy,' said Martin – and this was a wild, hopeful guess, which he was conjuring up from the back of his brain, believing his own improvisation – 'You're still a minor. You don't have to be interviewed alone. Surely?'

She didn't respond.

'What I'm saying is, I'll come with you, if you want.'

'Would you? Would you really? You think that would be alright?'

'I think that would be reasonable.'

'Oh yes, please, that would be better.' He heard her breath loosen and knew he had been right to offer.

'Then I will.'

'And the other thing is... I need to get him a lawyer. They won't let him home on bail. Only where do I get a lawyer? And do you have to, like, pay up front?'

'You don't need to worry about that, Wendy. He might have one already. They'll get him one.'

'Who will? Are you sure?'

Wheeling around with the phone in one hand, he caught himself in the big square mirror. What would Wendy think if she could see him? He had the receiver wedged between his shoulder and his ear, his elbows sticking out; his expression was one of startled concentration, his brow casting a deep shadow. Bent, but still tall enough to fill the space, he was a dark, sharp, twisted figure in the lamp lit room; except that he had a kingfisher blue silk scarf coiled about his neck. The colour sang out against the downy grey of the walls, as when his Julia used to wear it. It had her perfume, just, but not her scent. He ought to take the handset to the sofa and sit down. He was too much of a distraction to himself, stood oddly here.

'Yes,' he said to Wendy. 'And don't forget. A man's innocent until they prove him guilty.'

*Tuesday November 30*

MARTIN FELT SAFEST in the places Julia had been; it seemed somehow easier to access her. Whenever he found himself in new surroundings, or when things were happening quickly, Julia was never there. The Police Station was a case in point. Immediately he entered the reception area, it was already alien territory, a small, smooth, clean room, all straight lines and laminate, which partition walls had created inside a Victorian building. His gaze was embarrassed by the variety of small posters, drink driving, drug abuse, Samaritans and opening times, nothing the eye would want to settle on; they all looked fresh, which suggested the refurbishment was very recent. The flat surfaces were different shades of lemon and off-white, not far from Wendy's pallor now; an oddly shaped red blotch had risen on her sallow neck, to rival the colour of the warning notices, and she was uncharacteristically quiet. Two officers were behind the glass, a young man who took their details, and an older woman who had her back to them and was busy at a filing cabinet. The young officer was almost obsequiously polite, and listened as Martin explained why they were there, and who they were; then told him, 'She's over seventeen. She doesn't need to be accompanied, sir.'

'But anyone would be anxious. I do have a legitimate concern for her welfare. She's already had a terrible year before this lot started.'

The older officer turned and said, 'I think in the circumstances it might help to have Mr Harper here.' Of course, thought Martin; they wanted evidence they could use in court, didn't they?

It was this older officer who led the questioning, in another partition-created interview room, which had a slight smell of bleach. She seemed to take most of what Wendy said at face value, about Jack's routines, his friends, and so on. Martin watched the red blotch on Wendy's neck merge with others. Her hair looked darker in this light. She spoke unusually slowly, and her answers were straight and to the point. Her brother had always spent a lot of time online, and she had no idea what he was up to or whether he'd made new contacts in recent months. She hadn't been interested. She'd had other things to think about. What things? Her mum had relied on her. For? Housework. Shopping. Personal care. And there was school work: she'd just got eleven GCSEs. (At that point they all smiled.) The officer asked her about her brother's visits to the hospital where her mother had been treated, whose systems he'd targeted. (Unsuccessfully, as it had turned out; he was a mere script kiddie, as they called them, and had only got himself caught.)

'Wendy, did you know that your brother held a grievance against Adderhead General?'

'Yes. He thought they'd let her out too soon.'

'Is that all?'

She breathed out loudly, then pursed her lips. 'Look,' she said, with the tremor of anger in her voice, and a shake of those strange curls, 'All those weeks when I was looking after mum, he was never there. He was upstairs at the computer like he always had been, ignoring us both. And after she'd gone, his habits didn't change. That's all I know.'

The whole thing was over in less than half an hour, and they would be back before the end of morning school, in time for Martin's year 10 Maths. He was pleased with himself; she would be getting her phone back soon, and maybe the laptop in a couple of weeks, but they wouldn't have told her that if he hadn't been there to ask on her behalf.

'Well done, Wendy,' he said, once they were seated in the car.

'Mm,' she murmured, staring ahead. He prompted her: 'Seatbelt?'

'He hardly ever visited. When she was in hospital. That's what makes me mad.'

That night, stretched out on their soft warm bed, he ran over the day to share it with his wife. *I think I helped her just by being there. She's a great kid. It was odd to see her so nervous, because that's not her normal way.*

*If I'm honest, it's done me good. For the first time in ages, I've achieved something worthwhile. I feel I've made a difference, and the right sort of difference, as if there could be a purpose to this job. Because all I've been doing this year is to go through the routines and hope that if I keep turning the key, the engine will fire.*

At the start of the day, Martin hadn't so much asked the Deputy Head's permission to be out of school as informed him what needed to happen. It was legitimate pastoral business. Of course, Gareth let him go, and agreed to arrange cover, but not without remarking that it was beyond the call of duty. With an eye on the clock and lots to do, Martin hadn't stopped to think about it at the time, but now he reflected on that minor chord in the modulations of Gareth's voice, that was, unmistakably, warning him to be careful. *I think he was suggesting I shouldn't get too involved. It's a funny world, teaching. We're meant to care, but we mustn't get involved. How involved is too involved? Will I get more involved? Should I?* He knew what Julia's answer would be. Do what you can, do what needs to be done. *Why not,* he concluded: *what have I to lose?*

*Wednesday December 1*

MARTIN COULD HEAR the crudely amplified music from far down the corridor. Shannon's tinselly singing was strangely flimsy for someone whose speaking voice was so hard and loud, and she struggled against the band: *I... I... I... will fix you*. Constipated chords from the keyboard, and a drummer who somehow limped unpredictably behind his own beat. But as Martin pushed the heavy double doors open, another noise, thrashed from wall to wall and back again by the breeze blocks, came crashing towards him; angry voices, from a whole bunch of kids who hadn't been there at the start of the band practice. The knot of girls sitting in front of the musicians and with their backs to him had obviously come to listen, or gawp; but there was also a loose group of Catsea kids, girls and some boys. It happened sometimes that if they hadn't all got on the bus, they would take refuge there, where it was warm, to wait for the next one in an hour's time. Wendy was one of them.

Pupils came from miles around to Hanningford Grammar. Friendships depended on the bus you got, and the place you lived more or less reflected your parents' income, with Hanningford village (a fine wool church, a common, and cricket on the green) at the top and Catsea (semis backed tight up to the estuary, standing water on concrete roads in winter, odours of barbecue fluid and low tide in summer) at the opposite end of the economic scale. The Catsea kids were a minority at the Grammar, but they gelled in a way none of the others did; they would tell you they were proud to be loud. Martin liked them for their frank good humour. They reminded him of his home town in the north.

The band slumped to the end of the number and now all you could hear was the dispute. The boys had the floor. There were big, masculine shouts from lads keen to measure just how much more noise their journey through adolescence now allowed them to make. One thinner, higher voice carried over the top, and belonged to a tiny lad with greasy hair; he wore the uniform of a junior, maybe year 10 or 11. Martin didn't know him. He looked a bit like a mouse, with little darting eyes, but he was not intimidated by the older kids, and he kept squealing something. *He must be mental. No. I'm telling you. He's gotta be mental. No.* Every repeat wound the pitch up a semitone. Opposite him stood another lad, Connor, who was a prefect in year 13, well known as serious guy whose ambition was to work at CERN. His posture was that of one too tall for his own comfort, and the oversize school shirt flapped over a concave chest; he slouched and lowered his head to bellow back, which made him look like a great big question mark. His huge beak of a nose was curtained by long, lank hair. Martin heard him say, *Jack wasn't weird, he was clever. He could've done anything.* The mouse boy shrieked, fearless, *So look what he did, then. He was mental.'*

Martin homed in, and did his best to shut them up. They all fell silent except the rodent boy, who turned on Wendy now, yelling, *fucking mental, your brother*. He told her she ought to watch out. They all ought to watch out. Jack would've hacked into her contacts for a start, he'd have all her passwords. He'd have hacked her Facebook, and all her mates', too.

Wendy sneered as if he'd crept from under a stone, and told him Jack wasn't some little kid like him; he shouldn't judge other people by himself. She stood her ground.

An ash blonde sitting on one of the stools in front of the performing space turned round. Whisper, with Ari Clay. Danny, the lead guitarist, had put his Fender down and stepped over next to her. From the body language, Martin guessed that Whisper was soft on him – not surprising, as with his blue eyes and well-cut fair hair he was far better looking than the rest; plus, he had more than the usual three chords. Whisper told the squealer that you shouldn't call anybody mental, and added that there was no need to swear. At this, she caught Martin's eye, deliberately, and held his gaze just a second too long for comfort. She was prim, but oddly, they all seemed to take it from her. She must have a high cool quotient with the boys. Martin talked to them all, conciliatory; *come on guys, tone it down, let's not get carried away.*

Whisper congratulated her guitarist friend with a smile that showed her little white incisors, and which was followed by a snigger and grimace: *shame about the vocals...* Danny really ought to sing. *Yeah, you really ought to sing,* said Ari. The boy cast a look behind him to say he didn't want to discuss it here; so Whisper changed the subject. How awful it was that people were so ignorant, and so unsympathetic, about other people's problems. She sighed. She wanted to become an Educational Psychologist, actually. *That's why I'm going to do Psychology. It's like,* years *of training. But you get to help people.*

That lit the blue touch paper with the squealer, who had overheard perhaps more than she'd intended. *Who are you kidding. It's all right for you lot with your big houses in Hanningford. It's different rules for us in Catsea. We have to wait months and months just to get an assessment. Your parents pay to get you tested outside school, and you get your extra time in exams, just like that. You said it yourself, your mum even told the woman what to write. It's just business. I mean, fair play to you, if you can geddit, go for it. Budif I was a psychologist, I'd wanna help people who were really sick.*

He rounded off the diatribe by turning to Wendy to say, *No offence.* Martin understood this rapid change of attitude towards her; it was a higher allegiance. Wendy's brother might be a nutter, but at least he was a nutter who lived on the same street, metaphorically and who knows, maybe physically. Shannon too was a Catsea girl, and this was her cue to pitch in from the stage. Suddenly the tinsel voice was packed away, and the puckered little mouth re-established connection with her lungs. *He's right about that. It's not a level playin' field is it? If all the mummies and daddies in Hanningford village didn't shell out for tutors and psychologists, you'd all be crap like us.*

Martin had to sit on that: 'Nobody's crap.' But Whisper didn't want to leave it there. She was scathing: what was wrong with parents wanting to do the best for their kids? It was a basic responsibility, she said. The tide turned; with the implication that their parents somehow didn't care enough, she'd managed to offend them all. She looked so prissy, so sure that if you don't like it you can take it back, can't you?

Then somebody asked, Sir, was Jack really sick? Squealer and Whisper both snapped, 'Yes,' while Connor said, 'No,' and they all set off arguing again. Why target a hospital, unless you were a sicko, like that nurse who poisoned her patients? If the computers went down you'd kill all the patients wouldn't you?' Then Connor, who seemed the best informed, said Vulcan had a mission, it was all about being objective, so they must have had a reason. Most of the others didn't know what he was talking about. *What? Vulcan? What's Vulcan? Mr Spock? Told you he was weird. Seen the ears? I rest my case.*

In the silence after Martin's shout – *just stop it, now* – Whisper reminded the squealer that he shouldn't judge criminals, instead he ought to try to understand them, because they don't all have a good start in life. Did he realise, for example, that only yesterday Wendy had to get Mr Harper to go to the police station with her about her brother, because her mum was dead and they didn't have a dad? Wendy shot an accusing glance at Shannon, who went even redder in the face; then she threw her coppery head back and hissed, *For God's sake*, and Whisper said, *What? What?*

'Will you stop using me as an example for your sociology coursework.'

'I don't do sociology. It's *Psy*chology. I'm only saying.'

The guitarist pushed the squealer, who was now laughing and pointing at both Wendy and Whisper. He fell onto a chair and knocked it over, onto the amp; so the drummer came and pushed him into the nearest lad, who happened to be one of the Catsea gang, which meant they all pitched in. You could hardly call it a serious fist fight, and it could only have lasted a few seconds; once Martin shouted at them again they all just stopped.

Connor the human question mark asked, 'Why are we all arguing?'

'Because it's one rule for us, and another rule for them.' Shannon's jagged voice again.

He said, 'What do you think, sir?' Martin Harper had become the referee. They all turned towards him and waited for an answer.

He knew quite well that, since Julia had travelled to the underworld, he didn't always do what he ought to do. The protocols didn't seem to matter. He did the strangest thing. In the moment, he didn't know if it was his finest hour or his worst, although he sensed it could be either. The fact was, he could only hear one answer to give them. It became pure theatre. He stretched out his hand to the fair haired boy and said, *lend me your guitar a minute*. He pulled up a stool, took his time to check the tuning, then righted the amp and plugged in; he checked the volume with a few broken chords, and lowered it appreciably. He was milking the silence now. This was a *performance,* goddamit. He gave them a song that Julia loved, but which they had probably never heard at all.

> *'Cos Momma may have,*
> *And Poppa may have,*
> *But God bless the child who's got his own,*
> *Who's got his own.*

He got to the end and told them, simply, *that's what I think*. Shannon was the first to break the silence: *Sir, that was lovely.* They all murmured. Some of them clapped.

Wendy was staring at him, with a funny little grin on her face, the sort that might lead to tears any minute. Then Whisper asked, in all seriousness, *Sir, have I got my own?* He told them they all had. Shannon asked was he going to sing that in the Christmas concert and he answered no, he had just wanted to sing it for them, and just tonight, because it felt right. In a public concert, it wouldn't be the same. As the band started to pack up, he noticed that Ari Clay was looking puzzled. He asked her what was the matter, and she asked, 'His own *what?*'

*Thursday December 2*

NEXT DAY, the rumour in the staffroom was that boys had got into the common room after school and trashed the place, until Martin Harper stopped it all by singing at them.

'Gross exaggeration,' Martin told Paddy Clancy, 'It wasn't a real fight. More symbolic.' Paddy had taken the trouble to seek him out at morning break, partly in a gesture of solidarity, but also so as to hear it from the horse's mouth. Before the coffee was even into the thick-rimmed mug, he had to ask: was it true that music calmed the savage breast, then? Martin couldn't help grinning. 'I wish, Paddy. I wish.'

Not far behind them in the queue, Mary Parry was shrill to ask, if somebody was supervising, why were things allowed to escalate in the first place? 'Oh God,' mumbled Paddy as he deftly lifted two bourbons from the biscuit tin. Now Mary was asking, why did the conquering hero walk away and leave other people to clear up the mess? Martin kept his head down. 'What she means is, a chair fell over and I didn't put it back.'

The room was filling, and they shuffled sideways into a couple of seats next to the dark eyed language assistants. They were working pretty hard at understanding each other's English across the buzz of conversation, so they wouldn't eavesdrop or interrupt. Martin protested he'd only been at the band practice because they needed a Responsible Adult.

'Yeah, right,' said Paddy, and they both laughed. Paddy had an easy way about him. He brushed chocolate coloured crumbs from the white shirt which was stretched tight over his paunch, and flapped the blue nylon tie to show he was done.

'You know Shannon Matthews? Year 12? She sings in a band with some of the lads. One of their dads is a parent governor. So, he suggested they should do a spot in the Christmas Concert. Well of course they couldn't say no, but the only available rehearsal time clashed with the choir…'

'Oh my God,' said Paddy, sounding a bit Irish now as he entered further into mirth.

'…and the two groups couldn't possibly share the same building. Amplified music.'

'Devil's music, I'd say.'

'So Shannon says, it's a student band, it belongs in the common room, we've got a common room, Mr Harper is in charge of that, and he plays the guitar, so he'll be cool with it.'

'Faultless logic.'

'Once they'd set up, I disappeared and left them to it.'

'Ooh, dodgy ground there, Martin my old mucker. In hindsight.'

'I did go back to check on them, after maybe half an hour. Pandemonium. And that was just the band. They were doing *I will fix you*, and my God they needed bloody fixing.

Crimes against music.' He shook his head and they both chuckled. For them, that was the essence and the pleasure of the job: to watch the kids mess up in a million little ways, because if you let them practise, one day they'd get it right.

Paddy wanted the detail now. 'What was the argument about?'

'Oh... Catsea versus Hanningford Village, you know. They'd cancelled a bus or something, that's why they were all hanging around.'

'So cut to the fight: what happened?'

'That's just what I want to know.' Somehow Gareth Whittaker had wormed his way through the crowding room, and was standing over them, grey-suited and with a curious expression on his face; a closed, tidy little smile, his eyebrows — pale almost to the point of invisibility — raised in apparent expectation of good things; it looked like something he'd learnt on a management course. 'Martin, I've had a delegation from Shannon Matthews. She says there was a fight about Jack Mundy.' He nodded to acknowledge Paddy, who nodded back and turned to scrutinise Martin. 'She says you sorted them all out. Also that you treated them to a musical performance. She was singing your praises, on both counts.' His smile flickered into new life. Difficult time for Wendy, of course. Thanks for your help on this. Look, we've got a couple of things to talk about, haven't we? So could you swing by my way some time this afternoon? You're free at two, I think.'

'Yes. Sure.' Whittaker edged backwards-sideways through a stand of teachers, and disappeared towards the middle of the room.

'Would this be an important meeting coming up?' sang Paddy, who had been obliged to make his own contribution to the monitoring process the Head had put in place a month ago. 'You know you're all straight as far as the Maths is concerned. Last night… you didn't do anything daft, did you?'

All Martin could say was that he'd done what felt right at the time. Paddy checked his friend over for signs of trouble: he'd lost that haggard look, the frown; he was close shaven, haircut neat enough; a soft dark shirt, the sort Paddy would never buy, the sort you had to iron, but immaculate; there was a crease in his trousers, the jacket was clean, and he was wearing the brightest of his four famous square-cut ties, the terrible yellow one, which come to think of it they hadn't seen for months. Clean shoes, brushed suede, though why he couldn't just settle for ordinary black leather Paddy didn't know, it might have helped professionally. All in all, he didn't look like someone who'd lost control. The singing business was maybe a bit eccentric, maybe a bit inspired. Paddy's heavy watch showed eight minutes till the end of break. Five minutes, then, to find out what he could, and not be late for lesson three himself.

'So tell me about Wendy. The cover worked out fine, by the way, apart from your year 12 classics, Daph says they whinged a bit at being set work but then they would… How did she get on with the police interview?'

'OK I think. She couldn't tell them much. She doesn't know anything. She has such candour, anyone could see, she couldn't tell a lie.'

Paddy reserved judgment on that. His friend was just a micron too emphatic. He could be off on Gullible's Travels again. It wouldn't be the first time.

'What did you have to do?'

'Just be there. Well, I gave her a lift and I brought her back to school. I did get a chance to ask them about giving her laptop back. She really needs it. I told them it was essential to her education, and they said they'd do what they could. She's more upset about her phone, because of the pictures on it. Her mum.'

Paddy was surprised. 'No cloud backup, then?'

'It's big brother who's the computer wiz, not Wendy.'

'Fair point,' he conceded. 'Let's hope it's all straightforward now. You've got enough on your plate already.'

'I don't know what you mean.'

'You do. You know quite well they've got their eye on you. The question of your competency, remember? Don't let Wendy's home life make you take your eye off that ball.'

Martin stared at the carpet and shook his head.

'OK, I know. But the thing is, Paddy, she's got nobody to look out for her. Nobody at all.'

Paddy never doubted the sincerity of Martin's purpose, but he didn't trust his wisdom when it came to needy pupils.

'That's not your problem. Just be careful. Don't get too involved.'

*Monday 6 December*

THE FIRST THING Martin did when he got home was to open a bottle of red in celebration. He spent a few minutes selecting music, something loose enough to stay safely in the background; there had to be no words because his head was full of all the things he wanted to tell Julia; Coltrane would do. Settled on the sofa, he could pick up with his wife again, and review the day with her.

'Cheers my love. First today. That was a good one.' Apart from the first sizeable fall of Christmas cards which he'd trampled opening the door; he had always hated those bloody things. They used to have the same argument every year. He'd say, if you want to send them, you write them. And she'd say fine, I like to write a personal note anyway. Then by the last week of term she'd be so knackered they'd loom like another set of reports; so the deal became, she'd sit in front of the telly and he'd keep her company and ply her with red wine for a couple of evenings whilst she went through the address book. In the end they'd all have to go first class. And if Julia should be unwise enough to ask his opinion on what to write, he'd tell her, look, all you're doing is reminding the people we haven't seen – *which is not always an accident* – that we're still alive, in which case, your message might as well be "Not dead yet. Hope you're not either. Love Martin and Julia." She said if it was left to him they might as well have a rubber stamp made. He protested: it was like a bloody census, though, the Christmas card thing, as if you were clocking on with the family firm. But God, it had made him cross for a moment just now, to pick up from the mat an envelope addressed to both of them.

'I know, I know,' he told her, 'if some people still don't know you've gone, it's because I didn't inform them. And I could have told them if I'd known who was on the Christmas list you kept in your head. Which I was never interested in.' Anyway, he hated sending cards almost as much as he hated it when you didn't receive any.

'But we had a good day, didn't we? Mm? The meeting with Whittaker was sweet. Case dropped for lack of evidence. Ha. Lesson planning *tick*, preparation *tick*, resources *tick*, classroom management *tick*, accurate implementation of assessment policy *tick*, homeworks hunky dory and rapidly returned. *Tick, tick, tick.* Made his day, of course, because now he can tell the Head *he's dealt with it.* Even if there never was a problem in the first place, Gareth's the man who *dealt with it*. Manfully dismantled the bomb with no fuse. Gareth was pleased as Punch, because it was just the sort of evidence he wanted for inspection too, proof that he had his finger on the racing pulse of School Improvement. Although they could have the four horsemen of the apocalypse running amok in year 10 and it wouldn't matter so long as they'd signed in and got a badge from reception. Anyway, procedures have been followed, and everyone's a winner.' Martin raised his glass again.

Such a ridiculous look had come over Gareth's face, though, when Martin asked him straight what he intended to do about Timothy Slipman. Like a baby who'd swallowed a gob-stopper. Recounting this, Martin spoke out with vicious emphasis: 'You could see he hadn't given it a minute's thought. Hn. And he left it to *me* to tell *him* what to do. Which is, block him on the system, mark his email spam. As the kids say, *end of.* End of.'

But Gareth had been full of bonhomie and Christmas cheer, hadn't he, with all that guff about the band, and how that had all been down to Martin, and his light touch, as he'd called it, with the boys. All boys were aliens as far as Mary Parry was concerned.

'I think he was mightily relieved. So, well done and thank you, Shannon Matthews for your youthful exaggeration, which has done me no harm. Well done me. And well done, Inspector Gareth. God bless us, every one.'

And the best thing, the very best thing, was, yes, Gareth Whittaker had said, there was no reason why Martin Harper should not accompany the Pompeii trip. What he meant was, it had been shoved in a filing tray all term and nobody else had volunteered.

'Can you hear them?' he asked Julia. '*Ooh yes, me please, antiquity and culture for me every time, ooh please let me go in that bad man's place.* Naah. So it was less a vote of confidence than a massive crossing of simian fingers, but so what? I don't care. It comes to the same result... I like this Negroamaro, you would approve. Funny how our overall consumption hasn't gone down. Drinking for two.'

## 5

### *The Vicar's daughter*

THE FLOWER LADIES are busy with their hands in the half-lit church. Water has slopped over the quarry tiles. Mindless chatter: *Who does she take after, do you think? – Oh, didn't you know?* Adopted is a word that's barely voiced, but she hears it coming in the dip of their sing-song, and always knows it's there. Julia is rueful: if Satan exists, he's an old lady talking for talking's sake, looking for somebody to talk about, anyone, so obviously, she'll do. *Who does she take after, do you think?* It's a thing people say. Well, they shouldn't. As if we don't know who you are unless we can attach you, right now, to someone else. She recently heard a teacher tell the class, *you are what you do*. So let's wait and see what she does. What would happen if you added this magnesium to water. If you left the eggs to boil dry. If you stayed out all night. If you smashed the glass. If you smoked. If you brought a boy home. If you didn't wipe that smile off your face. If you told the flower arrangers to mind their own business. Who would you take after then?

AS SHE GROWS TALLER it gets harder to pretend not to hear all that her vicar's wife mother has to say about her to the neighbours. She stands there on the pavement, third person present wishing to be away: Julia this, Julia that, about her last report and guide camp and university one day, all things being equal… You're lucky to have a girl who's so sensible. Reliable Julia, consistent Julia, Julia always looks so tidy, not like my… whoever. That's when the demon jumps inside Julia's head, and she wonders: could she summon up the fire to swear out loud in front of Mrs Harris outside the post office? What words to use? Bloody hell Mrs Harris my mother does go on. Fuck me Mrs Harris my mother does go on. Fuck me she is such a pain and so are you and so is your pyramid baked bean display. That would shut them up. It would be worth it to put them straight. She starts to practise in front of the white-painted mirror but succeeds in shocking only herself. It would be so hurtful, after all her mum has done for her! Every now and then she cries her eyes out, what an evil, what an ungrateful piece of dirt she is. For a day she is contrite, and prays a lot: thank You God for stopping me just in time, and showing me the error of my ways. Gradually she uses that tidy long thin mirror to make herself as different as possible from her frayed and quilted mum. She will be sleek and certain, well-defined. Her hair will be scraped back. Her colours will be clear, not muddled by patterns which don't go. They did a thing in English: If person X were a piece of furniture, what piece of furniture would they be? Her mum would be a squidgy old sofa, obviously. She must make every effort, then, to become a filing cabinet. And if she were an animal? Puma, not Labrador like her mum. A plant? A perfect tulip, or an orchid. Definitely not a privet bush.

The roadside conversations continue, until one day at the school gate she and her mother stand eye-to-eye. Some random parent has struck up a conversation: '…And this must be your daughter.' With slow deliberation, she turns a blank face full to the vicar's wife who has raised her as her own since she was two months old. The familiar stranger she is staring at is mousy – alright, maybe fair – with grey eyes, a shapeless sort of cushion of a face, small uneven teeth, white skin that burns easily and makes pink-dappled gooseflesh on her arms; someone whose ambitions can be contained on a scrap of paper in an apron pocket. Her life is a series of small things. Any success, any failure is one she's borrowed either from her daughter or her husband. This week in Biology they did parasites and saprophytes. A parasite depends on a living host, as she depends on her family.

'...And this must be your daughter.'

Julia turns her head deliberately to the other child's parent and tells her, 'No, actually, I'm not.'

It doesn't hit the mark. Her mother raises smiling eyebrows in a show of unconcern, gives a tiny nod, and reaches out to pick a loose thread, or maybe a hair, from her school jumper, in that proprietary way which so annoys her.

'No, she's not.'

She is astonished by her mother's sudden energy. It's like a bite, or a cuff from a lioness. Once they are back home, though, Julia is sure she's going to cry and make a scene. Perhaps her mother has reached a funny age. She's read about this sort of thing. Older women get emotional, irrational. Unpredictable. It's hormones.


A LOW SPRING SUN shines through the windows of the Parish Hall, revealing motes of dust that wander, separate, in random directions. The day has been full and Julia's energy is already spent; her insides have been wringing themselves out all day; hunger and a headache nag, although she doesn't mind the extra obligation of the confirmation class, because it's warm and quiet here and nothing much will be demanded of her for the next hour. They have set their chairs to form a circle: Elaine and Jenny to her left, Beverley and John to her right, her father opposite. He has started to run through the confirmation service, this is where you'll sit, at this point you stand, you come up with your sponsor, and this is how it will be.

The Bishop will put his hand on your head and say, Julia Dawn, God has called you by name and made you His own

She wonders out loud: 'Is Julia my real name?' It sends a shockwave through the group. A chair scrapes against the boards; the teenagers exchange glances. Elaine looks sideways at her from under a fringe. The others are all staring at her vicar dad now, to know what he will say, and to see how he will say it. His cheeks take on the colour of crushed strawberries, as they do when someone swears or has a go at him. She hadn't meant to challenge him; the idea walked into her vacant mind for the first time a moment ago. It was the words. God has called you by name and made you his own. They had a power sweet and terrible at once, they had shaken her from her torpor; they touched her and made her tremble, as if they filled a hollow in her heart. She tries to clarify, but makes things worse: 'I mean, is there a name I didn't know I had?'

'You mean like a code name?' says John. She likes John. He's trying to be helpful and smooth things over. She ought not to have brought up this question of her birth at all; she would have lashed out at anyone else who had. This is the big, big thing about her, too big a thing to conceal, and too big to talk about. But her father, unperturbed, answers as if the question is one he's heard a hundred times, as if it comes up every confirmation class: 'Perhaps God has a name for you that nobody else can know.' Something has hold of her now and she is sobbing, hating her own tactlessness, moved by his answer, and sure there is something, some fact out there still to be discovered and which she might grope towards and find one day. For the first time, she senses the reality of her own true mother: she must have been just another girl who did a lot of crying too. Julia strains the ears of memory to hear this half-discerned frail creature, not much older than herself; childbirth has drained her of blood, and she is calling her now by a name... What name? It has been there, she knows it has, whispered in her ear, breathed on her baby cheek, and it must be there, recorded deep within her brain... her real name... listen for it... listen... And even though she cannot summon it back now, perhaps one day she'll recognise it on someone else's tongue, the tongue of a stranger. Or perhaps of the man she's going to marry, the one who'll claim her for his own. Flooding, wet, sticky, she feels full and empty all at once.

# 6

*Monday 13 December*

'IS THAT MARTIN HARPER?' A clear, almost clipped, formal voice over the telephone which never rang these days in the felted quiet of their soft grey sitting room.

'Speaking. Who's there?'

'My name's Timothy Slipman. I believe we met once, at a JACT event.'

Martin's anger was immediate and convulsive. This was outrageous, calling him at home... and where on earth had he obtained the number? Martin asked, 'Did you want something?' deliberately, in a tone as cold as he could make it, but what he felt was heat, and sickness; his guts were twisting, and he wanted to hit this man he couldn't see. There was a pause, then the voice went on: 'I wanted to say that I'm sorry. I'm really very sorry.'

'So you should be.' So he should be, thought Martin, for getting me that wrong, making me out to be a total shit, failing to see that Ariadne Clay is a deeply shallow little girl. One snide word to mummy and he's turned himself into a saviour, all at my expense.

'I didn't realise,' said the voice. 'I did wonder, though. Then when I heard, I thought I should say something.'

It was no use; any pretence of cool superiority had eluded Martin, now that the kindling tongue of anger was at work. He let his voice fill the room. 'Well I hope you're bloody satisfied. Who've you been speaking to, then?'

'Nobody!'

'OK, so you don't actually *talk* to people. Who've you emailed?'

If he had been in the room, Martin knew, he would have had him by the throat. But for all that, he could hear that the man was genuinely confused. He protested that he had no idea at all what Martin meant. He said, 'Look, I think we're at cross-purposes. Let's start again. I'm calling about Julia. To say I'm sorry. I was sorry to hear about your wife. She was… special.'

They were silent for a moment. 'My wife was remarkable,' said Martin. 'It's over a year. Why are you calling now?'

'I didn't know. I've only just found out. Look, to be honest, I thought she might have left you.'

Why would he think that? Was he delusional? That was possible. Martin's neck was suddenly too hot. Even if the guy was sick, he still wanted to hit him.

'When she wasn't there… I thought she'd left you.'

Wasn't where? What was he getting at?

'She, she was, very, special and, um, I'd like to offer, um, my condolences.'

'I don't need your condolences. We're just fine.'

'I need to ask you something…. Could you tell me… Where is she now?'

'What do you mean?'

'I assume there is a grave? I just want to, you know, pay my respects. I feel I should.'

'No. No. You don't respect me, and I don't respect you. You don't have to pay your respects. And I don't have to talk to you. Please don't call again.'

Martin dropped the receiver on his protestations, then cried aloud: *Julia, what's he talking about?*

Half uttered, half in thought, he picked up that dialogue with her which had never really closed. Now more than ever it had urgency. *He wasn't calling about work or Ari Clay. It was about you. What does he know about you? What did he say exactly... he thought you'd left me... 'when she wasn't there'. Where, Julia? Where were you meant to be? And why would he think that? What does he know about you? How dare he. How dare he. Filth. He wasn't calling to apologise for trying to lose me my job. He said you were special, bloody awful turn of phrase, shows the calibre of the man. Inadequate. This is disgusting, to hear him talk about you like that... But why would you be special to him? Love, you're going to have to tell me, if you know. And I think you must. But whatever the reason, it makes no difference to this: I swear, he won't find out from me. I won't ever tell him where you are.*

FOR DAYS, that telephone conversation played on a loop in his head. Or rather, it was broken down into samples that rattled and repeated but seemed to have no sense, like a hateful tune that couldn't be banished. He would wake with questions and beat them down one by one. What did Slipman know about Julia? Because whatever he knew, Martin knew infinitely more. Slipman couldn't have known, for example, about the way she used the night. She would sometimes get up to mark or plan, because she said she worked best then. Half the time Martin hadn't noticed she was up, he just rolled over and slept on, but now here he was, awake and ready for the night shift with her, like most nights nowadays.

Not that he achieved much in the small hours. The school didn't deserve his overtime and besides, he couldn't fathom more than the crossword. Did Slipman know about the way she wrapped stuff twice – bacon, eggs, left overs in the fridge – because she had this perception that everything was going to taint everything else? No. He couldn't have known that. Martin was party to a myriad of tiny habits, foibles, gestures, things only a husband knows. In all likelihood the only thing that had happened was, Slipman once heard Julia give that talk at JACT and fell for her. Julia was so at ease in that kind of formal situation, it would have been impossible not to be enchanted by her delivery. She picked her words so well, weighed them beautifully, and her voice, her sweet chestnut voice, was always so poised, so warm, no squeaks or ugly inflections; any man would fall in love with that. But that was the public face. Martin wondered if Slipman knew how, by contrast, in everyday conversation, she spewed out words; sometimes she got too excited, and suddenly nobody would be listening. *I loved you for that. You were all energy. And you loved an argument.* Maybe Slipman remembered Julia because she had argued with him, and if so, he hoped she had made him eat dirt. That was probably it.

*The people who didn't really know you remember you so well. Each according to his ignorance. Or his weakness. Mary thought you were hard as nails. Paddy thought you were soft as butter.*

There were a million things about Julia that Slipman could not know. But however much Martin soothed himself with that thought, there remained a splinter of a question, a cruel shard in his flesh. Did they ever, possibly, get closer than an argument? Surely it was unthinkable that anyone but

Martin could have known that frenzy that came on her when they lay together… And she would say, it was the scent of lime blossom, when it might be April and no linden tree in sight. Martin knew what she meant. *You cannot, ever, surely, have shared that with another man. There was no opportunity. I gave you none. I see as yesterday that look which came upon you, as if of hopelessness, an emptying you said, but I'd have said, you filled yourself, you gorged on me, and you sucked away the space between us, and as yesterday I feel your tender heat, but I search and search and cannot ever quite bring it fully back to mind, the scent of you, the scent of you, the scent of you, lost to me. Lost.*

*Tuesday 14 December*

DAYLIGHT WAS NIGGARDLY at this time of year, but at least school days were brisk and full of their own fluorescent importance, as the last full week of term was hurtling to its end. Martin was occupied with the year 11s, who were already planning their options for the Sixth Form next September, and he had the comfort of a clear set of familiar tasks – putting the information out, getting the forms ready for next term – and the illusion of usefulness as they trooped in looking for advice. This was, apparently, the one thing he was good for. One by one, bidden and unbidden, a trickle of wonderers had found their way to his office. The students were so tender at this time, it seemed to him; as they worked out what they might want to do, and might be able to do, they were busy with that job of making themselves, and all of this was new, meaningful, and urgent to them. Some were the waverers, the switherers, the hoverers, those had no sense of direction and had heard that he might help them find one. A second group knew quite precisely what they wanted, to wit, everything their parents disapproved of. Or so they claimed. He would rather talk these hotheads through their martyrdom than attend to his marking, or write reports for the year 9s (due tomorrow), or update the Higher Ed list (deadline end of term). School time was absorbing, almost pleasant, if you spent it talking about stuff that mattered. Besides, if you could get them excited, interested, they would stay put at Hanningford and not move to the College down the road. Retention was everything to Senior Management, and Martin knew that Gareth Whittaker and the Head would have their ear to the ground.

And then there were preparations for the trip. Amy had called a lunchtime meeting. As well as the kids who were already signed up, she'd rounded up the rest of the Sixth Form classicists, plus the Drama lot and anyone else who was half interested, because not one but all three of the year 11s had dropped out. If they didn't fill the places, the school would take a serious financial hit. They met in the library, at Martin's suggestion; the fug of overheated classrooms was unbearable in the winter months, and the way the steamed up windows overlaid their grey mist on an aluminium sky just added insult to injury. Mrs Hammer had told the students succinctly how things stood, and dismissed them in good time for period 5, exiting dutifully herself and expecting them all to follow her. Predictably, though, they lingered and discussed. The year 12s had Class Civ next anyway, and that was with Mr Harper, who was standing right there and not inclined to hurry.

Shannon remarked that Mrs Hammer looked well narked about it all. 'Well is that my problem?' said Ariadne

Clay, and Martin recognised one of Whisper's stock retorts. Wendy spoke up, from under clown-arched brows which suggested she had had an idea; and in a clear voice she announced that she'd always wanted to see Pompeii, ever since she was little. It wasn't a wistful voice, more a voice that recognised a possibility. So why hadn't she put her name down for the trip in the first place, asked Shannon? Wendy claimed she'd thought it was too expensive, but Martin knew that when the letters first went out, she'd had other things to think about and was missing lots of school anyway. Then Whisper reminded them all that technically, the contributions were voluntary – that was the law. Another girl said, 'Yeah, but if there aren't enough voluntary contributions, they're allowed to cancel the trip, aren't they? So it comes to the same thing.' A mutter rippled through the group. Martin felt now was the time to intervene, and assured them, 'Well it's definitely going ahead now, because everything's already booked.'

'Exactly,' said Wendy. 'Which makes now the time to ask.'

Martin was momentarily surprised; he hadn't thought she was that calculating. And she sounded slightly brassy, as if she was making a point, and maybe a bit impatient with them all. It was an unspoken *why shouldn't I?* Good for her, he thought; maybe she was starting to live as a girl of her age should, having fun and trips and a school life unbroken by housework or nursing. If you knew what you wanted, all you had to do was work out how to make it happen, that was what he always told them. He saw immediately how he could help Wendy make this happen, and get her to Pompeii; he knew there was a hardship fund, and if that failed, he would subsidise her himself, if the school would let him. They could hardly say no in the circumstances.

Then he that noticed that Ari was staring at Wendy's cardigan. It was one of those shapeless ones they all seemed to go for at the moment, not strictly dress code when you stopped to look. There was one button, near the top, which was the wrong colour – blue, not black – and it was different in shape, slightly square instead of round. He wondered what Ari was thinking. Was she remembering that Wendy didn't have a mum to fix things for her? Or acknowledging her creativity? Or maybe asking herself, *who mends buttons these days, don't you just buy a new cardigan?* But Ari's expression betrayed no enquiry at all; in fact, her face was just a picture of blank affront. A simple, stupid registering that something wasn't quite as it was meant to be. Martin had always thought that if the devil existed, that look which Ariadne Clay wore now would be one of the ways that you would recognise him. By his dullness.


EVERY HOMECOMING had been the same that week. He pushed open the door, turned on the light, and was met by the gaze of an Indian girl, maybe 12 years old and in a bright pink sari, peering from a glossy flyer which lay flat on the little table in the hallway. Sponsor a Child. For just 75p a day. It took so little to turn around a life, he read. Martin couldn't quite throw this piece of paper away, but hadn't acted on it either. Perhaps he was a very wicked man. If it were simply a question of money, then yes, they could have a contribution, gladly; but to take that step of sponsoring an individual was so much greater. However clean the direct debit, the arrangement could not fail to signify something much more than money to each party. *His* neediness would become explicit, his need to matter somewhere, to influence, to have a life-changing tie with one chosen person; but one who was chosen utterly at random. And for her part, the child might expect letters, something personal; guidance, love... he didn't know what... Any meeting would be so frankly asymmetrical as to be unkind. And how could you ever admit to that child that thanks were inappropriate, that it had all come down to this: that one day, aware that Christmas was approaching and feeling rather lonely, he, Martin Harper, had conducted his own moral audit; this had revealed that he was turning into a crusty old Scrooge who needed to do some good in the world, and so he let a microchip choose you, nothing personal you understand. *No,* he said out loud that Friday. *I'll send a cheque to the Red Cross instead.* They did good in all the dirtiest places and they'd understand a godless sinner who intended to lurk safely in the shadows.

And then there was Wendy. Before he had taken his coat off, he found himself telling Julia, *there's one small thing that I can do for this girl, and I'm going to do it. She's coming on our trip, Julia. I'll find a way.*

He wondered now if he and Julia had been good for each other, in respect of having children. He hadn't cared enough. He had dealt with it as if it were some problem of algebra, where x can be any child, your own or another's, if need be. Maybe there were still brooding aristocratic males out there who fretted about the blood line. But Martin's guess was that most men didn't go looking for children any more than they went looking for a wife.

*It was you I wanted, Julia, not any third party who might come as part of the deal.* Once he had Julia, and once they'd lived together long enough to deepen in love, once they'd shown everybody that they didn't fight and this would last: then, and only then, they knew a child was right. If it had happened, it would have seemed, quite simply, appropriate. A tepid word.

*But it was not something I sought. I think I wanted a child because you began to, and I wanted this most, if I'm honest – can I tell you this now? – I wanted it most when you became possessed by the idea. I thought a baby was the cure, do you see? The cure for your pain.*

*Friday December 24*

IT WAS GOOD of Julia's parents to have Martin to stay, good for them all to meet up. There he was again, albeit alone this time, snug in the spare room, where he and his wife had spent so many Christmas nights together. The couple always arrived on Christmas Eve in darkness; waking the next morning, they would admire the hollies at the splendid old Georgian rectory across the lane, and kid themselves that they were better off in the properly heated modern vicarage. It certainly had the better view. On the other side of this floral papered wall was her mother's fluff and glitter version of Julia's teenage years, the white fairy tale bed and all those silly, girly objects, once pushed to the back of the wardrobe, but now back on show and dusted every week. He whispered: *We won't open that door, there's nothing there we'd recognise.*

Martin and Julia's home in Hanningford was on the edges of a built-up area, washed with sodium light which sluiced the stars away; but there were no street lamps here in this north Essex village, so on a clear, frosty night such as this, the sky promised to be a beauty. Martin switched off the light, and drew aside the curtain a little. From his first floor window, he could make out the irregular dark shapes of trees hunched around the west end of the churchyard, and sure enough, there were the heavens: all the dancing constellations, all the myths entwined; there was Hercules, heaving himself up from behind the yew; and did that bright star in the north west sky reveal the lyre of Orpheus? Orpheus, the wondrous musician, the only human ever to have travelled to the underworld, granted permission by the gods to retrieve his dead wife Eurydice. He led her back, to within sight of upper earth; then famously forgot the injunction always to walk in front of her. As Orpheus turned to look on the face he loved, she shrank back, lost forever. So there was a lesson for you, Martin Harper, over-faithful widower.

From his place at the cold window, the outline of the church grew steadily sharper, and more and more stars formed as he stared. All those stories. Since Saxon times, so many tales of holiness had rattled underneath those beams; as many as the pagan myths that tripped across its roof night after night. His own family were not great churchgoers and it had all felt so strange, that first year at Great Chapham. He couldn't even get a carol right. *The cattle are lowing, the baby awaits,* he had sung to the shaving mirror, their first Christmas. '*Awakes*, you bloody heathen. The baby *awakes*,' she'd said. Every year they heard her father preach on that story in the half-lit church. Julia took communion, Martin bent for a blessing, and when they were alone afterwards he would ask her, what was all that about then? It used to be a gentle, funny time, when she'd put him straight about the nativity, how this thing symbolised that. Then over the years their childlessness became apparent and Julia started to snap at her mother. Martin stopped asking facetious questions about the Christmas story because he could hear his wife listening to it.

One occasion in particular still stung in his memory. It happened four, or maybe five years ago. Geoffrey's brief homily considered the consecration of this church to Saint Mary the Virgin in the 13$^{th}$ century, how the virgin birth had crept into belief, and whether it mattered. He seemed to be saying to a congregation wearing bubble jackets, woolly scarves and novelty ear muffs, believe this if you need to; if you find it unbelievable, then perhaps, for you, it doesn't matter, so don't worry. To Martin it was all the usual vicar-talk, no more. But once at home, Julia had rounded on her father, on some spurious pretext. Out came such a torrent.

'What it comes down to, Dad, is everybody can go home believing what they want. What they already believed when they walked in. And everyone in the parish can feel smug with the thought they all got in on the act. The farmers can say, we were there, the intellectuals can say, we were there, the retailers can say, we were there, we saw an opportunity in the market. And of course even the village idiot can say, ooh, *we've* had a baby. I mean the baby really is the *lowest* common denominator. So we're all OK. Aren't we. Jolly good for us. The massacre of the innocents was just collateral damage and you can bet the retired brigadier in the Old Rectory understands that. In fact, probably the one historical truth was the nastiness of Herod.'

Her meek dad had gone scarlet. He stared at the carpet and found that slow, serious voice which Martin imagined he might use to debate with the Archdeacon, punctuated with little breaths. He said something like, 'If I understand you correctly, you seem to be saying, firstly, that Christmas makes people feel good about themselves; and second, that this is wrong-headed.'

Martin recalled the way Julia had rolled her eyes at her father. She used to say he was a typical Anglican, he had such a knack of turning wine into water. To Martin's way of looking at it, he just took his time to unfold things properly, that was all.

Geoffrey had said – what was it? – he had an academic way of phrasing things... That her inference was false. 'But your observation is key. The Christmas story allows us, most precisely, to feel good about ourselves. To feel hopeful that there is a place for us. A role in the world.' He raised his eyes deliberately to meet his daughter's, and made an observation which Martin recalled verbatim: 'Feeling good about ourselves is something many of us find curiously hard to do.' At that, Julia had begun sobbing and would not be comforted. There was always a demon on her shoulder, in the vicarage.

The window pane reflected an icy coldness which was starting to make his nostrils hurt. His breath beat on the glass, and muddied it with little, temporary pulses of condensation. Now that Martin's eyes had adjusted to the light, he investigated all the subtle qualities of black in the churchyard opposite. Blackest was the yew. The smooth-leaved ivy shone as it strove up the tree trunks and over the boundary wall; the dimpled flints of the building, so hard by day, now looked as soft as the very wool that paid to build them all those centuries ago. He knew that there were simple, low gravestones by the west door, but they seemed to be hidden from this vantage point by trees and the stone wall. Martin would never tell Julia's parents what she had spat and gasped to him from her hospital bed, the day she was admitted that last time: *Leave me anywhere but that churchyard. I won't lie peaceful there.* He'd thought she was hysterical at the time, but once she'd gone, those words were an injunction.

There were things that Julia had told him over the years about her time at Great Chapham, things she said maybe for effect during an argument, then never wished to be reminded of. She had been deliberately promiscuous for a while, as a teenager, she told him more than once, because it irked her so to be the vicar's daughter. Meanwhile, her Mum believed those grades had gone to her head and that was why she became so aloof – her favourite epithet for Julia. Long before Martin ever met her, a pregnancy led to a termination which led, Julia believed – and he never could dissuade her – to that chain of medical disasters which made her now so very hard to find.

Rational, Martin blamed their childlessness on the endometriosis which descended as soon as she came off the pill. He lost her to that for days on end. It perplexed and troubled him, this pain he couldn't ever know himself. Months of consultations and tests turned into years. There was no link between the severity of the pain and the severity of the disease; her case was mild, and she should keep on trying, they said at first. Finally she had the surgery which seemed to offer the best chance of improvement both for her symptoms and for her fertility; it was a matter of waiting patiently and giving nature a good chance before the next option of IVF. But Julia blamed herself. It was one November, when she had been in pain all day; Martin had woken up to an empty bed and a light along the way, and the strangest noise, a whine, spun out in a long thin skein. Julia had been sitting in her dressing gown on the edge of the bath; the frost echoed off the white tiles. When at last she spoke, her voice was as cold and hard as the chrome – 'It's my own fault, Martin. I had a child. When I was still a student. Only I killed it. When it was still inside me.'

*Love...* he whispered now, and listened for her exhalation. Nothing.

There was a bustling downstairs and the front door closed. That would be Geoffrey leaving. And sure enough, there he was crossing the road in that long cape which covered his cassock, ready for midnight mass. The little wiry man with his fleshy nose and crab-apple cheekbones, his grey hair thinning and slightly disobedient, was transformed into a superhero by distance, darkness and the heavy costume of his calling.


HE WAS A FUNNY BLOKE, Julia's dad. Always rationalising. He could find a sense to anything, pick up meaning just as easily from a toenail clipping as a star. Martin wondered if they taught them that at vicar school. Vicar improv: *now Geoffrey you have 2 minutes to consider the place of the cracker joke in God's plan*. But it must have been a strain, for a clever guy like him to spend his life encouraging others to believe the impossible – in fact worse than that, it wasn't an abstract impossible, it was a myriad of quite specific impossibilities – without ever betraying a doubt. Another thing they must teach you at vicar school was to be circumspect about the people you confided in. Geoffrey's public discourse proclaimed there was sense to grief and dignity to misery, and the sheer grinding discipline of it all – of never being able to drop your guard – would have crushed a lesser man. Because the thing was, for all his mastery of the concessive clause, for all his ponderous circumlocutions, his larding with conjunctions, his insulating layers of example and hypothesis, he was one of the most emotional blokes Martin had ever met. His cheeks flushed, his eyes filled, ten times a day. Anything might touch him, everything was raw; his neck would fall between his shoulders and his hands would grow slack as he puzzled at suicide bombings, homelessness, or a parishioner's harsh remark about bringing in Romanians for the berry picking. There was one obvious reason why he so postponed the full stop: daily life had no satisfied amen, did it?

This year, at least, and perhaps for the very reason of Julia's absence, there was no blazing row after midnight mass. A plate of warm mince pies appeared, the gift of a parishioner, their lids deliciously askew as only homemade pies could be, leaking sticky mincemeat; they ate and stared wordlessly, gratefully at the tidy spruce Christmas tree with its many-coloured lights and ageing, familiar decorations. Julia's mother Dorothy took pains to impose cool, non-committal colour schemes throughout the vicarage, with nothing stronger than forest green, and you knew that anything which fell outside that spectrum had to be a gift. When it came to decorating the tree, however, it was all misrule: red, gold, blue, emerald, anything went anywhere, and multicoloured tinsel was admitted. She even allowed the overhead lighting to be switched off for the festive season, in order to appreciate the sparkle and the glow. Only the vicar and his wife were living here, but the seating was disproportionately generous and arranged to accommodate constant visitors. Now, the day over, the empty chairs somehow got in the way. This was a busy time of year for a priest. As Dorothy quit the room for bed, she drew attention to her husband's lazy eye; you could tell that he needed a rest, she said, because the lid had dropped like a playhouse curtain. It was a heavy hint that Martin should leave him be and let him go to bed, but Martin didn't buy that. Geoffrey happened to have one eye that showed the hurt more, that was all, and if his hurt eye was looking especially hurt tonight, it was because he wanted to talk something out. The two of them sat up with a bottle of single malt, a sad pair, propping each other up, and wanting to talk about Julia. Although Martin was sure that when the vicar of Great Chapham had invited his son-in-law for Christmas *to support him and Dorothy*, what he had meant was, he didn't think that Martin should be alone. He knew this trick, and used it all the time professionally himself: if you had a pupil who was going off the rails, you gave them a responsibility, something or someone to take care of. *Look after us*, was what Geoffrey had seemed to say, meaning, *take care of yourself, Martin*. It was a double bluff, but who could say that it felt wrong?

'I know it's early days yet,' said Geoffrey, 'but you do know... if you were to find somebody else, we'd understand. Both of us, Dorothy and I.'

Martin balked, remembering what Shannon Matthews had told the kids up in the library: *Mr Harper ought to get married again.* Was this a general expectation now? All he could tell his father-in-law was, 'I can't imagine.'

Geoffrey was tired but the patter set off fluent as ever. He asked about school, and Martin told him he was going to make the Pompeii trip again in the Easter holidays.

The two men shared their weariness, eyes fixed on the tree; and as the shadow of their silence lengthened, Martin spoke inwardly to his wife.

*We'll go to Italy.*

After a while, tilting his empty crystal glass, her father said, 'Insofar as I can tell, it makes no difference that she was adopted. I can't imagine feeling worse. And I know it's the same for her mother.' He fished a handkerchief from his pocket and used it to polish his rimless glasses, which was a way of avoiding Martin's gaze. 'Dorothy still feels she needs a place to go. That's what's difficult for her. She's one of those who need a grave to visit. For my part… I've lost my daughter now. We won't meet on this earth.'

'I'm sorry. I didn't mean to hurt her.'

'I know that.' His puddle eyes were confirmation. Last year, Julia's mother had been stung that there was no burial in the churchyard. She suspected Martin of some caprice, some snub to keep her from her daughter. There had been, if not a row, an awkward falling-out.

'I have cast the ashes now, Geoffrey. I know I should have told you, but it was something I needed to do alone. I went up to Burnham, there's a field there by the river, where we used to walk.' He couldn't tell Geoffrey that this had been a righting of wrongs, the counterweight to the church funeral, where he hadn't known or even understood the hymns, and the Archdeacon's eulogy described someone he hadn't recognised – a woman far too serene to be beautiful.

Geoffrey said, 'We would have come, if you'd wished it, of course.'

'Yes. But it would have turned into something else.'

'A ritual? Or more properly, a rite.'

'Mm. Something public.'

'Something shared.' Martin pondered: shared, like this hideous Christmas tree?

'Sometimes I wonder, would it be any different if we'd had a child,' he said.

'Different, yes, but not easier.' Geoffrey spoke awkwardly; this was not the fusty modal melody he sang in church, which damn well should be tuneful because it was entirely scripted. This was uneven, almost rasping. 'She was happy with you, Martin. Much happier with you than she was with us. I have to thank you for that. Of course, she chose you, you see. Whereas she never let us forget that she wouldn't have chosen us. We chose her.'

'That told her she was special, surely.'

'When she was a teenager, she used to say, *you picked me from a catalogue*. Julia felt she'd been the object of a transaction, do you see? If ever we had a difference, or had to exercise what used to be called discipline. Training, you could say. The simplest thing, not to drop litter, doing your own laundry. Anything that irked her. *You picked me from a catalogue, but now you're cross because you can't just send me back.*'

'I quite like wilful kids.'

'Me too.' Geoffrey positively glistened now, and his smile was broad.

'At least they have the energy to want. Which means you can try to make sure they harness that want to something good. But don't forget, I only knew Julia when she was quite grown up. Didn't drop litter, great with laundry. You and Dorothy saw her through the tough bit, Geoffrey, and you did a great job.'

Was it the scotch, or the season, or the tiredness? Martin had never disliked his father in law, although they had nothing much in common. But at that moment he realised in a surge that he really, really loved the guy, and the thought warmed through him, liquid, magical. Another thought was forming, here at the dark of the year; and before he had shaped a statement, it welled up as question in his mind: what should he do for Wendy? Then the statements came. Because he could do something positive, to help her.

'Geoffrey,' he said, 'We were wondering about fostering someone.'

'I know.'

'No, now, I mean. I have a student who really does need help, and I'm wondering if I can maybe arrange something. '

'How old is he?'

'She's seventeen.'

Geoffrey let out a breath fit to extinguish every candle on Jesus' birthday cake.

'No, Martin,' he said, kindly, 'You can't. In the first place she's too old. Also, the mechanics would be impossible to work out. And Martin, it's not just that you can't. You mustn't try. She's your pupil. People wouldn't understand.'

'You would.'

'*I* would. I know you. But you're a man.'

*Sunday December 26*

THE FLITCH had kept its stone flags and must surely have a proper, old, cool cellar; the ale was always good. It was a favourite with Martin on his visits. Nowhere could be less like the vicarage. On every side you were jostled by dark oak beams, and irregular plaster lozenges painted ox blood red and flaking at the edges; there must be dust about the inglenook, there must be cobwebs in the crooked joints, and yet Dorothy always seemed delighted to find herself there. The sweet dry wood smoke irritated the throat and enchanted the nose in equal measure. Perhaps she found the pub exotic in its quaintness. Martin and Dorothy seated themselves behind a scored and venerable table which a card proclaimed *reserved*, ready for her treat of someone else's cooking Boxing Day lunch, while Geoffrey headed for the bar. He was out of his dog-collar now after the morning's service, and swaddled in a thick hand-knitted sweater over jeans. The pub was full of diners. He waited, under incongruous mistletoe, then turned to talk to someone next to him, a younger man whom Martin dimly recognised and who looked across to their table and smiled.

He was an odd-looking chap, about Martin's age, quite striking; he had the sort of face you'd remember, the sort of face you'd look at twice because you couldn't quite believe that it was real. A massive, dark head, bizarrely square from the front, features almost symmetrical; bulging forehead and low fleshy brow, heavy black-rimmed glasses – retro-chic – wide, downturned mouth, and a thumbprint cleft in his darkening chin. He turned to talk to the barman, and sideways on, you had to marvel at his cartoon nose, which was unfeasibly upturned, yet chiselled, almost trumpet-shaped; and you realised that the slicked-back hair, which drew receding arches on his forehead, was actually scraped into a tiny ponytail. He was heavy, solid looking, stiff, and held his arm awkwardly across his chest. It looked as though he worked out; the black lightweight roll-neck under the tight-fitting v neck sweater showed that off. Maybe this was ski gear, Martin wouldn't know. When Julia's dad was served, the man helped him carry drinks and menus over to their table. On seeing him approach, Dorothy let out a surprised 'Bless me!'

'You remember Timmy, don't you?' said Geoffrey, now they were looming over the table. And to Martin: 'Tim was one of Julia's friends, way back. They were at school together.'

The man smiled at Julia's mother, and held out a massive hand. 'Timothy,' he said. 'Timothy Slipman. And you're Martin. We spoke on the telephone quite recently.'

There were two speech-strands going on now. At the table, the exclamations, Timothy visiting his parents, how long must it have been, *you were only a boy, yes, another classicist, what a coincidence, coincidence upon coincidence, two classics teachers from the same school, and that was all down to the excellent Miss Finch, yes, such an inspiring woman*, and *now here's a third, Martin*, and where they met and how they met and conferences and such and whatever happened to Timothy's magnum opus, and not to trust the internet. But the over-writing, the urgent, of-the-moment palimpsest for Martin, was this: *I ask you, Julia, why did you never once mention that you two had been at school together, had grown up in the same village, had tested each other on your conjugations?* The babble lulled as Slipman remembered to tell Julia's parents, he was so sorry to hear about their daughter.

Martin grasped for her now. *My wife. You, Julia.*

*What do you prefer, I used to say, to conjugate or to decline?*

*To conjugate, every time, you used to answer.*

*Monday December 27*

IT WAS THE DREAM of a strange bed. Martin was glad to be out of it, but drawn back to remember it. It took a while to come round, which he did in a measured way, as one who checks his limbs after an accident.

'It was you.'

He didn't dream *about* his wife – he had dreamed that he *was* her, lying in a place that smelled of crushed stems and wet leaves. The last, most vivid moment of the dream was a numb scraping feeling; his knee was being grazed against something hard or dry; it hurt, rasped, and he knew he was sobering up, and he/she said '*I've had you now, you're done with. You're dumped,*' and slid off the hard stone ... which was a bed... Which was a tombstone in her father's churchyard. The weight on him/her was Timothy Slipman, but he was much, much younger, with a full head of lank brown hair which fell down over his eyes in dark stripes next to the massive bosses of the forehead. The waking Martin knew that he had never seen Slipman as a young man, but felt sure that this was what he looked like. He wasn't wearing glasses then; he probably didn't. In the dream, Martin/Julia felt faintly bored now, and proud to be the one who was walking away. He/she was thinking, 'I can take this or leave it.' Too much store was set by all this, that's what he/she thought, and here was the proof: to have sex with a person you disliked, in a place where you shouldn't do it, then walk away. Just walk away.

Martin roused to a sense of where he was, his in-laws' chaste spare room with its chintz curtains, all acid pastel sprigs. He reached to touch his left knee, where he could feel a bruise and recalled a clumsy leave-taking from behind the table in the pub yesterday.

*Was it you, Julia, come to me to answer my question? Or was it my imagining?*

As the wintry daylight fumbled its way into the room, his rational self took over. *Whether you loved him or you hated him – and I think you hated him – he mattered, and you had to bury that... He troubled you, and now he's come to trouble me.*

*Tuesday December 28*

HOME. MARTIN'S FIRST MORNING back was spent in bed, reading. To read by day was a luxury, and now, a way of sheltering. He learned that after the Romans departed, the Britons built their turf huts right on top of the crumbling country villas which nobody left had the skill to maintain. That was the sort of find he customarily shared with his wife. *Imagine, Julia, what this might have looked like – a hairy equivalent of Catsea, with its strange architectural add-ons and quasi-classical features, as they call them, its army of cowboy builders and home improvers. They have this expression, don't they, retro-fitting; that's neat, because the word describes itself, the vernacular with a classy bit of Latin stapled on.*

He was forced downstairs to switch the heating back on. It had timed out and the whole room had descended into a chill which he didn't notice until the very bones of his nose began to ache. Lunch was a mis-shapen offering in cling film, from Dorothy's kitchen, which fell into separate items when he warmed it in the microwave, but tasted good. In the afternoon, he went up to the study. It was starting to look untidy, because so many dumped and forgotten objects had accumulated there since half term, including a bag with his unused gym kit, and now Christmas gifts in transit for the charity shop.

He was looking for something quite specific, a particularly clear street plan of ancient Pompeii, which he wanted to scan and send to Amy, who was putting together a booklet for the trip. But he was searching for his wife at the same time, tracing her handwriting on the labels, investigating her absurdly tidy filing, smiling as he ran his finger over one tab, then the next. The alphabet led him to a file marked miscellaneous, and it struck Martin that this was out of character, because his Julia could find a category for most things; so he had to see for himself what, in her world, this miscellaneous might be.

It was a postcard, still in its Italian-stamped envelope, addressed to Julia at school. It showed in close-up the little bronze statue in the Tuscan atrium, which gave the House of the Faun its modern name, and made it one of the most visited sites of Pompeii. *Here I am again, hoping you are feeling better.* Signed *Tim*, *x*, in an almost childish, oafish hand. Martin's mind rocked and swung and struggled to find level ground. When? The postmark was illegible. After her accident? How did he know she'd had an accident? Or was it from long before that? She had kept it. And then he thought, a post card though, how quaint. And then he thought, an email? Did he ever send you an email? But he was afraid to look. A stupor claimed him for the rest of the day.

*Do you remember, on the road which snakes up the side of the volcano, those ghastly pleasure palaces? Quite true to the Roman spirit, in their way. White columns, blinding statuary, sun beds, fountains, outside lights, and frozen, giant beasts beside the pools? A great big plastic dare.*

*I wait for you to inhabit me again. Afraid you will, afraid you won't.*


*Wednesday December 29*

IN THE ANCIENT WORLD, dreams might foretell the future. For Martin, they had long become a distorted reconstruction of the past, and now in the lonely trough between Christmas and New Year – the anniversary of Julia's death – they were turning into grotesque riffs on every fear he had ever had about her.

In one dream, the doorbell rang in Julia's old flat in Hanningford village. Martin went to the door. He'd always liked that door, solid, Edwardian, with two half lights of leaded glass. Behind the glass there was a heavy outline. It was Slipman, a grown man, with slick hair tied back, in running gear and trainers from a jog, saying he was just passing by and could he have a minute. Martin didn't want to let him in, and searched for a reason not to. But he had taken up an armchair in the sitting room, in the bay of the window, with the light behind him, which meant his features were a blur. Martin and Julia sat side by side on the sofa opposite.

In fact, Martin didn't remember the furniture arranged like that, and if this detail was something he had imagined, then surely none of it was true.

In Martin's dream Slipman had flattened to two dimensions, yet somehow this was more disturbing than the real man in the pub the other day. The greyness was curdled but stark at the same time, silhouetted against the white light at the window, and both Martin and Julia were uneasy. Slipman spoke very quietly and sat immobile with his knees together, and his hands in his lap. Intent. He said... what did he say exactly? Something like: 'I have to tell you, Julia, you're making a terrible mistake. As a friend, I have to tell you.' Then: 'No good will come of this. You mustn't marry him. He's not right for you.'

Awake and safe in his own bed, Martin struggled to remember Julia's answer, but he did remember how Slipman had listed his reasons. At first, they were vague and trite – he'll never make you happy, he doesn't understand you; but the longer he spoke, the more his observations sharpened... he became more venomous, more penetrating... The things he said... *Some of them were true, Julia.*

'He's a sniper, not a fighter.'

'He lacks ambition.'

'You can't rely on him, he fears responsibility, so don't expect he'll give you children.'

'He's a coward. He's all talk. He's weak, weak, weak. He's not your equal, and he knows it. He'll always be the one who leans on you. He's a child himself, he can't make space for anybody else.'

Then Julia spoke, very distinctly, with that slight curl of her lip: 'I want sex. But I need love. If I can't have both, then I'll have neither.'

And Slipman said: 'I can make you come until your whole body cries. He'll fall back. He'll slump. He'll abandon you when you most need him. Believe me, he'll walk away.'

Julia said, 'So be it.'

Then Slipman's dark head shook, because he knew that he was beaten.

The next thing, in this dream, Timothy Slipman was nowhere to be seen, and Martin lay with his wife in the warmth of this very bed, the bed they'd bought together for this their marital home, and her whole body gripped him in the tightest of embraces, and he felt her as he used to do, and he was full of joy, and his eyes were closed on inner brightness, because now he was in possession of everything he had ever wanted; because he had won her, and he heard her say, 'Martin, I want no-one else, whatever happens, know I'll always love you.'

It was his love-starved brain. The Julia who allowed Timothy Slipman to lecture from the armchair was unlike the Julia he knew, too terse, too passive. But the Julia who only seconds ago had accepted all his fears tied in a knot, and loosened that knot by her love – that was the Julia he needed now, and who, surely, might stay near at hand.

YET SHE ELUDED HIM. The more he said, and the more he raved, as he ranged from room to room, the further she seemed to have retreated, and his attempts to re-kindle that last warm visitation grew feebler. Thin light did no more than seep into the house as the year expired, and since nothing had colour now, a dull pall of dust about the house was tolerated. Martin was pinned down by the weight of time. Rubbish piled against the door in the kitchen, sorted for recycling but not put out.

*Thursday December 30*

SPONSOR A CHILD. Here she was again, bright and shiny on the telephone table, the universal orphan, overseas, smiling, innocent; her intent was not reproachful, and yet Martin took it badly. It was kind of Julia's dad to ring him on the morning of this, the anniversary of Julia's death. He wouldn't have called Geoffrey, but it was good to hear his voice, like a warm bath that you didn't realise you needed. He cared for Martin, that was what it was. When Geoffrey Chamberlain cared, he always did something. That's why he's a better man than I am, thought Martin. Martin asked after Dorothy, and Geoffrey said, 'It's a hard time for her.'

They talked a bit about books and all the TV spin-offs this Christmas, and picked over Angus Strang's latest offering on Saturnalia, speculating why the media had this current fascination for the Romans. Was it political, the moral to be drawn from tales of empire? And that flush of classics in the world of education, was it truly training for the brain as Martin used to like to think, or did it reflect nostalgia for the norms of public school, no more strategic than a taste for sponge puddings? Then Geoffrey said, 'I wonder, how has your young student fared this Christmas? I've prayed for her.' Martin had to tell him he had no idea, and his father-in-law replied quickly, 'No, no, of course, why would you have?' Geoffrey was checking that he hadn't acted on his rash impulse to look after Wendy. Martin thought, he's worried for me, but he doesn't need to be. It shocked him to think how quickly he had forgotten his pupil, though, and all because of Slipman and the dreams and this torment which was blotting out everything real. *It is, Julia. It's stamping everything with black, black, black. Filthying everything.* So the next thing Martin said – without thinking and without connection – was 'I don't like that Slipman guy.' It was another of his blurtings out. Incongruous, but it was true. And what did Julia's dad say? He said, 'Neither did I.' And he didn't miss a beat.

Martin told him Julia had never mentioned that she'd known Slipman at school, and that it seemed strange to him.

'Don't let it trouble you, Martin. You hardly knew him.'

'All the more reason.'

He fell silent. Martin said, 'I think Julia knew him very well indeed.'

'Let her go, Martin. She's at peace.'

'I'm not. You do understand that, don't you? I'm not at peace.'

More silence. So Martin pressed him: 'Geoffrey, why did you dislike him?'

'Do *you* have a reason?'

'Work. He's caused me a bit of grief at work. So what was he like?'

'He was quite a lot older than her. They went to the same school, it's true, but they barely overlapped.'

'They went out together.'

'Not officially. But in the holidays, when she came back from university, he was always... hovering. But look, I didn't really know him.'

'So was it just your instinct? Because I can tell you, it's definitely mine.'

When Geoffrey sighed, it was the sigh of a naturally candid man who didn't like to deal out dirt.

'Perhaps it was coincidence... Look, how do you know when someone really loves you? Hm?'. Martin recognised a closed question by its tune, and had no answer. 'I'll tell you how. When they've passed by, they leave a shine on you. I just noticed that whenever Timmy Slipman passed by, he seemed to cast a shadow.'

MARTIN KEPT THINKING about this long afterwards. *Did I leave a shine on you? I mean, did I always?*

*I didn't know then what losing was. First I lost you to pain, then to the hospital, and now the warm and pulsing you has separated out to this... Dust in a bag.*

*I fear sleep now. I'm afraid that in my next dream, you'll have no love for me at all.*


HE NEEDED the next term to start. He used to think the holidays were worth thousands on his salary – the freedom to read and play guitar and be with Julia. But something worse than loneliness was gnawing at him now. He tried to fix on that last flood of light, and the feeling of the two of them fused again, but it won't hold. Instead, Tim Slipman kept coming back to his mind's eye. He turned over all the things the strange-looking man had said in the dreams, and worse, the apparently innocent phrases he had uttered for real, in the Flitch at Great Chapham on Boxing Day.

Sick of his own company, and knowing he was doing himself no good, at last Martin forced himself to stir. There was nowhere he really wanted to go, but with nothing much in the fridge and a second bank holiday imminent, it was logical to make a visit to the supermarket. He shaved and dressed so as to be fit to be seen, which occupied him for the best part of an hour; he had to clean the village mud off his boots, then he noticed that the same matt grey-brown clay had caked the hems of his favoured jeans, which sent him searching for a fresh pair, in the suitcase he had abandoned in the unheated spare room. It was about time he dealt with that bag. It would be a bad thing to start the new year with clothes unpacked. Laundry was overdue. He should change the bed linen. On his return he would attend to these jobs. He would snap out of it. *Sort himself out,* as Paddy would say.

The trip to the supermarket surprised him: he had forgotten what these places were like in the run up to New Year's Eve. He drove to the most up-market store around, the nearest thing to a cathedral that this part of the estuary could offer: a handsome, modern building, with pale floor tiles, ample warm lighting, glossy blond wood and even modern textile hangings in its coffee shop. Normally, he liked the place for its calmness, but today it was impossibly busy, and extra goods had been stacked which narrowed the aisles and hampered progress. They obviously anticipated the whole town partying tonight. Some of the shoppers were purposeful and urgent in their movements, darting about to pick up objects from a list, but more were slow, and steered loaded trollies with difficulty, dazed by all the decisions of consumerism, blinking at overcrowded shelves; they, like him, had just emerged from a sort of drunken hibernation.

He stepped into a space which happened to open up by a chiller cabinet full of fresh meat, and scanned the glistening flesh, bloody steaks and ghastly chicken portions, trying to find something he might want to cook and eat. Nothing appealed. There was a man behind him, standing so close that he could hear air whistle in the stranger's nostrils, as he craned his neck to see what Martin was buying. At least, that was how it felt. This unknown man was just a random idiot. It made him realise, though. Slipman had been stalking her. All those years. He knew it now, he knew it for a fact.

*Saturday January 1*

THE PREVIOUS YEAR, New Year's Day had broken on a numb white mist as Martin struggled to comprehend that life would now go on without her. He had been locked in that mist, dazzled by its opaque brightness and troubled by the sudden two-dimensionality of a sunless world. There had been conversations on the telephone, and Geoffrey and Dorothy had come down, but he could not recall the detail of anything they said.

This year the cloud was higher, the sky was greyer, and you could see further, to the houses and the trees across the street and beyond. Martin stripped the bed and loaded the washing machine. He intended to unpack but sat at his desk, took a black pen and wrote instead:

*People say* the New Year *when they just mean the next one. But that was, truly, a new year, because it brought new ways of marking time.*

*You were well aware you should have healed by now; the surgery had been on the 19th. You were re-admitted two days after Boxing Day, Sunday 28th, with severe abdominal pain and all the concomitant misery. Going down that road again was fearsome, because it was familiar.*

*'What am I digesting?' you said, and you gripped my arm. It was some days since you had held food down. You whispered, like a mad woman: 'Martin, I'm eating myself alive.'*

*When I was a boy, hospitals used to smell like hospitals. Aggressively clean. The antiseptic clung to people's clothes and cut through everything; you might catch a whiff from the stranger next to you on the bus, and wonder – out-patient or visitor? You knew exactly where they'd been. And when you stepped into a hospital, the odour said, you are through the portal, approach with reverence, this is a serious place, here miracles may happen, but fearsome rules and rituals must be observed. The very first time I entered the glossy marble lobby at Adderhead General, I approved the absence of that smell. But by the time you were re-admitted, I had learned to long for it. I knew there may, or may not, be a stench on entering the surgical ward. It had so shocked me the first time. How could I leave my Julia living here? How could anyone work, think, sleep, lie sick alongside this? It came I think from the toilet or the sluice room, I don't know, I never wanted to investigate, but on a bad day it hit you as soon as you got inside the double doors, just where they'd fixed the hand-sanitisers. Further down into the cramped and overheated ward, it was more of a miasma. Some poor soul might have soiled themselves or used the bedpan, and the smell smeared everybody. Television screens on massive insect-jointed brackets lowered over every bed, all permanently on, it seemed, twitching, nervy. The window looked onto another wing of the flat concrete building, and reminded you that the modern entrance had been grafted on to an ugly sixties cenotaph. Flowers were banned for danger of infection. We visitors wore a common expression of embarrassed fright: where was the eye to rest? A cough ripped from the woman opposite, and she was too weakened by it, too ill-mannered or too out of love with life to cover her mouth. Crazed with dread, you snarled:* there are people here with open wounds. *Even in the quiet times the air was thick with the hum of electronics, the clink of small movements against metal, and the soughing and sighing of all those bodies. Humans whose physical needs had bloated to fill the space where personality had been; at least, that's how it looked to the observer. If I was terrified to witness it from that grey plastic chair, how were you to thrive? Apollo flared at the window, but the lights were always on, as if to say, it's not as bright as you might think.*

*Moira, the staff nurse that we liked so much, beamed a smile of recognition, and made happy welcome noises, but her eyes were shocked to see the state of you, back again. Bloods were taken. You were seen by Mr Jones. It was possible, he said, that they might need to operate again, to drain the infection. You were not on the next day's list. Nor the next. All the time I was bringing in titbits, foods I knew you liked, potted shrimps once, lime pickle, devilled eggs; they said it really didn't matter, you should try whatever tempted you; the thing you must remember, they told me, is that she can smell herself, and she can smell her wound, and she smells horrible to herself, and this makes her less inclined to eat. Wednesday morning would be the last list before New Year, and we watched the ward empty: anybody that they could discharge was gently ushered on. Waiting became our occupation. That, and scrutinising professional faces for a sign that might betray some judgement. You had a gadget to control the flow of morphine; I watched your use of it, and speculated what it meant, asked at the nursing station, was this normal, and learned nothing much; but they always took you seriously, I could see that. My ears strove to pick up signals of harmonious resolution; all my will was straining to the future. They checked you time and again for this and that. Your mood went up and down, through passing fevers, flitting pains, vile evacuations, and terrors which we loyally hid from each other. At midnight on the 31st, I sat by your side: about to watch the past become, precisely, that.*

I can't write this down. I am too ashamed.

There was no tight grip on my arm that night, just a patting hand that searched for mine. The dipping line on her forehead was back as in the classroom: that little mark which said, here's what we're going to do, get ready now for action, get ready to receive your orders.

Come here. No, here. Put your head here by mine. I love you, Martin.

I love you Julia. Our cheeks were brushing.

Where's the champagne?

Champagne?

A whisper through a half-smile: We have to make a toast.

Of course, the New Year.

Martin… This has been lovely… You're going to have to let me go, Martin.

Something I'd often heard her say. I thought, she's rambling, nothing here has been lovely, how can I let her go, this is a lame embrace, I barely have hold of her. It's another fever. I panicked. I sensed something had changed and I still can't say just what it was. A colour, an expression? But I was too close to see. Something hidden in the hollow of the hand I chafed? Something's going wrong here, and I can't fix it, but this is a hospital and someone else will know just what to do, I'll get help. And God forgive me, I left her side and went to find a nurse.

Shame on me. Shame on me.

*Monday January 3*

ON THE VERY LAST NIGHT of the Christmas holiday, he woke with a start.

It started with her tender voice on the pillow – quite distinctly, her voice. He was not mistaken. There could be no mistaking such a thing.

'Martin. I can explain. I want to tell you everything.' To hear her say his name was magical. But then she wailed at him: 'How do you expect me to forgive you? How can I forgive you, Martin? If you won't forgive me?'

When his eyes opened, they opened to pitch black. The bed was warm. He could feel the tension in her limbs beside him, hear another human breath drawn from the darkness; he was straining to make it out, sure she was there, sure she couldn't be. She had become a plus-or-minus value in these latter days. It used to be a sinking, sickening disappointment, to wake up to the loss of her. But now, her voice was clear, and he began to understand she had both a presence and a purpose.

He asked her: 'Why did Slipman write to you?'

The voice was caught by sobbing, and she said, 'See, how he still torments me! I never wanted him. I never did. And everything is his fault, all of it! All of it!' Where did her voice come from? At that moment, she was not beside him, but he didn't know where else she was. Everywhere. She filled the room.

'Julia,' he said, 'I can't forgive you all those things you never told me.'

At that, she began to rage: 'There's nothing to forgive. That man just doesn't signify. I don't need your pardon for anything that happened with Tim. And in any case, Martin, there's one much bigger thing you can't forgive. You can't forgive me for leaving you. But look, I haven't. I won't.'

They wanted to comfort each other, their arms were searching, fingers outstretched, but he could no more touch than see his wife, who seemed to fill every corner of the darkness. Then she calmed and said, 'I want there to be no space between us. I always wanted it that way.'

The next morning, Julia remained a stubborn breakfast absence, but her voice had been as full and real to him as any sound was now, the kettle or the radio.

# 7

*Friday January 7*

IN THE DAYTIME WORLD of school, the tempo of life picked up. Martin was learning to like this world better because it gave him the illusion he could act, even if it was only over trivial things. He went to Gareth Whittaker and secured the promise of funding for Wendy on the trip. Two days later, beaming, there she was in his office, Wendy with her straightforward, here and now needs. She had a form and two little photos in a poly pocket and said 'Please sir, could you sign this for my passport, to say it's a good likeness. Only please tell me it's not.' That made him laugh. He duly signed and told her, no, it wasn't a good likeness, although it was, it couldn't have been anybody else. Her hair was an odd cut at the best of times, wavy yet shaped against her head, slightly fluffed like a seventies footballer with stray bits round the neck, and on the photo it was flattened somehow, which with her long face made her whole head look like a rusty nail sticking up. 'Well, he said, what can you expect, they don't let you smile, do they?' It wasn't Wendy without a smile. So, Pompeii then…

'Also, sir, can I have time off school.' This was the matter-of-fact opener to a much more serious conversation. Her brother should be coming to trial at Chelmsford Crown Court sometime in the next couple of weeks, and she was going to have to give evidence for the defence. They ended up talking about the whole procedure. She smiled and shrugged a lot, trying to make light of things, but her eyes could not pretend, and she looked scared. Martin swung his chair round to face the computer screen and found the web page for her, which at least gave them something concrete to work on, and they agreed she ought to contact the solicitor to see a copy of the statement she'd made back in November; she was worried about what she might have said, because of course she couldn't remember, it all seemed so long ago. Martin reminded her there was a counsellor at school, and she could always talk to her. She sighed and answered yeah, the counsellor was very nice, but that was all talking about how you felt, they weren't allowed to tell you what to do. Martin suggested that when she got the statement from the solicitor, she should bring it in so that they could look at it together. Then came an accelerating stream of quite specific questions. She asked her teacher's opinion of what might get into the papers, and which papers, and what day the Echo came out, and whether you could stop people you knew from attending court. They were going to cite her mother's illness as mitigating circumstances. Martin hadn't fully appreciated how badly she had wanted to conceal all this from the other kids at school, how much she dreaded *it all coming out*, as she put it. That seemed to be upsetting her every bit as much as the prospect of her brother in the dock. Martin told her she could be very proud of what she'd done, caring for her mother, and she grinned, all flame for a moment: 'Oh I am. But I know it isn't normal. I don't like people knowing all my business.' He told her they wouldn't, that wouldn't be the focus, and just hoped that this was true. She seemed satisfied and listed on her fingers the things she now knew she had to do: one, tell the office when you have the date, two, don't panic, find out exactly where you're going, call the solicitor, bring in the statement, and – one important point of her own – work out what you're going to wear and get it ready the day before. They sat quietly for a minute, until Martin felt it was time to close this interview, so he thanked her for coming to see him.

Then she said, 'I nearly didn't.' She acknowledged it was none of her business, but he was looking tired and she reckoned maybe he wasn't well, so she'd thought twice. She said, 'I didn't want to bother you. Only I did,' and she gave a little shrug and grinned and raised the henna eyebrows in a *what-am-I-like* sort of gesture. He couldn't help smiling back. Then she added, 'Only sir if you don't mind me saying... You've gone all quiet, everybody's noticed.'

Martin said surely that was an improvement; he would have thought people would be pleased. 'Oh they are,' she said, innocently. 'But it's not you, is it?'

He told her he was in perfect health, but thanks all the same for her concern. And then she told him he should make sure he was eating properly. Oh, yes, and the counsellor was nice so long as you didn't expect miracles.

# 8

## *The Dice*

'I CAN TELL ANYBODY, any time, about you coming here. I can tell your father.'

'He's not my father.'

'Or maybe I'll tell a couple of his parishioners. That old biddy who polishes the candlesticks. She'd be interested.'

Timothy Slipman's long lank hair keeps falling in front of his eyes, and every time he flicks it back, he wrinkles his snub nose and blinks.

The sun is warming, filtered through nascent beech leaves behind them, but brazen here where Julia has been lying half naked; her pale olive skin craves the easy tan which is her mysterious, un-English birthright. Now she is sitting upright, hands clasped round her knees, feeling the cool in the air – you have to be horizontal to believe an April sun is warm. But if every girl knows you must offer yourself up to it whenever you get the chance, it matters even more for her. While they talk, she turns to present as much of her body to the sunshine as she decently can, and she's straining so as to cast the smallest shadow possible. What was Timothy Slipman ever doing here, in this hidden outer corner of the churchyard, behind the bins where they stack the fallen leaves, behind the fence, behind the blackthorn and beyond the dead tree trunk? This has always been a private place; she's never ever seen anybody here before.

'You want to do it,' he says. 'You want to be normal, don't you?'

She weighs the proposition up. He's not really her type, although her type has yet to be discovered. It makes her quiver, though, to have somebody so much older look at her like that, and then – without trying to kiss her, without ever touching her at all – to hear him say, *I'm going to have you*, in a tone of voice which meant, I know you will say yes, sooner or later. The boys in her year wouldn't talk like that. He shaves. He has a smell she hasn't smelt before, a mix of after-shave and something that must just be him.

She tells him she *is* normal, and he says, 'You're just a kid. But you are one beautiful chick.' Nobody says that word, it belongs to another time, another older world than his; but the oddness of it flatters, even while she shrugs laughter at him and tells him, no way José. She knows she is one beautiful chick. She measures his distance from her, fearing he will make a move, because if he does, she'll prove him right and show herself up as just a kid who doesn't have the first idea, and also because she really doesn't want him to lay his hand on her. He waits an age, staring her in the face; then her throat tightens as his hand goes to the zip of his jeans. He turns his back on her, and he pisses noisily against a tree.

'Maybe next time,' he says as he goes, without even turning round.

JULIA FINDS HERSELF thinking a lot about that hidden part of her body which is a she, and which is pretty noisy for a silent thing. She ought to have a name, but not a biological one like you are taught at school. Not one of the names the boys use, either. This she has a life. She purrs under the pressure of a hand. She sings and trembles like a violin. She cries for joy. She is a part of all the pain, not the seat of it, but implicated. Perhaps, one day, if ever she were satisfied, the pain would stop; because a pregnancy would stop it, everyone knows that. Not to be countenanced right now. The two of them together, Julia and her sex, wonder a lot about Tim Slipman and in what way he is attractive; because if he isn't, they wouldn't be thinking about him the way they did, would they? One night she dreams that Tim lies with her, locked as a man locks with a woman; so this is sex, she thinks, it's calm and still and an easy, comfortable feeling. He said maybe next time.


DOWN THE TWILIT LANE, the warm air is thick with the scent of honeysuckle; she treads heavily, and fast, to the drumbeat of the argument in her head. *Why should I help to clear their things away? I barely know these people, they're just strangers who happen to invade the place I live every Wednesday evening. I've got better things to do than table settings for the parish hall. Why does everyone assume I want to do the things they want to do? Why on earth would I want to join them for a talk on patchwork?* She has a million other worthwhile things to occupy her mind, homework, music, stuff to read... but she's so maddened now that reading would be impossible. They are stealing her time from her. They never take their eyes off her. They never stop enquiring about her. They are living off her. Her mother had pretended to be shocked: 'Julia, what's got into you? I hardly recognise you.' And she had screamed back, 'well I don't recognise you, but then I never did.' Thinking about it makes her start to cry again, her head aches and aches, she's hot, her hands make a fist and her arms are stiff and shaking. She knows she ought to be grateful, and she is, but she longs to be in nobody's debt. *I love her, of course I do; I just don't like her much.* She doesn't want to turn into her mother, some pastel, insipid thing, and promises herself she never will. At the side of the churchyard, she lunges through the kissing gate, so clumsily that the iron clangs before and behind, and heads for her private place, through the graves, past the compost bins, minding the thorns, and over the dead tree trunk. She drops to the ground and folds herself to earth. Here the shaking takes over, and it becomes a wild percussion; the teeth chatter, the right foot taps, the side of the arm starts thumping against a stone, bang, bang, numb, numb, *be numb, be black tomorrow, and I won't care*; she forces air through clenched teeth to beat out a long thin wire of sound, *out out out out*; she's listening to her own alien sound intently, and trying to creep inside it, so that the sound will be everything and nothing else will be. You could call it hysteria. But to feel it... it's splendid. Splendid to be taken over.

Then something – some huge physical force outside herself – hauls her back up to her feet, and she chokes with fright to be in the sudden grip of arms which pin her elbows to her sides, and to feel her face drawn against the body of some solid living thing so close she can't see it. She recognises the smell. Someone else's words, a boy's, repeated: *it's alright.* Time passes but the pressure never wavers, his hold is still and good, until all the turbulence begins to trickle out of her, the spasms end, her breathing slows, and a primal memory tells her, this is familiar. This is how it was when she was tiny, this was how her real mother soothed her, this was how she calmed her down when she was still an infant.

The secret is, you have to hold her very tight. A wholesome feeling of release washes through her now. The smell is Timmy Slipman. He has charmed her. He knows the secret. That grip has charmed her back to life and to the daylight world onto which her eyes opened again, where sun is filtering through the fresh green beech; she is suddenly lighter, glad and able to go forward. At the same time there is the clench of a mean fist deep in her belly which twists her guts about; a dull awareness: so that's what this was all about, so here it comes again, so this will be the heaviness of waiting over, ready for the sharper pain to start.

There was no scene when she got back, although she'd left the house in a terrible rage; instead her borrower mother made her chocolate and sat next to her on the bed. 'Look,' she said with a simplicity and sweetness which shook all Julia's expectations, 'You shouldn't have to go through this each month.'

THE GP WEARS that practised smile her father sometimes uses. Nothing must be seen to embarrass him, and perhaps nothing does; but that's not enough, he has to make that same effort all the time to look interested. He asks about her periods, and when she's answered his questions, he says, 'Rather too frequent then, heavy and very painful,' and writes something down. Julia is surprised to hear her mother's observations. She tells the Doctor that her daughter is basically a sweet-natured girl but these days she's up and down, there are times when she will argue black is white. Which is normal for a teenager, but not like this, the way she works herself into frenzy over nothing; her whole body shakes, and – she discovers – it's upsetting for everybody.

Apparently it's the discomfort and the pain which drive her mad. Julia wonders: why didn't she say any of this to me, before we came? The vicar's wife, who's never good at sticking to the point, strays into reminiscence: when Julia was a toddler she had such temper tantrums, the only thing that calmed her was to hold her tight. She describes the rigid child in her arms. The GP nods and makes no comment, as if that's all incidental. The prescription pad is under his hand. When he says, 'I think we can put you on the pill, with your mother's agreement,' he glances at her mother, who smiles, and actually looks grateful. This is about as confusing an outcome as the girl can imagine. She doesn't really hear much else, as he moves on to the grey stuff, the instructions, the warnings, the stuff a doctor has to say. Her mum is listening on her behalf, and nodding.

Julia leaves the room thinking, *so, the vicar's daughter's on the pill,* and wondering what that might mean.

A FRIDAY NIGHT. Her mum has said why not invite John over for supper on Fridays, which was nice of her in a way because on Fridays she goes to badminton and dad is usually busy, so they get some time alone in front of the TV. They've been going out for weeks now, if you can call it going out, when there's nowhere much to go except the youth group; John walks her the fifty yards back to the vicarage and kisses her at the gate, and goes no further; and they sit together on the school bus. This particular Friday, her dad is at a meeting of the Parish Council, and there's nobody home. They've half-watched TV, starting with *Look East*, through *Top of the Pops* and beyond, and now there's only rubbish, because it's summer schedules; their eyes have quit the screen completely. Jagged background music and intermittent shouting from the set annoy, but not enough to make them turn it off; besides, their hands are busy. Eyes closed, their world is touch, and the throb of twin bloods pumping. If you are kissing, you don't have to worry how you look. Soon they are in each other's pants – this has happened the last couple of times, it's going to become usual, she knows – and that secret part of her is singing, singing, and wanting something more. Abruptly – and this is today's new step – he takes his hand away from her, sits up, and curls damp fingers over hers, around the silky-thin skin of his penis. She's surprised enough to open her eyes and look at him, wondering what to do. He pauses, looks her in the eye – neither of them will look down at the hot thing in their hands – that's one thing which will not happen – and tells her, 'I love you.' Julia replies, 'I love you.' Obviously, she must. Or this would not be happening. They kiss and she is happy, grown up, real. The closing theme music says they have another forty minutes before anybody will come home, and John says, 'Can we go upstairs?' She hadn't envisaged this, and she has no immediate answer. He says, 'I won't… you know. I'll be sensible.' Which sounds lame. But then he *is* sensible, a good Christian boy, and this is why her parents like him. A kind and thoughtful boy, and this is why she likes him. She has just discovered that she loves John, so she must behave as one who loves, and bare herself as one who's loved, and be fearless. He will see her bedroom now. Is it OK? She hasn't tidied up. There are still things left from this morning. Has she left clothes on the floor, is her concealer on display? She can't remember; but there is definitely all that junk from when she was little; her stomach lurches at the thought of a doll seated with arms outstretched in one corner. If he notices, she'll have to say, sorry but that's my mum's idea, and just hope he likes the Michael Jackson poster. No, love will make her bigger than all this. She rises from the sofa and extends her hand to pull him up. He is gorgeous, after all; those blue eyes are looking dreamier than ever now, he looks so vulnerable; her eyes flit to the long bare neck above his tee shirt.

She leads the way. Just as they approach the bedroom door, she has a brainwave: if she turns on the bedside lamp, instead of the overhead light, he might not see the doll, or anything else much. So this is what she does. He takes his tee shirt off, and starts to undress her, then off come his jeans, then they are on the bed and she learns that touch is not just about the fingers, but the skin, and that outwardly a body is, all, skin. They rock from side to side and she is bright with extraordinary pleasure; they share a quiet laughter, grinning. They are like two otters playing, rolling in the sea; they roll right over, once, twice, then suddenly he stops stock still. She sits up, terrified: did he hear a noise? Has somebody come back?

His face is distorted in a terrible grimace. Is he in pain? She hardly knows him, stares and wonders: can John's jaw really be that shape? It hasn't looked so awkward before. Has she hurt him somehow, or is he ill? His eyes dart to the bedside table, and back to her.

'How long?' he says. 'How long have you been on the pill?'

Underneath the lamp, the brittle, weightless blister pack is in full illumination. Her mouth is dry as cotton wool, and she starts to explain: 'No, it isn't that.'

'I never believed him. But he was right, wasn't he?' The boy is close to tears, his voice even more grotesque than his face.

'Who?'

'Tim Slipman. He told me. He said... what you were like. I never believed him.'

'*What* did he say?' She is bewildered, her voice a twisting skein.

'About you in the churchyard. '

She is all protestation and her *no* spirals upwards and far away. This is impossibly wrong, it can't be happening, none of this was ever meant to be. It takes seconds for the fair-haired John to gather up his things, to dress, and disappear. She cries, and rocks, and rocking becomes trembling, while downstairs the television rages to itself.

BY THE TIME her mum gets back, though, she is lying calm and still in the dark, and slowly, dully, piecing it together. Why did John run away? Because he thought she slept around? Or because he was scared? *Now he knows I'm on the pill, he's going to need a good excuse not to have sex with me. That's why. Most boys would have been delighted.* John was the sort of match her borrowed parents had in mind, a good match for a nice girl. *But I'm not their child; I'm not a nice girl, I'm another mother's child. I'm of another blood.* She has just told John she loved him and for a minute thought she did, but it wasn't true. Maybe it could have been anybody. Maybe she wanted him to touch her more: she wanted the shocking things to go on happening, to push all the doors open, one after another. Maybe it could have been anyone. The truth is she's been thinking about Tim Slipman ever since he turned his back on her; Tim's the one she had the dream about. He's the one on her wavelength, who knows her best. He's the one who held her fast and made her still. If she was lying motionless now, it's because she had conjured him in her imagination. Tim's grip is unwavering. He has a musky smell she wants to smell again. Tim knows her. *He has told me, he will have me, maybe next time, and I want him to, because I know he's bad, and so am I.*

She reasons it this way: the main argument for not actually having sex is not to bring unwanted children into the world. She's not so stupid as to want to leave school and end up with no qualifications and no job. But she doesn't have to worry about that now. The mother who gave birth to her is growing more real by the day, unknown and yet familiar. If Julia went to Tim Slipman tomorrow, he would look at her and say, 'You belong to me now,' and hold her gaze every bit as firmly as he'd held her arms, and that certainty in his look would make her want to do it. To step outside herself. To know something her parents couldn't guess, to carve her own privacy where no busybody could go looking for it.

Yesterday, she had been sure I wouldn't. But today she thought she might.

*IF I CAN'T HAVE a nice boy, I'll have a bad one.* It felt like a rebellion, but if so, it was pretty lame, because Julia never wanted anyone to find out. Although at school they did. It felt inevitable, something she had to do. Maybe she only started to have sex with Tim Slipman because she could. Something made her do bad things.

By the end of the summer holidays she is grown used to it. He'll be off to Exeter in October, and the certainty creeps up on her that she won't miss him. Not him as a person. It made her feel more real, for a day, to let him have her; she still liked the badness of him, but not the way he hovered round the vicarage and smarmed up to her parents and asked her dad fake questions on the Vulgate Bible. And she still likes the sex, she likes it, in the warmth of an afternoon, to be covered and uncovered by a lick of air, a breeze. But the weekend after results, there's a big party at his parents' house, and everybody has too much to drink, especially her; her cheeks are numb and tight, that's how far gone she is, but even then she knows, he's making sure that everybody sees just where they're going and what they're going to do, as he leads her tottering by the wrist down to the bottom of the garden, with everybody cheering behind them. They do it on the grass in the paddock, and she freaks because she suddenly gets this idea, where there is grass, there must be grass snakes.

The next day she sobers up with just one thought: he thinks he has the upper hand. Well, she can take the sex or leave it. It matters more to him – much more. She can walk away from all this right now. Step out of the summer heat, into the shade. Go back to school, get her A levels, get on with her life. It will all be easier when he's gone.

She practises seeing Tim Slipman as an object. Now she needs to drink before they do it, to get outside herself; she needs not to look too much at him, because she hadn't ever found him an attractive boy in any way – muscular and stocky, not her type. But he has this scent about him which really turns her on. Plus if she asks him, he will hold her boa-constrictor tight, and she *wants* that. So the day comes when she knows for certain it will be the very last time, and she knows exactly what she's going to say; she gets a bottle of cider and gulps it down as best she can, in between practising her lines. Then when it happens it's pretty horrible really but she doesn't care because it's worth it to tell him: *Fuck this and fuck you, I've had you now, you're done with. You're dumped.* Worth it to prove to herself that she could use him, then just turn her back on him and walk away. Which she does. She takes a long detour right round the lane, circling the church, and by the time she's within sight of home, the zigzag has become a good straight line. Or so she tells herself.

TIMOTHY SLIPMAN became part of the past.

Julia learned from her mother, who got it straight from Marjory Slipman on the bus, that Timmy had graduated with an upper second. 'You used to be fond of him. It was a shame you two lost touch.' 'We didn't lose touch,' she said. 'I dumped him.' That didn't stop him calling round every vacation for a year. He'd plonked himself next to her at the village panto, invited her to parties with the mates from his year group, and that first summer he had even turned up at the vicarage again, because, he told them all, he knew she'd be making her university applications soon, and maybe he could help out with advice.

'He still hasn't found the right girl. None of them seem to last long.'

'He's a cradle-snatcher, Mum. He likes to stick with the fifth form.'

'Marjory says he's never brought anybody home.'

'That's because they're all under age.' It was a regular topic of reunion gossip now his friends had all left school and gone away to study. All sightings were reported.

'From university, I mean,' said her mother. 'You never bring anybody home, either.'

'Funny thing, Mum, but nobody wants to spend a week with the vicar.' She squeezed her mother's shoulder and brushed a kiss. She meant well, God bless her.

Julia wasn't short of boyfriends, and they had all been in a different league from Timothy Slipman, with his great bossed forehead and his greasy hair. That summer she had met him in her secret place at the back of the churchyard was now three years past, and safely filed under the category *A Phase,* a necessary working out of immaturity. Like being horrible to her poor old mum. She had been just... pupating. An ugly thing in every way. Now at last her wings were full and colourful and caught the sun; she could flit about wherever she pleased. Whereas Timothy had barely developed, if the village rumours of his love life were anything to go by.

'Well, anyway, Marjory asked me to tell you, he'll be getting together with all the old gang from school this Saturday in the Half Moon.'

'Thanks, Mum.' *His* gang, that would be. Nothing would drive her there.

IT WAS ALMOST two years before she saw him again, and that was by chance. It was the Easter vacation of her final year, close to the start of term and the submission date for her dissertation. The weather had been good; it was that heady season when warmth coaxed every forgotten scent out into the open, so that even objects, a cardboard box, a handbag, took on new life. She breathed in the library odour of wood and leather, in the farthest corner of the room, with her back to the wall. It was her favourite seat: she only had to lift her head to survey all the comings and goings. The clamour on the page – the passions and poisonings of the Republic – was all the more exciting for the surrounding coolness of library routines. Julia commuted easily between these two distant worlds.

A group of visitors hummed through the double doors, all wearing large plastic tags on lanyards, and evidently on a guided tour. She recognised him by a movement, something in his walk that was familiar, and was shocked to find herself alert, as if she *wanted* it to be Tim Slipman. The style of dress was similar – dark colours and drainpipe trousers, with the addition of a shaggy afghan coat – but this man's dark hair was scraped back into a pigtail. A tidy sort of hippy. Quite a throwback. The guide waved a hand, and the whole group turned obediently to gaze across the library in Julia's direction. At that point there was no mistaking him, with his full, wide forehead and his constant smile. He seemed not to notice her, as if she had disappeared into the book-lined wall. She stared outwards, daring him to action. The positive click of a date-stamp tapped, heel-toe, and the delegates left.

Her thoughts scattered. She had been so near to finishing her task, excited by the pressure of closing in, sure she would complete the final draft that day, read it through the next, and submit. Had Slipman failed to recognise her? Or just chosen not to acknowledge her? Was it his way of saying, *I'm over you*? Of course, it shouldn't matter either way. Julia made a deal with herself: she'd find out what the group was, and what he was doing here, just to satisfy her own curiosity, then get back to her desk. She allowed herself to go down to the entrance hall and ask at reception. There were often conferences going on during the vacation. This one was a Symposium on the Golden Age, it had started that morning and they had one more day to go. It would be up on the board again tomorrow. They were staying on campus. Having settled this, she went back to her post in the library and wrote straight through the afternoon, following the plan easily and faithfully, until she reached the very end of the conclusion.

Her flatmates weren't up for going out. Jen was chasing a deadline too, but had spent most of the afternoon arguing her way through a band practice, and now she was way behind and in too much of a stew. Cassie had to work her shift in the Union. 'Come on anyway,' she said, 'I'll stand you a drink. There's bound to be somebody there. You can prop up the bar and keep me company. So she did. The Union bar was a dingy, sticky, noisy place, where a steady thudding bass bullied every conversation; once you'd had a couple of drinks, it tried its best to parasitise your brain. There had been a sudden, ordinary rush on the bar, a crush at her back, and a body pressed behind her, which then elbowed its way to her left side; the man's forearm was bare and covered in ripples of dark hair; his brown fist held a folded ten-pound note almost in her face, and she caught the scent she had never been able to recall, appetising, spiced, narcotic. Potent. Timothy Slipman. She might have made no movement, but instead turned around and stared straight at him for the second time that day. Coldly, deliberately, she summoned an insolence to equal his, on that first warm day in the churchyard, when she'd been just a kid.

But once it began to unravel, it unravelled fast. She asked what was he doing here? And he said, down for the Symposium. No, she said, I mean the Union Bar, why drink here of all places? Now that you're a grown-up? He made no answer, except to say that he'd completely forgotten she'd been here, and what was she doing? Celebrating. Just finished my dissertation. On? Poison. Poison in Roman life and literature. He'd love to read it. Some other time. What was she drinking? House red. Christ, he said, we can do better than that, but not here, come on, come with me, I won't bite, let me at least buy you a drink. She didn't say yes, she didn't say no, just stared at the horizontal wrinkles between his eyes, thinking, I *will* say no, and breathing in that scent again, and remembering how good it could feel to be held fast. Look, he said, I can see you're not sure. Let's leave it up to these. Then he brought out of his pocket two small objects and placed them on the bar; two irregular cubes inscribed with whorls, the concentric circles of Roman gaming dice. She wanted to know, was this real bone, the real thing, or a replica? Odd you come with me, he answered, even I leave you here. She said she'd throw, then, and scooped them up. A six and a one. They left the bar and walked the short distance into town, shared a bottle of Chianti, and when he said, Christ Julia you are one beautiful woman, and cupped the back of her head with one hand, she told him straight he was mistaken. Then he laid his hands on her shoulders, and his fingers flexed and kneaded; we can stop any time, he said, looking grave and excited all at once. We can stop any time. But she couldn't.

The next day Julia re-read the typescript and checked her references methodically. She had an uneasy feeling that there was something she had missed out, but couldn't work out what was the important thing that she'd forgotten. The dissertation was parcelled up, submitted and sitting in the faculty office before she remembered that the last time they had been together, all those years ago, she had been on the pill. Momentarily, a chasm opened: a stupid, stupid thing to do, a stupid risk to take, and to do it for Tim Slipman of all men! He was bad for her, he had always been bad for her; he had called her dark side back and she had frightened herself by the sight of her own reflection. How could she have let this happen? But it wouldn't matter, because they'd never need to meet again.

Then he wrote to her, care of the faculty, in the most extraordinary terms: *Julia, I am so happy to have got you back. I realise now that you were special all along. You always wanted me, didn't you?* And so on, laughable, pitiable really, ending with a reminder she should give him an address and phone number. She didn't. A week later, he had obtained them, simply by phoning the vicarage and asking.

SIX WEEKS ON, and she went home for a long weekend after finals. Her tiredness didn't surprise anyone, after all those weeks of effort and all the hours of concentration. Her mum thumbed easily through the old ways of spoiling her, lemon pudding, cushions, the first sweet peas. But she didn't have a lot of conversation. She overheard her parents talking about her; they assumed the exams had gone badly, because she hadn't said a word about any of the papers, and she heard her dad say, 'She's not going to relax until she's got those results.' On the Monday morning he found her sitting half way up the stairs. It was only this that was unusual; otherwise she was her everyday self, wearing her jeans tidily and with her chestnut hair tied back. When Geoffrey asked what she was doing there, she looked up and answered, 'Deciding.' Wary, he smiled and listened, waiting for her to tell him more.

Those were the only outward signs of Julia's pregnancy that anybody might have glimpsed. Two days later, back in

Bristol, there were none. By the time she phoned home to say she had an upper second, she sounded her old self again. 'There,' said Dorothy, 'I knew she'd be OK.'

# PART TWO

*CAMPANIA*

## DAY 1 YOUR RESORT

RIGHT FROM THE JOURNEY OUT, Wendy should have read the signs. Quite apart from the fuss about Mr Harper getting stopped at airport security, which she hadn't really witnessed (just heard the bitching afterwards about *no wonder they stopped him, carrying a bag like that which made him look like a hippy*) Whisper Blake had been all over her on the plane. You couldn't really escape on a plane, could you? Whisper kept going on about Jack, asked all sorts of questions about him, first like she cared, then just nosey. Because she was one nosey cow. So was it true that Jack had apologised to the hospital for trying to hack their network? Was he still on Facebook? So, if they'd banned him from the net, couldn't he just use an alias? Whisper thought he must be banned from the hospital too, and she asked, if he was sick, would they make him go somewhere else for treatment? Did Wendy have a photograph of her brother on her phone? Oh yeah, and his star sign... turned out it was the same as Whisper's dad's. Then she wanted to know his actual birthday. In the end, Wendy said, 'It sounds like you fancy him or something, and how can you fancy somebody you've never met?'

She answered, 'No I don't.' So Wendy asked 'Why all the questions?' and she said 'You're my friend.' And Wendy said 'Am I?' and Whisper went 'Yeah!' and she did her holy Virgin Mary face. It would have been nice to believe her but like they say, where's your evidence, and show your workings out. Then on the coach she just ignored Wendy and sat with Ari Clay. So what was all that about?

Wendy had picked the rubbish side as it turned out; most of the way she had stone walls and rusty railings for a view because the road was squashed against the cliffs. The others had the sea. The Mediterranean, which she'd never seen before: it was just *so* bright, turquoise like you'd never see in Catsea. And not a single cloud. The sky was almost royal blue at the top. Amazing. If Wendy wanted to see it, though, she had to look in their direction. Which was annoying.

The coach from Naples to the hotel was *so* slow. Mrs Hammer made the Hanningford group sit together, and what was even more embarrassing, she wouldn't let the other groups on the bus until she'd counted them all in, like they were still in primary: eleven students, Mr Harper, Mrs Hammer, and Whisper's mum. Mrs Hammer had told them all to call her Mrs Blake, but Mrs Blake said to call her Barbara, or even Barb; so whatever you did, you were bound to be wrong. That was when Wendy first realised that there was a problem between the two women and Mr Harper, because he positioned himself as far away from them as he could, behind the whole group. Right behind Wendy, in fact. She sat on her own. She thought about saying hi and making friends with the guys from the other schools, but they didn't look very friendly. Losers, flopping about, messing with their water bottles, only with a face like they were handling guns; a load of couples joined at the headset. When she did look round at one point, Mr Harper had his head in his hands, and Wendy wondered whether he was travel sick or it was just that their courier, Carol, was getting on his nerves. Seated at the front, and deafened by her own microphone,

Carol didn't seem to notice the kids sniggering or the teachers rolling their eyes as she informed them Rome was a place in Italy, the overhead storage was above their heads, and the sea was on their right. As if you might not have clocked all that incredible blue.

Mrs Blake and Mrs Hammer claimed the seats at the front of the bus, and they made a funny looking pair. In the aisle seat was Amy Hammer with her pussy-cat spectacles and her zipped-up dolly mixture fleece, and her funny little face all white and pink like strawberries and cream; while window-side, Barb, tanned and made up to the colour of a Danish, was wearing a beige outfit that was casual, oh yes, casual, but the kind of casual that had *dry clean only* written all over it. And you could always tell a lot about people by the hair. So, Mrs Hammer had a flat haircut which told you either she hated the hairdresser or the hairdresser hated her. But Barb had BIG hair, a bit like poodle hair. At first Wendy thought it was a wig, but you could see the skin at the front. And she had these big round shiny black sunglasses so that you couldn't see her eyes, except when she pushed the glasses up onto the hair, which made her look like a film star, but couldn't be very hygienic. Anyway, the point was, the hair said *look at me* but the glasses said *ah but you can't see me can you?*

The two of them rabbited on all the way from Naples airport. Yak-yak-yak, really annoying, especially Barbara; the whole coach could hear everything she said. Then the traffic got so bad that eventually they were hardly moving. Stop, start. Stop, start. Stop. You could hear each time a car came past from the opposite direction, wwwhhoosh, and there was a strobe effect as the sunlight struck its roof and reflected on the bus's windscreen. Over and over again. The coach driver kept making a particular gesture which Wendy thought must be really Italian: if you wanted to shrug your shoulders, you had to take both hands off the wheel at the same time. Passengers never like it when a coach stops for too long, and the hostess Carol felt the need to say something over the microphone. She told them that last week there had been a landslide on this road. She said good news bad news: good news, they had built a tunnel, which took you past all this; and bad news, they closed it in the winter for maintenance, so it wasn't due to re-open until next week. Wendy said to anybody listening, 'April isn't winter, though, is it?'

The hostess on the microphone said there'd probably been an accident and it had blocked the road ahead. So then Barbara Blake started mouthing off about how would they get the ambulance through, or the fire engine? Then they all had to gawp at the tunnel entrance like it was the Eiffel tower or something, as if they'd never seen the Dartford crossing, and then a bit further on the coach just stopped and that was it. Only the place it stopped couldn't've been worse. It was high up on a viaduct, right by the sea with absolutely nothing either side (you couldn't see the bottom) and a big gap between the road and the cliffs. Carol started going on about the sheer drop from the church in the town just up ahead. So that was a good thing to think about when you're staring into nothing on both sides. And the driver showed Carol a text he'd got and she said again there'd been an accident, and Barb shouted out that there was no sign of the emergency services, and the pair of them started a double act. There was a big smash there last week, said our hostess, there were *fatalities;* so Barbara said you'd think they'd sort this out in this day and age and where was the nearest A and

E anyway? She was so loud, all the kids behind were staring. Then next thing Wendy knew, Mr Harper was out of his seat and down to the front of the bus starting an argument. The mic picked him up and the woman had to switch it off. He said something like, *If you say one more thing about*, but they never heard what. Then he turned round to Mrs Hammer and she definitely heard him say *You'd think they'd know better. Why scare the kids?* Wendy couldn't hear what she said for sure, but it sounded like, *Martin, the kids are OK,* and she definitely saw her touch his arm, and he nodded and went *I know, I know.* So now Barbara was looking daggers at him, and when he walked back to his seat she said something about *unprocessed anger* so everyone could hear. And of course Whisper and Ari looked daggers at him too.

Then Wendy heard Shannon Matthews, who was sitting behind Mrs Hammer, say *'Is this where it happened? Mrs Hammer? I bet this is where it happened, isn't it?'* Shannon must have been able to follow most of the argument, and now she was leaning round the aisle pestering Mrs Hammer, and Barb craned forward to hear. Mrs Hammer lowered her voice and said she didn't know and it wasn't their business. She wanted Shannon to drop it, anyway. Then Barbara Blake's voice cut through like a knife, asking '*What* happened?'

Mrs Hammer got up and said, 'I'll just check on the students. Whilst we're stationary.'

Barbara looked round, then pulled her sunglasses back down to look out of the window, and you could tell that she was really annoyed. When Mrs Hammer asked, 'All right, guys?' a pathetic little voice answered, 'No. I'm going to be sick.'

'Are you sure?'

'Well, yes.'

'Alright, Whisper. Put your head between your knees.'

'There isn't room! And that's for fainting. Can we stop the coach?'

'Well, we *have* stopped, really, haven't we?'

'I need to get out so I can be sick.'

Then Wendy heard Mr Harper say, 'If you're going to be sick, be sick in this.'

'I need to get off the coach so I can be sick.'

'Look,' said Amy Hammer, we can't let you out of the coach here, it isn't safe.'

Then Ari Clay joined in and said, 'She needs fresh air.'

'Why isn't it safe?'

'Because of the oncoming traffic.'

'There isn't any?' Which was the one thing that was true.

Ari Clay chipped in again: 'She could stand by the side of the road.'

'I need to get off this freaking coach.'

Mr Harper said: 'We all do, Whisper.' He wasn't cross with her, although he should have been. And he tried to get her to concentrate on breathing slowly. Fat chance. She just shook her head and frowned.

Barbara Blake started on at the hostess, asking if they could all stop and freshen up and let her daughter get some air, but you could see that Carol wasn't having any, and the driver just waved his arms about. It was definitely looking like a no. Then Barb said, 'What? It is *always* possible to stop a vehicle. Or aren't the adults in control here?'

Everyone had been drowsy, but the whole bus was awake now. Even Hal and Jessica managed to prise themselves apart, and his big head bobbed from side to side above the seat as he strained to see what was going on. People shifted in their seats, and you could see that the teachers from the other groups were sympathetic towards the Hanningford staff, but mostly they thought it was hilarious. They all tuned in to the entertainment, especially when Barbara got up and stepped down the coach to comfort her little girl. Mrs Hammer stared at the luggage rack for a moment, like she wished something heavy was going to fall down and straighten the poodle hair, before brushing past to get back to her seat.

In time the traffic moved again, everyone sat down and the coach began to climb. There was a ridiculous sound of dry retching which carried on some while, but that stopped eventually. Then Whisper walked to the front of the coach and asked her mum if they could get a taxi. Amy asked how that would help, if you were travel sick? But Barb seemed to warm to the idea, because her daughter had always found group travel stressful, apparently (this was the first Wendy had heard of it) and *she'd done so well on the plane. She'd been so positive.* I mean, honestly, what rubbish.

'It's the same road, the same traffic. It won't be any faster.'

'Have you been sick, honey?'

'No, I can't be sick in front of other people. But I feel awful.' She made her voice trail away. Her mum sounded to be nagging at Mrs Hammer, and Mrs Hammer came back to talk to Mr Harper; Wendy couldn't catch what they were saying, although she tried hard, because you could see they were in a kind of huddle. A few minutes later the driver turned off the main road, made a detour into the town and stopped outside a train station, and Whisper and her mum got off the coach. Everyone groaned and the kids behind said, *oh, man*. They dragged their cases towards a taxi rank. Nobody waved, obviously, except Ari Clay.

Mrs Hammer came back to sit with Mr Harper, right behind Wendy, so this time she heard most of their conversation. There was a really good view of Mount Vesuvius now, and Wendy drank it in, grey, definitely cone-shaped, most definitely a volcano, not a mountain. How could the Romans have got that so wrong? So what if it did look different then, anyone could see, it was an unfriendly place. Amy Hammer said she'd swing for that woman before the week was out, God help her. Mr Harper said shame they hadn't taken bloody Carol the courier off the bus with them, the two of them had been getting on so well, then some rude things, and he sounded really cross. Then Mrs Hammer told him what Whisper's mum had said about empowerment, by which she meant Whisper needed to be involved in deciding what happened to her, which made him do one of his famous laughs. Mr Harper was famous for his laughs. His students could all do it: two notes, a bit like a siren, *he-hah*. A lot of people thought he was sarcastic, but Wendy had never heard it that way; he just liked to laugh, that was all. Weird things made him laugh. Mrs Hammer said what's so funny? And he said what *tosh* that woman talked, *complete bloody psychobabble*. And he did another laugh, and said he bet this wasn't on the risk assessment, losing not only a pupil but also a parent before you'd got as far as the hotel, and what if they were never seen again? Mrs Hammer said she didn't feel good about it, actually. She sounded quite peeved. And he said sorry Amy, don't worry, it'll all be fine. Then he said it a second time, only this time like he meant it.

Mrs Hammer did sound stressed out, but of course, she didn't know Whisper that well, did she, so maybe she didn't realise... Whereas the rest of them had all known Whisper since year 7. So Wendy popped her head over the top of the seat and just told her.

'Honestly Mrs Hammer, you should take no notice. She's just a drama queen.'

The two teachers glanced at each other, and Mrs Hammer looked particularly embarrassed. Then Mr Harper smiled straight back at Wendy and said, 'So, you OK, then, Wendy? Not going to puke all over me and Mrs Hammer?' Which was just like him. He looked strange, though. Even then, right at the start of the trip and before anything had started to go wrong. More than just tired. The little muscles round his mouth (there are hundreds of them, Wendy had seen this on the telly) were sitting all wrong. Whatever he said, he looked basically annoyed.

'I'm cool,' said Wendy. 'Cool.' And she slithered back down into her seat, and plugged her earphones in, to show she wasn't one to eavesdrop.

THE FIRST THING Barbara Blake saw as she stepped from the taxi was Amy Hammer, hovering grotesquely behind the plate glass of the hotel reception – or rather, a seemingly headless light pink fleece which bobbed about and gesticulated, and which she knew had Amy in it. It was a trick of the light: faces don't reflect, bad leisurewear sure does. The hotel, on the other hand, looked smart. It was nicely proportioned, with a grand staircase leading up to the central door, a modern terrace bar perched above the pavement, and stucco walls which positively sparkled white. Its old-style casement windows were dressed by shallow balconies, and the lacework of white-painted wrought iron was simply charming and so Italian. This sort of balcony was more for show than for use, but Barbara hoped their room would have one. Amy stepped forward to help as mother and daughter swung their suitcases up the marble steps.

'Thank goodness, I was just starting to worry...'

'Really? You didn't need to worry on our account. It was no big deal.' Please God, thought Barbara, this wouldn't be the start of one whole week of being counted out and counted in, and causing a commotion if you strayed from the herd. Barbara Blake was not a herding animal. Anyone who knew her knew that.

Introducing herself at reception, she looked around, and took in the internal decor with prompt relief; you could feel quite at home here in the Hotel Proserpina. Behind the traditional facade, its ground floor was open plan, a large, airy space with reception to her left and a bar in its centre, chic, minimalist, carrying through the white theme but with rich ultramarine lending accent notes. The furniture was classically modern, a mixture of nicely disposed sofas and inviting armchairs, with nothing too high backed of course, so as to maintain that sense of breadth and space. To the right of the bar was a wide screen TV, which was great just there, where it didn't have to dominate. She noticed that several of the Hanningford girls were already changed and starting to explore, hooking up to Wi-Fi, ordering drinks, wandering from the heaven-white lobby on to the terrace where the two boys, Hal and George, were taking photos of Vesuvius. Just one key was left on the counter; mother and daughter would be sharing. Whisper was glum about that, but then, she didn't travel well; it made her mother the more purposeful. Barbara pushed her sunglasses back on her head and grabbed her turquoise suitcase; she had energy enough for both of them. She headed for the lift. She was about to tell Amy they were fine now, thank you, and brush her off, but thought better of it: her curiosity about Martin Harper had been roused, and Amy was the one who had the gen. She ought to strike while the iron was hot. So she turned and said, 'What about a drink, Amy? Give me twenty minutes, I'll meet you here and buy you a Bellini.' Behind the candy-floss woman, back through the open doorway, she saw a greyish cone on the other side of the bay: the whole mass of the volcano, two-dimensional, outlined against a sky of perfect blue. It was extraordinary, flat and distant. There would be plenty of time to look at that again.

Barbara didn't check her watch, just took the time she needed to deposit bags and freshen up, trusting her judgement that it would take twenty minutes at her usual brisk pace. She found Amy in the bar, as agreed, and persuaded her to move to a sofa nearer the *terrazza* which overlooked the street, which was a much better place for them to take in the *atmosfera*; the sliding glass doors were half open, and a sea breeze wafted in. How wonderful that it would actually be warm enough to sit outside, if you wanted to. She ordered the drinks. Amy preferred a Limoncello. Sickly-acidic against the pink fleece. That thrillingly vibrant cobalt of the upholstery was doing her no favours, either. 'I noticed the *piazzetta* from my room,' Barbara volunteered, indicating the cute little square opposite them. 'It surprised me to see that we're way up above the shore. I hadn't realised, from the taxi.' The piazzetta in front of the hotel was set on a small promontory with cliffs dropping away below its three balustraded sides, and separated from it only by a narrow, fairly quiet road. It had old-fashioned benches, pollarded limes just coming into leaf, and a discreet café bar which stood at its farthest end, looking out to sea. There were one or two older, local people over there, walking dogs, and a few customers at the café.

'That looks like Hal and Jessica looking out to sea, joined at the hip, and yes, that's little George playing gooseberry as usual. See, I'm getting to know their names! And who they are. So, that's: Jessica who does Class Civ in little Ariadne's year, Hal the boyfriend who doesn't do Class Civ at all but hey, he paid, and who cares, he's a nice boy; and George the Token Male who does Class Civ with all the girls in year 12.' Amy said well done. Barbara studied the sky, an even, empty blue, scratched by the fingernail of a jet whose movement she traced from right to left. It was her first time in this part of Italy, she reminded Amy; she only really knew Tuscany. And Liguria. It was such a wonderful opportunity, to be able to come here and visit all this archaeology in the company of experts. People who really knew their way around. Amy smiled, a tidy little smile, kind of practised, thought Barbara, but pleasant enough. Amy's little white face was heart-shaped, with a pretty mouth, and she could be very nice looking if only she'd change that hairstyle.

'So then. What's the story with Martin Harper? First he gets stopped at security, then we have this ugly behaviour on the coach. What's eating him?'

'Well,' – Amy lowered her voice – 'I suppose it's only fair to tell you. Some of the pupils obviously know. Last time he did this trip, his wife was in a serious accident.'

Barbara adjusted her sunglasses: 'Mrs Harper.'

'It's hard for him. The last time he came here, with the school, they were together. But he lost her over a year ago now.'

'Tragic...' Barbara nodded; this was a major life event, and it would explain so much. But all the same... 'All the same, if it really did happen on that very road, what was he thinking of? Why wasn't he prepared? He must have known we'd be travelling this way.' She shook her head for a moment, and let her eyelids droop behind the dark lenses, while she took a moment to see it all. This clever man was not showing emotional intelligence as regards his own affairs, so what hope for his students? That was the root of it. 'So, what happened exactly?'

'She walked under a car as she was crossing the road. Only the thing was, it was a long time before they got her to the hospital. Well, you've seen the traffic. It was the same time of year, the Easter holidays, which is the best time for this trip. They had the same problem, with the tunnel being closed.'

'But she didn't die in Italy? Ariadne used to have Mrs Harper. Now, she was *good,* from what I hear.'

'No, no. It was much later. From what I understand, she had a lot of trouble after the internal injuries. She got better, or so it seemed. It took a long time. Paddy Clancy – you know Mr Clancy, Head of Maths? He was quite friendly with them both – Paddy told me she had major surgery more than once. Because she'd had medical problems before the accident, so it was a second lot of abdominal surgery, then afterwards she had adhesions – you know, like scar tissue? And they tried to fix it but she never really healed and finally she died of septicaemia.'

'That doesn't happen in the twenty-first century.' Barbara Blake shook her head and shrugged, sure that Amy was mistaken. It must have been something else. 'Don't you think it's strange, though, that he wanted to come back here? With a coach load of students?'

'Maybe he needs to lay some ghosts.' Amy was looking ever so slightly tight-lipped now, she thought. She was loyal to her colleague, which was all well and good, but you had to look at his behaviour from the students' point of view.

'He obviously hasn't. And there's all that anger backing up, why, anyone can see he isn't dealing with it... It's too bad for the students, they only have one chance. Of course, we feel much better now that we've found Whisper a tutor. Tim has been our saviour. He can't do enough to help. You know, filling the gaps? And he is such an enthusiast, you know, which is what young people need, isn't it? In fact he spends every summer holiday here. He knows all these ruins like the back of his hand. He has family out here, so he has a place to stay. It's a tad embarrassing, though, because he knows Martin Harper, in fact he knew them both. Still, that's too bad, I say, Whisper's needs come first. We don't want her to end up in some ex-polytechnic. So, were you with them when it happened? The accident?'

'Me? No. I came to Hanningford as Julia's replacement. That was temporary, part time, which suited me because my youngest was still in year 7.'

'Each to his own', said Barbara. 'Part time and temporary, not in my vocabulary... I guess I'm just a regular workaholic. I've trained my kids to do for themselves. But fair play to you, Amy, you have to go with what feels right for *you*.'

'I wouldn't say organising this trip has felt part-time.'

'Well I'm sure you've done a great job. And this is a neat little spot, with such a fabulous view.' Barbara had the sense to realise it was time for a positive stroke. The chill moment had passed, and Amy warmed again; she explained why she had chosen this hotel, when it would have been so easy to do what the other groups on their tour had done, and carry on to Sorrento itself, which was the obvious place, but with all those bars and shops, a nightmare to police. Besides, you couldn't be sure about the other groups – other schools had different ways of doing things. Different standards, different curfews. Sometimes the teachers were the worst. At least this was a safe place for the kids to hang out. Barbara conceded that they were comfortable in this quiet residential area.

'Oh, that's not all,' said Amy, pushing her oval spectacles up her nose, 'the hotel has its own private beach. There's a path goes down that little tunnel. It looks as though the kids have found it. There goes your daughter and her friend, just now, see?'

'You're quite the undercover cop.' Barbara made her point with a smile, but any irony was lost on Amy, who went on to explain that if she set up her office in the bar, the students would always know where she was, and find her if there was any problem. There was a pool, too, at the back of the hotel, although it wasn't really warm enough to swim yet. There was a garden. So they had everything. And Amy could watch TV from here, or read a book, or just look at the sea, depending on where she chose to position herself.

There was one more thing that Barbara remained mildly curious about.

'Why did they stop Martin Harper at the airport, then?'

'They didn't really stop him as such, did they?' said Amy, rather too defensively, she thought.

'You know what I mean. I guess maybe it was his wild expression!' Barbara laughed. Share a joke, and you can share a confidence. When they had gone through airport security back at Stansted, the Hanningford group had split up across several parallel queues. Harper had been just ahead of Amy in one. In another, Whisper had already gone through, then Ari and finally Barbara behind, and the three of them had seen that Harper had been stopped, and they'd made him take something out of his bag. There had been quite a conversation with the security staff, and everybody in that queue had been held up. Amy had been right behind him – she'd gone through the electronic gate but couldn't pick up her own hand luggage because he was stuck there talking, so she must have seen what the offending object was, and overheard them too.

'So, what was it in his bag, that got them so excited?'

'Nothing.'

'Oh come on, it can't be such a secret.'

'Nothing. None of our business.' These were exactly the words she'd used to that girl Shannon on the coach. Barbara smelled a rat.

'Because, you see, Whisper said she was sure they held up a polythene bag, with something powdery in it, only I've told her, it couldn't have been drugs, because they let him keep it.'

'It was nothing.'

'Well I'll just ask him myself, then. It can't be such a big deal, can it?'

'Don't,' said Amy, and her voice had dropped right to her chest. 'You mustn't. Please don't intrude.'

Intrude? That was an interesting choice of words, and Barbara told her so. Amy didn't like that one bit. What was she hiding, asked Barbara with a chuckle, why all the mystery? There was a little verbal tussle between them which pulled back and forth, back and forth, but Barbara knew that she could hold out longest. In the end, Amy, exasperated, told her: 'Look, this is a really personal matter, right? I didn't know myself. He carries it with him all the time, a small bag with the last of his wife's ashes. They were just checking it out. He told them what it was and they said sorry to have troubled you sir. And that was that. OK? Satisfied?'

'Why didn't you just say?' said Barbara, with a smile and a shrug. Amy was red-faced and upset, which was a shame, but whose problem was that, if she couldn't just be open about the facts? 'I'm sorry to have upset you, Amy.'

'That's fine,' said Amy, and stared at the street. Barbara followed her gaze to where a youth was trying to start his motor bike. It wouldn't catch, and he kept kicking downwards with ever bigger and more energetic movements, until he was jumping down on the saddle and slamming his foot on the pedal, like a puppet whose whole body was lifted by the shoulders and dropped, lifted and dropped again and again, by an unseen hand.

The pair sat in silence for a couple of minutes. There was the scraping of a heavy chair leg, and Martin Harper was in front of them, stooping towards the coffee table, where he set down a double espresso. He was long-limbed; suddenly the furniture didn't look so generous. He sat down opposite them, gave a polite hello, and blocked the view. Or rather, changed it. He wanted to talk to Amy about arrangements for the next day. She had flushed an even deeper crimson now. As he talked, Barbara looked and listened, purely as a dispassionate professional. You could pick up a lot from watching the client interact with a third party, unawares, and Martin was certainly oblivious to her. He'd made virtually no eye contact all day, to the point of rudeness, really. The warm hazelnut skin tones indicated he'd spent a fair bit of time outdoors, maybe abroad; in fact, he looked in his element here, with the familiar sun picking out every little line on his gaunt face. The furrows above the eyes gave it all away, of course: the habit of anger. There were laughter lines too. What made him laugh? She hadn't really seen. He had nice eyes, now that he wasn't looking stern. He trusted Amy, you could see that. He didn't interrupt or talk over her, didn't seem to be the dominant partner, even. Intelligent, definitely; attractive, yes, lips not too full, not too thin, fine teeth, nice chiselled canines, and the mouth set level. Straight. A straight sort of guy, generally. You weren't dealing with a lop-sided personality as such. So the mitigating circumstances all made sense; something had happened in this last year or so to throw things out of kilter for him. Depression meant chemical changes, and inexorably, chemical changes in the brain led to aberrant behaviours. However wild, however negligent this man had been, particularly in respect of her daughter, and her schoolmates, there was a reason: she would bet he hadn't always been like that. Which meant that he had every chance of a complete recovery. To understand was to forgive.

The teachers' talk was all about the itty-bitty details and what-ifs, mealtimes, ground rules concerning the hotel and its environs, tomorrow's itinerary, what they'd do if somebody overslept. He didn't sound uncaring or disengaged, although it was clear that Amy was calling the shots. He asked were the students OK with their rooms, and Amy said no complaints so far; then he said, 'Wendy and Ari sharing, though. Don't think that's going to work.' He looked troubled, over-solicitous. Maybe he was a secret worrier, or maybe he just wanted more control. Barbara interrupted to confess: 'If Mommy hadn't been here, Ari would have shared with Whisper, which I'm sure they both would have preferred. So that's my fault, sorry!' and she smiled and flopped her open hands towards herself so as to say, *lay that one on me*, as lightheartedly as she could. 'All I can say is, Ari's an easy enough girl to get on with, that's for sure.' Amy agreed, pointing out, ' Perhaps it might do Wendy good not to be the one who gets left out all the time.' Martin Harper raised an eyebrow and said, 'Perhaps,' but his tone was sceptical. So maybe Wendy really was as challenging as Whisper made her sound.

'HE OUGHT TO BE over her by now. It isn't natural.'

'Plenty more fish,' said Ariadne Clay.

'Yeah, plenty more fish.'

The two girls stared out across the bay, deliciously aware that nobody could see them from the hotel. Ari had a bad feeling about the route they'd taken and was glad to be back in daylight. From the nice little square right opposite the hotel, Whisper had led the way down a sort of ramp, and soon they had found themselves in a creepy tunnel which was actually carved into the rock, paved with flat black slabs like she'd never seen, sort of 50p shaped. If it had been down to her, Ari would have gone no further. But they had found the light again, on a kind of balcony, with two curving paths which led down to the beach; you were soon in shadow; the beach turned out to be so narrow a strip that it was hardly a beach at all, and the sand was so grey it looked more like cement, like when they did the patio. Whisper said the wooden platforms all around the tiny space were for sunbathing, not boats, and there was some sort of bar or kiosk stuck between the water and the cliff. It was shut up, and the whole place deserted. The season hadn't started, Whisper said; she had been to Italy before, so she knew these things; another couple of weeks, she said, and there would be parasols and sun loungers on the platforms, and you wouldn't be able to move, and it would be so cool. But they'd be back at school by then. The place had given Ari the creeps, it was like being in the bottom of a pit, with the steep cliffs curving round them, and nowhere to go if the tide came in. And they'd lost the sun. So they didn't hang about at the water's edge. They had wound their way back up to a bright landing where the parallel paths had met at the mouth of the tunnel; green lizards scurried into the wall.

At this point, leaning over the rough stone masonry, they were half way down the cliff; you couldn't see any sand at all from this height, but you could hear the splash of waves below. The sky and the sea were just so blue. They had a perfect view of Mount Vesuvius, the big triangle exactly opposite them on the other side of the bay. You couldn't miss it. A shame it wasn't smoking, a little curl of smoke would just complete the post card, but Mrs Hammer had told them that Vesuvius wasn't like Etna, you didn't see much activity here, although when they visited the crater, in a couple of days' time, they would get close enough to see little puffs of steam. Vesuvius was dormant. Hammer had been quite interesting about this. She could be. Apparently, people said, the longer you went between eruptions, the bigger the next one would be. So, the last one was during the second world war. But even if their volcano was being very boring, the stone was hot against the flat of her arm, and Ari was excited to be here, by the Mediterranean – just say that word, *Mediterranean!* – soaking up the sun.

'He's got a thing about Wendy,' said Whisper.

'Oh my God, your mind, what are you like?'

'You can tell by the eye contact. He always looks at her too long.'

'Well yeah, she is like, not normal in the looks department, so you can understand anybody wanting to stare. I mean, do you think maybe she broke her nose? She does look weird. Like a man.' Ariadne Clay snorted.

'He's got a thing about Wendy. Otherwise she wouldn't be here at all. He made sure. Because, who paid for her? I don't think she can have, or her skanky brother in prison.'

'On probation.'

'Whatever. I think he paid for her. Harper did. Now they've got the opportunity.'

'Opportunity?'

'To be together.' Whisper said this with a laugh, half-joking.

'How? Where would they go to be private?'

'It's private right here. Maybe they've already been seeing each other.'

'In Hanningford?'

'Well he lives on his own, doesn't he? Or Catsea. Jack wouldn't care. And there's nobody else home now, is there? No-one's to know.'

'More romantic here though.' A warm sun had begun to set behind pink feather clouds.

Whisper turned her back to the sea. 'Neat Piaggio. Wonder whose it is. I wouldn't say no to a ride on that.'

There was a shiny wine-red scooter parked just inside the tunnel. The scooter was gleaming but the stone wall it leant against was splashed with graffiti, in every colour of the rainbow, one thing over another. Everything was so neat and tidy round the hotel and on the square, and then you got something like this. A mess. So there must be bad people who came here and painted on the walls. What sort of people would come out at night? Whisper went back to talking about Harper.

'Tim says he just lost it when his wife died.'

'Ooh, Tim is it?'

'He told my mum. He said that anyway, Harper depended on her for everything. She was the brains.'

'He never told my mum anything like that,' said Ari. She was piqued, but interested all the same. Ari had always called him Mr Slipman. Sometimes she wondered if Whisper made things up.

'Mrs Harper was a good teacher,' added Whisper. 'Everybody said.'

'Yeah. I had her. Everybody said. Only she was off sick for ages.' Ariadne knew she was more nervous than she ought to be about these exams waiting for her back in England, and couldn't help thinking that somehow it was Mrs Harper's fault.

'Why did she marry him? That's what I don't get….And why did he marry her? I mean, someone you work with, someone you see all day every day, and then there they are at home every night. It isn't normal. Couples need distance.'

'Distance, yeah.'

Eventually they walked back up the tunnel and onto the piazza.

'I thought I was going to share with you,' said Ari Clay as they waited to cross the street opposite the marble steps of the hotel. 'I'm not looking forward to bedtime. I bet Wendy snores.'

'I bet her feet smell. She looks like they do. Anyway, I have to sleep with my mom. Who is, like, totally, my best friend. But even best friends need time out, sometimes.'

'Distance.'

Wendy was sitting on the little terrace by the entrance, fiddling with her phone. Whisper said it was an act, she was texting her imaginary friends... or maybe Martin Harper. Wendy smiled her big-tooth smile but didn't get up to greet them. They walked past and inside.

'So what's your room like, then?' asked Whisper.

'Come and see.'

Ari and Wendy's room was on the first floor and Whisper said it was very like the one she shared with her mother, except that it overlooked the garden at the back of the hotel: you could see palm trees and brightly coloured climbing plants she couldn't name, and loungers along the fringe of a large swimming pool, most of which was hidden. There was a heady floral scent at the open window, mid-way between nice and nasty, definitely foreign-smelling. The marble tiled floors were icy cold and slippery under foot, but the colour scheme, sea blues with pale grey and yellow, was pleasant. Ari passed no comment, watching her friend walk around the room. Whisper looked at herself in the mirror – they'd agreed it was too early in the season for a real tan, but maybe they'd get a head start for the summer now – opened up the notepad on the desk, which hadn't been used yet, and set it down again; she checked the minibar, peered inside the wardrobe, and pointed out that the safe was open.

'Yeah,' said Ari, 'I can't make it work. Stupid thing.'

Whisper snorted and said, 'Pointless anyway. Like as if we're gonna get robbed.'

'Yeah, as if. Only it's good for your passport. My dad knows how to make them work. We always get my dad to do it.'

Whisper went back to the wardrobe and considered the contents. 'God,' she said, 'You can tell straight away whose clothes are whose. This is your side, right? The normal side.' It was true. Ari's things were pink, blue, white, clean looking. Wendy's were all brown and orange.

'Flower-pot colours,' Whisper pronounced. 'She dresses weird.'

An ugly black canvas holdall sagged against the wall. It had a kicked-in look already, even before Whisper hit out with her foot.

## DAY 2 POMPEII

THE TEXT TO JACK was meant to say *Hi bro 2days th day I go 2 pmpii, yay*. Ever since she was a little kid Wendy had wanted to see this, and now that she'd finally made it, the whole day was being soured because she'd lost her phone. When she was the one who never, ever, lost anything. That morning, Ari had tripped over her bag in their room, a bit melodramatically really, so it must have slipped out then. It would be there waiting when she got back. Might her brother worry? He seemed not to care whether she messaged him or not, didn't always answer, never texted first. But who else was there to care about him?

It was quite a walk from where the coach had set the group down. They made the ascent up a road paved with flat black stones, and came under the sudden shadow of a massive arched gateway. Their party gathered on the pavement opposite a dark high wall, which was tagged by a slender sign: *Basilica*. Behind them a honeycomb of small, square, ruined buildings, all single storied, sprouted weeds, but they were sunlit, so Wendy turned her gaze that way while she listened.

Whisper was unimpressed. 'Where are the bodies? On TV, they always show you the bodies.'

'They're plaster casts,' said Mrs Hammer. 'There are some on show, some by the forum. And a dog.' Someone murmured, *aww*…

'They think most of the population had already evacuated,' said Mr Harper in his lecture voice. It carried better than Mrs Hammer's creaky squeak. 'They can tell that from the relatively low number of bodies. Volcanoes like this one don't just blow overnight; there would have been a series of earthquakes before the eruption, so plenty of warning. They were still doing repairs from a big eruption in 62 AD.'

Ari Clay said, 'It wasn't all that bad then. If most people escaped.' As they crossed the street, Wendy moved alongside Mr Harper, but had to wait until they had entered the basilica and heard his ten minute revision lecture on Roman justice before she could ask her question.

'Who would have stayed behind? Sick people, right?'

'Sick people and their families… the elderly… maybe a few religious maniacs. People who believed they were protected.'

Wendy imagined Catsea, completely emptied of all its noisy inhabitants apart from herself, Jack, her mum, and the Jehovah's witnesses. Her mum had been sick at home and nobody had called apart from the nurse and the carers. She imagined what it would be like to be stuck in Pompeii if you were too sick to move; and wondered how long it would have been before her mum would have told her and Jack to go. Or would she just have told Jack to go, because he was already in his own world? Not because he didn't help (that didn't matter) but because somehow Jack and his mum couldn't look each other in the eye. It was as if he started to be afraid of her, once he knew she was going to die. Whenever he wasn't at college, he was on the computer. Wendy still didn't know when all the dodgy stuff began, though. Maybe he'd been hacking for years.

By the afternoon, when they had still only covered half of the city, she realised the enormity of its emptiness. In spite of the fantastic things she'd seen now for real (the little fountains on street corners, the mosaic dog on the doorstep, the scooped shop counters, the amphitheatre) she found she hated the place, because where once its inhabitants had chewed up life, now its roofless dwellings ached like so many hollow teeth.

The group halted opposite the snack bar at the forum baths to open their packed lunches, and Wendy sat next to Mr Harper, because he was looking serious, and maybe he was lonely. He wouldn't annoy her, and he wouldn't mind her sitting there either.

'You alright?' she said.

'Mm. You?'

'I've lost my phone. Well, probably it's in the hotel. I haven't texted Jack today.'

'Is he allowed a phone?'

'Phone yes. Internet no.'

'You can borrow mine,' said Whisper, who had appeared from nowhere; carrying drinks on a tray from the snack bar. How long had she been standing behind them?

'Were you listening?'

The blond girl's shoulders met her ears, and she gaped: 'You just shouted it out for anyone to hear, so I'm only saying, why don't you borrow mine? I was only trying to help. I mean, was this meant to be *confidential*? Only I'm sorry if it was.' She shot a funny look at Mr Harper, then straightened her neck backwards and tilted her head in a gesture that Wendy always thought ridiculous. Like a gawky puppet.

Mr Harper told her it sounded like a good offer. So she gave her sorry thank you and accepted Whisper's little white-rimmed phone. She texted as quickly as she could, to get it over with, because nothing annoys you like a favour from somebody you hate: *this wispas phon. gone 2 pmpii its a mess. Am Ok tho howru 2day?xx W*

From that moment, and for the rest of the day, it seemed to Wendy, Whisper walked round with a smirk on her face.

IT WAS TRUE that Mr Harper spent a lot of time talking to Wendy on the trip generally. She liked talking to him and besides, Wendy suspected he probably got more sense out of her than the other muppets. The photograph that Whisper later said was *evidence* showed the two of them involved in a conversation which she remembered pretty well, except for the actual words they used. It had been after lunch, in a place called the House of the Faun, which was quite an amazing place really because it was a proper big villa and you could imagine how it used to be, with lots of people, living more or less outdoors and walking in and out of the rooms around these courtyards all the time. One step from the bedroom to the patio, like a posh hotel. It only made sense in a hot place, though. Mrs Hammer had done a lecture about the architecture. Nowadays they made you enter the house from the back gate so you really only got to see the statue of the Faun at the very end, and you approached it from behind, when actually it was meant to greet you at the entrance. Which they'd turned into the exit. So the whole thing was back to front.

When they'd found the Faun, Wendy had said, 'But it's really small,' meaning the statue. They had hyped it up with the house name, hadn't they, so she was expecting something bigger. The boys spluttered with laughter because they thought she meant the penis, which as a matter of fact was quite dainty and kind of dancing about. When she thought about it afterwards, being laughed at again was the thing she most keenly re-lived. As for Whisper's photo, it showed Wendy and Mr Harper staring at the statue, with nobody else around; he was caught with a funny look on his face, the way that happens with photos, say if you're just about to speak. The rest of the group had moved on and it was true that the two of them had stayed behind for a while talking. But they weren't far behind, and they were talking about Jack, not the naked man. They weren't really looking at it, either, it was just there in front of them, and if they hadn't been looking at some random object, they'd have been looking at each other, wouldn't they, which would have been worse really. If you wanted to twist things.

If you had to ask, as they later did in their investigations, was it a personal conversation she was having with Mr Harper when this photograph was taken in the House of the Faun, well yes it was. Very personal. Mr Harper was being kind. He was checking she was OK, and that Jack was OK too. The whole business with Jack and the police had settled down, the media lost interest once they'd realised he'd come nowhere near to bringing the hospital to a standstill. He hadn't even got past their firewalls, just got himself caught trying. It was, like her Mum used to say, all something and nothing. But now Jack was on probation and under a restraining order. Strictly no internet access. She hadn't talked to anyone else about all this, because who was there to talk to? Not Whisper Blake, although she had told Wendy she was *there for her* (*You ought to talk to my mum, she's a therapist, she'll, like, just listen. It gives you a perspective? - Yeah, I bet*). Shannon said that Whisper said to Ari that Jack was a real criminal. Anyway, at the House of the Faun, in this personal conversation, with Mr Harper, they were talking about messaging, and how you get more from a phone call, and how Jack never used to text her before. Or phone. In a way, she and Jack were closer now than they had ever been, but that wasn't saying much. She told Mr Harper how she had fallen out with Jack over visiting their mum in hospital, because those places made him feel sick; she thought he was pathetic, and it got to a point where they were barely on speaking terms, he was such a wuss. Mr Harper said Adderhead General was upsetting enough for the visitors let alone the patients. Wendy told him how she had really lost patience with Jack when the hospital discharged her mum: he turned round and accused them of giving up on her just because they wanted to clear the ward for the bank holiday. Which was rich, coming from him. He blamed them for sending her home instead of making her better, but by that point, they couldn't've. And she was happier at home. You couldn't be yourself in hospital, could you? Whatever you did, there was somebody watching.

So what else would she remember about Pompeii? They all visited the brothel, of course, shuffling past the alcoves in a cramped single file, goggling at the painted menu-frieze, showing all those different sexual positions. A row of neatly dressed Japanese ladies sat on the kerb outside the exit, their faces flat and smacked-looking from the visit. Wendy knew how they felt. If it hadn't been educational, you wouldn't want to see it, would you? They were still and tired in the afternoon sun. The whole day, the whole place, was just too much.

BACK AT THE HOTEL, Wendy got Ari to call her number, sure that it would ring somewhere in the room. Not a sound; it went straight to voicemail, which meant the power had run down. She searched on her hands and knees like a pantomime cat, shoved the furniture about, unpacked, re-packed her drawers, practically got inside the wardrobe, until Ari Clay told her she was making a complete idiot of herself. Clambering up from the waste bin, and catching sight of herself in the mirror, she could see that blotches of crimson were bruising her sallow face and neck. Typical. This always happened and it was always embarrassing.

'It's only a phone, for godssake.'
'Anyone could be using it.'
'Tell them then.'
'*Who* do I tell? And anyway, I need it.'
'You can always borrow mine again,' said Whisper, but Wendy had slammed the door and headed downstairs. She had a feeling it was somehow all their fault.


THE RESTRICTION ORDER which banned Jack from using the internet meant there was now no fixed connection at the house in Catsea, so he relied on the mobile networks and an anonymous pay-as-you-go smart phone.

That evening in Essex, Jack's phone buzzed and shivered across the table. A faceless icon and a name told him it was from his sister. She must have got her phone back, then. It wasn't her normal kind of message, though.

Harpers gon wierd. tell u more laterx w
- ??
- I think he fancies me
- UOK?

- Y x

A few minutes later it buzzed again. This time it was from Whisper Blake, who must be Wendy's friend, the one who'd lent her phone.

Hi Jack. U on Klappa? Cant find you. Give username pls. Have something 4 U.

He didn't have a Klappa account, but knew it was a video and photo sharing platform that a lot of kids were into. He opened one as YoozerJ, and texted Whisper back with that.

A buzz, a friend invitation. Accepted. Jack entered her page, and saw a still photograph of his sister with a tall thin man in his late forties, in some ruins. They were both looking at a weird statue of a kind of naked man dancing, only he had horns and shaggy legs and cloven hooves. A second photo was taken from much further away. This time they looked like they were having an argument from the way Wendy was waving her arms about. There was a caption: *so where is everybody else?*

He added Whisper to his contacts, then messaged her WTFIGO. What was going on?

## Day 3 Naples

ON DAY 3 they went into Naples and spent what seemed to Ariadne Clay to be an age in the museum. All through the journey home they talked about free time, like, as in, when were they going to have some, and they got told off for not reading the information they'd been given which would have told them. Ari counted it out to everyone on the white squared off tips of her shiny nails: they were going up Vesuvius tomorrow, then a trip to Paestum which was Greek on Wednesday; Thursday was Herculaneum which was like Pompeii only more upmarket, and that meant it would be Friday morning before they were free, before a late afternoon flight. Not much, then. Once back in the hotel, and before the teachers disappeared into their rooms, they sent Shannon to argue their case with Hammer. The whole group stood in the lobby and waited for a plan. Shannon got them permission to go into town for the evening, provided they stayed in twos or threes and were back by 11. Whisper muttered to Ari that 11.30 would be fair enough. Mrs Hammer said she would stay in the lounge to check them in, and made it sound like a big favour, but what else would she be doing anyway, she was so boring? *Chatting up the barman*, said Whisper, *so no change there*. Which made Ari snort with laughter, because, unlike the geriatric waiters, the barmen were really pretty hot. Then somebody asked how far it was into town, and how would they get there. Hammer said they'd have to find their own way: keep the sea on your right and you couldn't go far wrong. Reception had maps. It was a couple of stops on the local train. They could walk. Well obviously, that would take ages. They could share a taxi. Ari wasn't sure about any of this, and she was the one who said, 'Can't somebody just take us?' Then the whole group – even Mrs Hammer and Whisper's mum – looked at Harper, who shrugged and said that was fine by him, he'd take them, but they'd have to find their own way back. They smiled and sang: *Oh, thanks Mr Harper, thank you sooo much, thanks Mr Harper*. Ariadne even joined in herself, in spite of hating him for being so full of his own cleverness. This was what you were meant to do, to make a song and dance about being grateful. Maybe it was a bit over the top. But the point was, of course they all wanted to go out. So you do what you have to do.

They got through the dining room as quickly as they could and were out of the door just in time to catch the local bus, feeling pretty pleased with themselves, even though the bus was full and they had to stand. Harper was in the aisle, between Shannon and Ari, with his crazy bag. They had already agreed that it could be a woman's bag; it was made of woven coloured canvas, crimson, blue, pink, green, what you'd call ethnic, deep, with a long wide fabric handles, like you could get on Camden market, Whisper said. The bus stopped with a jolt at the first crossroads, and that was when the multi-coloured bag fell from his shoulder to the crook of his elbow, then down to his wrist; the long fabric handles twisted around themselves and whole thing slapped Ari hard on the outside of the bottom of her leg, with such a force, it really stung. Harper made some awkward, jerky movements, and managed to free his wrist, but the bus juddered too, and now the bag fell heavily onto the gangway, and all of its contents spilled out. A bottle of water and a biro rolled far away under a seat, and a couple of guidebooks fell to the dusty deck, but the strangest thing, alongside them, was, unmistakably, a woman's make-up purse, a really pretty one, made of some sort of satin, a luscious red, very expensive looking, and shiny.

He grabbed that first, of course, and stuffed it back, then let people help him with the rest of the stuff, including the water bottle which somebody had managed to stop and pass forward. When he had done, he looked at Ari with such a horrible expression, it was as if she had been the one who'd assaulted him. Everybody noticed, and they all agreed afterwards, he looked totally mental, and there was no sign of him apologising. Shannon piped up, 'Sir, what have you got in there?' and his whole face just screwed up. He never even answered. Not a word. He just held the bag close to his body, with his arm over the opening so nobody could possibly peek inside. Anybody who saw it happen would tell you, there was something wrong with that man. As soon as they had got off the bus and he was out of earshot, they all had to discuss it.

Maybe he was gay, maybe he was a trannie. They sniggered, who'd have guessed, but then when you thought about it, there were all those statues of young men on his walls, and the diver ... Whisper said, it didn't matter what his sexual orientation was (which was right) but he was a pig for never saying sorry.

The eleven of them kept together that evening, and didn't stray too far from where the bus had dropped them off. Eventually they found a tourist bar with a huge wide terrace that overlooked the darkening sea. The sun had disappeared and you could make out little strings of lights which had come on, far over the other side of the bay; it looked so pretty, and it was a while before they noticed the shape of Harper, alone at a table on the other side, staring into space. There was a beer bottle in front of him, and his arms were hunched around the bag on his knee.

## Day 4 Vesuvius

THE TRAIN shook them all from side to side as it rattled and squealed its way in and out of tunnels, where dank air blew in in great unruly gusts, and the open windows sucked the battering echo of engine noise against brick back into the carriage. Four days into the trip, they were all used to the *Circumvesuviana* now, and although the brakes set everybody's teeth on edge and made them grimace, the girls gave themselves up to the fairground movement, swaying along exaggeratedly. They were curious to see the volcano, and desperate for a day without ruins. The teenagers chattered about everything and nothing; they talked across each other, they talked over everything. They filled the train with their estuary sing-song, which dipped but always rose again, and always ended on that high note; they could out-sing the family of Italians sitting alongside Martin now.

*You know, you said, I think I might be half Italian. I think this is my place. Maybe Julia was my real name after all.*

*What do you mean, your real name? Of course it's your real name. My Julia.*

*It sounds good when you say it.*

*You look a bit Italian.*

*I want to speak the language, I mean, properly, not just pasta talk. It's so musical.*

*No it's not. It's the sound of people nagging.* Nag-a-nag-a-nag-a, nag-a-nag-a-nag... *Like they can't let go. Like they're all obsessed. I want to tell them, OK, whatever it is you're banging on about, just drop it, can you? It's like a hacksaw on the ear.* Nag-a-na, nag-a-na, nag-a-na...

*You have no soul, you tepid Englishman. I want to be intense and passionate and* –issima *in everything. Way over the top. Obsessed is good.*

That was how they created the maybe myth and maybe truth that Julia was Italian; here, on honeymoon.

Martin didn't begrudge the kids their right to be loud and happy. He was just not going to let them catch his eye. So far, since they'd left the station, he had pressed his face against the window. Today, the sun rinsed memories of all his times with Julia here, and made them sparkle. From trips spent, both with students and without, came details he had forgotten: the single track, the order of the settlements they passed through, Meta, Scrajo, Pozzano, Castellammare di Stabia, Via Nocera; how fine the grey soil on this plain. The train sliced through dusty market gardens, and the buffeting air from overhead brought every feature of the landscape in for him to taste afresh – earth, ash, green shoots, fig, soot, cobweb dark of the tunnels, and beside the stations, all the trackside escapes: jasmine, wisteria, laundry.

They alighted at *Pompeii Scavi* again, then had a short walk over to the bus. He tasted pine woods, and scrub, and loyally imagined the scent of wild herbs which must surely still crouch there, as the bus followed the winding road up the wooded slopes of the mountain, past the brazen holiday residences which in April were still waiting, spring clean, for the season to start. Today, in their eerie, empty precincts, nothing moved. The white was an affront, the statuary more so, though the girls trilled at the enormous leopards and – was it really? – a six-foot polar bear. He and Julia had laughed at the fake palaces from that little Fiat Uno. A hire car, left hand drive. Left hand sinister. The bus stopped in the woods, and the party climbed onto the giant 4x4, which turned out to have huge balloon tyres which made it more a minibus on stilts, and as it lolloped and see-sawed up the track, it revealed the forest to be both dry and birdless. Martin had not remembered it so. He stared through the flat pane, numbed by the air con, knowing the warmth outside; and as he concentrated, each separate frame of now, as it sped by, was like a page he'd turned down at the corner, helping him to fold their future back against their past.

At last they were out in the dry air. The lads kicked dust in the car park, then they all shuffled up to the path. The way was steep, the mountainside much steeper; this wasn't earth beneath his feet, just grit, pumice, scoria which shifted with every step; the particles trickled down as if the whole thing were a sand hill, or a simple bowl of sugar; this fearsome mass, now seen up close, proved to be made up of so many small and weightless things. This was how it should be: upwards, all clarity; the sun should be crashing down like this, yes, it was the job of these red cinders underfoot to take that light and make it fizz and crackle, with so many little sparks of mica, glass, crystal, tiny, tiny, more than the stars in the night sky, all saying to the sun *see me, see me, I came from the dark, but look, look at me now...* A precious, cloudless, clear day. He lifted his head and looked onto the plain and knew that there was Ercolano, there Pompeii, there the Sorrentine peninsula... all Campania spread out, and stilled, but for the distant wink of plastic poly-tunnels to prove life had gone on.

He hung behind, to be alone with Julia, and watched the others snake uphill. The kids' lives would go on, whatever happened here. They didn't need him, and they didn't want him either. They'd all pass their exams. Ariadne Clay would never make the grades for Durham and that would be his fault. In five years' time, Whisper would have found some happy job that offered power without responsibility, and that too would be no thanks to him. *And Wendy,* Julia seemed to ask, *how would things turn out for her?* Under his breath, he answered: 'Wendy will flex to take whatever strain. I mean, she's one of those people who cope, isn't she?'

*Oh come on Martin. She's still just a funny looking kid who's lost her mum. You won't just walk away from her. She deserves somebody's care. Someone to believe in her. Some continuity. There's still a job for you to do.*

Julia came to him, often, in the shape of a thought. If anybody knew about this, they'd say it that it all came straight out of his own head, but they'd be wrong. Now that he had searched for her in the darkest places, the two of them were closer than ever. In these last months, she had shocked, and teased, and argued with him. She had the power to direct and to inspire. She was a creature quite distinct from the matt grey ash that he had scattered by the River Crouch, or that sat in the make-up bag he had so clumsily dropped the night before. Julia had fully separated from that now. She was diffuse, sublime.

The wooden fences alongside the path had shepherded the group ahead to the little snack bar, and through the turnstile, and now they were close enough to see the crater's edge. The terrain was rockier, and the path grew steadily narrower until it forced them almost into single file, but there were plenty of places where you could boulder up to look inside, and sea-side telescopes near the entrance gate, to help you. Some of the girls were eager to frighten themselves.

They pointed out the steam from fumaroles tucked amongst the crags inside, and took each other's photographs. There was a different purpose to Martin's looking. He overtook them easily, clambered up and looked down over the lip. It was a deep drop to the dusty floor, and even in the high late morning sun, the mountain seemed to hold its own shadow. Perhaps it was because the rock and ash were darker there, inside the crater. If you fell over the rim you'd likely be caught on the jagged rocks. Unless you walked over to the farther side, where the walls were smoother, and there'd be nothing much to stop your fall; you would break your neck and every bone in the tumble to the flat disc of scrub below. *But you would shock, and harm, a lot of people, if you did that.*

Suddenly there was a squeal and a rush of exclamations: 'Look, look. It's Tim.'

'It is!'

'Where?'

'Down there. Look, in the car park. Getting onto the moped.'

'I can't see.'

'Who?'

'To the left of the minibus.'

'You can't tell from here. How can you see to tell?'

'It is, it's him. I can tell by the pigtail.'

'But he wouldn't ride a moped. Surely he'd have a proper motor bike?'

'Who's Tim?'

'He ought to be wearing a helmet.'

'Her tutor.'

'Mr Slipman.'

'That's ridiculous, you can't possibly tell from here.'

'Well he walked like him.'

That was Ari and Whisper, waving, jumping up and down, and chanting, 'Mr Slipman, Mr Slipman!'

Martin found himself shouting, 'What do think you're doing?' He was enjoying it; he let the words in his mouth boil and fly like steam from an engine; but he knew he shouldn't be doing this, so he took the pressure of a shout and pushed it through the funnel of a whisper: 'What are you playing at? What's it about? What is it? What? What do you know?'

He had moved to reach the group with absurd speed – they had hardly progressed from the gate, and were gathered way down the slope, on the opposite side of the path from where he had been standing. The little stones were still skittering down where he had run. People were looking, tourists, the attendant. The school group had fallen silent, and Hal had drawn Jessica close to his side. Shannon and Sam were glancing at each other and sniggering, but Martin saw that most eyes were on him. Some of them look frightened, especially Ari. Why? What should she be frightened of? Wendy was frowning. He had over-reacted. Whisper Blake had no expression on her still, pale face at all. She stood with her head slightly tilted to one side; she was registering all this, like some machine. Taking it down to use in evidence. A footfall on the grit, and Amy was at his elbow.

'If you walk a bit further up,' she told the students, 'you have a brilliant view of Herculaneum. Come on, I'll show you.' She touched Martin lightly on the arm, once, twice. Ari gasped with theatrical disappointment and impatience, 'Oh! He's gone!' The high-pitched mosquito buzz of a motor thrashed up and down in the air, and a trail of dust, like a cartoon fuse, rippled out of the car park far below and chased the moped out of sight, into the pine trees and down the trail. The girls walked upwards, quietly complaining, quietly exclaiming, raking it all over. How Mr Harper lost it again.

*What's he on?* he heard. *I mean, what is he on?*


THANKS TO AMY'S INSISTENCE on an early start, they were off the mountain by mid-afternoon, so they took the Circumvesuviana back and carried on a couple of stops beyond the hotel, in order to give the girls free time in Sorrento. Barbara picked out the perfect bar for them all, with plenty of room for everyone to enjoy a drink outside, but Hal and Jessica walked on oblivious, while the rest of the students hovered on the pavement, then sat down for a moment, then all got up again and left the adults to it. Whisper vaguely waved goodbye to her mother. It seemed to Barbara that Amy too was unusually unresponsive, chewing at her lower lip in a most irritating manner, and no sooner had the waiter approached to take their order than Amy looked at her watch, claimed to have quite a bit she needed to get from the shops, and disappeared into a narrow street around the corner.

Barbara shrugged – 'just us two, then' – but her disappointment was fleeting; this was the first time she had really had an opportunity to draw the enigmatic Mr Harper out. She ordered peppermint tea and a double espresso for Martin – not a good idea for somebody in his state, but if she drew attention to the addiction to stimulants, he wouldn't want to open up about the bigger problem. It was best not to pass comment. She would come at this obliquely.

'This really is the ideal spot to sit back and take the whole world in,' she said, settling back in the wicker chair. Martin readily agreed, although his eyes did not, and all those little lines that had such great potential for laughter remained stubbornly set firm. The afternoon air was pleasantly warm, the scent of wisteria hung in the air, and there was movement all around them, from passers-by, cars stopping and starting, changing traffic lights and even a little white tourist train which rattled down the street with its bell ringing. It was the start of the season. The world was busy, busy, whereas their day's exertions were pretty much over, and they could savour the luxury of sitting still for a minute and relaxing a little while others hurried by. Barbara took her time. She knew quite well that she was one of life's givers. She had arrived at a mature understanding of her abilities, and her weaknesses too, and whilst she was never going to be one of those people who appeared with cups of tea or mopped up spills, she was second to none when it came to listening and – well, not giving advice exactly, that would be too patronising – helping others to recognise their needs. She was never one to shy away from a challenge, either; no client was negative enough to sap her legendary energy, no case was too complex for her holistic vision. She had channelled her gifts and honed her skills over the best part of two decades, and it hadn't taken her long to figure out what Martin Harper's problem was. Here was a man who needed help, and she was sufficiently generous of understanding to forgive his poor treatment of her daughter and do what she could. She was only too glad to be at hand. But timing was everything; and this might be her moment.

'You know, Martin,' – she stared across the piazza with practised nonchalance – 'I don't know how you teachers do it. I mean, you're with all these kids, 24/7; you're tour guide, lecturer, nurse, life coach...'

'Life coach? I don't think so.' The corners of his mouth tightened upwards - you could hardly call it a smile. It was followed by an equally superficial laugh. This humour, this persistent levity in his manner, wasn't it his way of discounting the compliment? Wasn't he rejecting the significance – and of course the responsibility – of his role, by denying it?

She cocked her head and said with a smile, 'Every teacher is a role model, don't you think?'

He gave another small laugh, polite, dry, and very close to a cough. 'What, all of us?' he answered. 'That must be confusing for the pupils. We're all so different.'

'Martin, you're on the button with that one.'

'And the kids. They all need different things from us. That's why you can't be the right teacher for all of them.' Now he made a point of looking her directly in the eye. He wasn't trying to deny that things had gone so badly between him and Whisper, and her friend Ariadne, too. He had some self-awareness, then.

'You know, you're quite a formidable guy. You're very clever, and you have such a strong personality... A tad scary, for them? You're in a difficult place, though. And – I hope you don't me saying this – I think sometimes you come over a bit fiercer than you realise.'

'You mean, this morning.'

'Well, yes. You yelled at those kids, Martin, but they hadn't done anything wrong. Or yesterday on the bus into town. You really hurt poor little Ari, you know, with your bag? It wasn't her fault. But the girls said you didn't even apologise. Sometimes it seems you're wrapped up in your own thoughts, and the rest of us mortals don't figure. Even on the coach coming out... you were just... well, rude. I don't say you meant it. There was a lot of anger there.'

He remained silent and frowned as if trying to recall it. Then he nodded slowly and said, 'Go on. I'm listening.'

'Amy tells me you lost your wife. Martin, I'm sorry for your loss. Tell me, how long ago did it happen?'

He looked at her warily: 'Did *what* happen?' Now this was wild. Extreme denial. She would have to guide him. A low, warm voice was needed. She told him: 'A year ago? Or is it more, since Julie passed away?'

'Julia.' Ouch, a bad mistake. The lines on his forehead made an extraordinary pattern, a set of deep horizontals now drawn down by two diagonals, like fractures on a rock face, all the way to the deep vertical cleft where the dark eyebrows met. It spoke to her of focus, yes, but also the habit of fury.

'Julia. Forgive me. My mistake.' A slight nod of the head, no more, by way of pardon. She thought, *whatever*. 'You know, Martin, that's quite some time to stay angry.' She paused. 'And look, you do have a future. It might sound crazy now, but I can see you in a relationship again, someday. Look at you, you've got so much going for you, smart, attractive, interesting…'

He turned his head away, fixing on an extravagant display of fruit in front of a greengrocer's opposite, the typical thing here – huge lemons hanging from the awning, oranges of several types, and strawberries already. Conveniently eye catching, for sure. So, let him make his inventory… 'You have to grieve. But when grief becomes a habit… well, we seldom stand back from our own lives, do we?' He remained silent. The frown grew deeper, if anything, but he hadn't stopped her, so perhaps he was ready to hear. 'What I'm saying, Martin, is… and I'm just making an objective observation, right, as someone who's not involved but who's seen this kind of thing many, many times before... What I'm saying is, that what you're going through... what you *present*... it isn't normative?'

'What *do* I *present*?'

She thought: tell him Barb. He's an intelligent man, grant him his dignity by telling him the truth, now's the time to share your insight and your knowledge. She took a careful breath and started to explain.

'There's a phenomenon we come across from time to time, when somebody has lost a loved one and the grieving just goes on beyond its natural course. When the person can't move on. Can't find resolution...'

'And this phenomenon would have a name?' He was making eye contact again; good. Good. Diagnosis was the first step to recovery. His eyes were really very attractive, a deep blue, almost indigo. That was an illusion; when you looked closer, the iris had a dark black rim. Quite a looker.

'Why, yes, you're right. It does have a name. We call it *Complicated Grief*.'

'And you can treat it? I'm guessing?'

'Why yes.'

'Barbara, let me tell you something.' This was the first time he had ever used her given name, and now he leaned across the table towards her, slowly, deliberately. She had been right to take the risk. He was connecting. At last.

'My grief, as you call it, is quite extraordinarily simple. Simple is what it is. Simple is its greatest attribute.' He emphasised each word as if she were an idiot.

'Martin, you're sounding hostile there.'

'I am,' he conceded, with a single brusque and heavy nod.

He got up and started to walk away, in precisely the opposite direction to the one Amy had taken, then turned only to say, 'Thank you for your concern. Maybe I need a little time to myself. I'm heading back to the hotel. Could you tell Amy, when you see her?' He looked embarrassed now. She chose to believe that he was sorry, and maybe even grateful. You should always think the best of people.

OFF THE LEASH, the teenagers took to the town. It was late afternoon, still daylight, and they were starting to know their way around; they soon fragmented into smaller groups. Shannon and Sam tagged along with Whisper and Ari. They found narrow lanes full of little shops open to the street, all completely touristy, it was true, but colourful and crammed full of fantastic things, expensive handbags and cheap fridge magnets, but also things you didn't see at home, lemons the size of grapefruit, salami that smelt like wet dog, bottles of Limoncello, more Limoncello, bowls designed for olives, cool clothes, terrible clothes, Limoncello. Shopping baskets, paintings, beach towels, bright printed tablecloths and aprons, scarlet chilli peppers strung together and cascading from the awnings, amazing leather sandals made to measure, bright ceramics, ice cream not kept in deep tubs like at home, but trowelled onto trays.

Like Shannon, Ari wanted to find something to take home for her parents, which gave their browsing a sort of purpose. They stopped at a store which sold leather goods, gloves, belts, bags, purses of all shapes, sizes and colours, and found that behind the narrow frontage and the displays on the street, there were shelves upon shelves running far back into the shop, looping round and back again, like a bag library. Whisper said, see how they put the biggest most beautiful things right up front, to catch your eye. That was marketing psychology. They know you can't afford it but you might want to buy a little bit of the experience, so you step inside, see how it worked? Shannon said she loved that smell. Ari had never really thought about the smell of leather before, but here it was so concentrated, you had to notice it. Amazing. This was serious leather. Everything seemed to smell stronger in Italy. They lingered and compared. They came upon a rail of leather jackets. Tim had one like that. Maybe this was where he'd bought it, Ari suggested, because after all, he spent every holiday somewhere round here. She was pleased to be in the know and to give the others some information. Which she and Whisper had known for *ages*.

'How come?' asked Shannon.

Whisper took over. 'Family. His grandparents live near here. He loves Italy. He's so passionate about his subject. He knows everything about the Romans, and he knows Pompeii like the back of his hand. He'd live here all year round if he could.'

'Do you know where his house is?' asked Shannon. They didn't. 'Shame. You could visit him.'

'It would be so great to see where he lives,' said Whisper, and the group hummed agreement. 'Mom says we're too busy. She says she doesn't want to miss any of the ancient sights. We've got his number and everything. She said maybe the day we go to Herculaneum, we could, you know, hook up, maybe meet for a pizza afterwards and find our own way back.'

'Your mum's great,' said Sam.

'She said about it to Hammer and Hammer said maybe but let's keep that to ourselves because it all gets hard to manage when people start peeling off. I think what she means is, don't tell Mr Harper.'

'Yeah 'cause he'd go mental probably. He's so unpredictable,' said Shannon.

'And anyway, we couldn't *all* go, because that would be taking advantage.' Then Whisper frowned and said, 'You know, it's so annoying. Tim could be showing us round. He could have taken us to Pompeii, and everything. He explains it better.'

'Yeah, he explains it better,' said Ari, realising how cheated she had been.

'What do you think it's like, his house?' asked Shannon.

Whisper said, 'Modern. Italian design is the best. Black and white. White leather sofa. Or maybe white carpet, black furniture.'

Ari wondered aloud how she could possibly know that, and Whisper told her it was just a matter of observation. 'That's what I think. That's what it would be.' But was that likely, if it was his grandparents' house? Ari kept that thought to herself.

Shannon bought two matching leather key fobs for her mum and dad, which were hideous, embossed and colour printed, completely gross, although you couldn't say so. For herself, Ari wondered about a little blue purse which made a nice click when you snapped it shut, but in the end she wasn't sure enough to buy.

They stepped out of the shop and Ari caught sight of Barbara Blake a few metres further down the cobbled lane, in front of a rotating stand full of sunglasses. She was just so chic in her classic denim. That was the thing about her: she wasn't particularly nice-looking, but she always looked nice.

She looked up and saw them. When Ari waved, Barbara responded energetically, and beckoned them across. Whisper sighed. 'Now we'll get the third degree.' 'Oh come on,' said Ari, 'don't be mean.' And Ari was right, because she was only taking an interest, and in fact she took an interest in all of them; she asked what they thought of Sorrento, swapped notes on the shops they'd seen and what might be worth taking home, and wanted to see what they'd all bought, which was just Shannon's manky key rings. And although you could absolutely know for a fact that she must hate anything so tacky (because she was so stylish, she had better taste than any of their mothers) she still found something nice to say which was at the same time probably true. She said, 'I'm sure your parents will love them.' She was so clever, like that. Tactful.

They talked about transport back, whether to make the two stops on the train, or to find the bus station. Ari favoured the train. 'It's ages till dinner,' said Shannon, 'I'm good here for a bit.' Barbara Blake said she was thinking of staying in town. She'd read about a trattoria in the old harbour where you could eat the most amazing seafood. As she talked about it, her face worked really hard; it always did, whenever she was being enthusiastic about something, or explaining why a thing was wrong. It was as if every muscle had a job to do, persuading you to listen. Which was great, although it was probably why the lines on her face were so deep, from folding and unfolding over and over again. She didn't have those little wrinkles that really old people had, mind you.

'Every time I come to the Mediterranean,' she announced, 'I have to have just one big tray of *frutti di mare*. Clams, mussels, oysters, crab, you know, the whole works.

And I've worked out that tonight is more or less my only chance.'

Ari winced. 'Rather you than me.' She'd been down to the cockle sheds often enough with family, and watched in disgust as her dad picked winkles from their shells or chewed his way through a bowl of whelks. She made it a rule not to eat anything from the sea that wasn't genuinely pink. Grey shrimps were out, the name told you they were filthy. And she knew that you ate oysters raw. You squeezed lemon on it, and it wriggled.

'So will you be going with the teachers then?' asked Whisper.

'Oh my God no… They're very lovely people, but I do think they need their space. Besides, we've spent the whole day together already, and they'll want to be getting back to the hotel for you. They're working. I'm on holiday!' She beamed at everybody and said, 'Whisper will keep me company, won't you, honey?'

She answered 'Sure,' as if it were a familiar routine that bored her.

IT TOOK MARTIN AN HOUR, but after turning his back on Barbara Blake and her bloody nonsense, he walked the whole way back to the hotel, at a good lick. His limbs felt the need to be on the move. *I could see you in a relationship again someday.* And had that really been Slipman on the mountain? Surely the girls only imagined it was him, but that showed how close he'd got to the surface of their consciousness. Why couldn't they have left the memory of him back in Essex? Or were they goading the inadequate Mr Harper, as he'd felt at the time? No, they were innocent, he reasoned, they didn't understand how the mere thought of this man had the power to sully everything, even on a day and in a place where the light had been so exceptionally, antiseptically clean. Surely, surely they knew nothing of his past with Julia. Martin found his way from the town's main street into suburbia, breasting an endless tide of hotels and houses, many lavish, many modest. He navigated crudely, by the sun and sea and glimpses of Vesuvius. It felt so good to take big strides away from everyone, it was good to spend the energy which might have fed a fight, in fact a fight could be a good thing for him now, a fist-fight, such as he hadn't had in years and years and not since he was a kid at Chantry Lane when fighting with your mates was what you did. This forward momentum felt good, it was what they called a good brisk walk, and it hardly mattered what he was walking towards. With every step, the weight of Julia's shoulder bag beat on the flat of his right thigh, a rhythmic tune, a muffled *tha, a tha, a tha, a tha*. He made up words. *We go, we go, together, so. We go, we go, together, so.* He soon felt sticky. The minute he got inside, he would take a good hot shower and wash this all away, the grime and the annoyance of the day. It was only when he reached the hotel and lifted his body up the steps that he measured the full weight of his tiredness.

Good, the lobby was empty, so with any luck everyone else was still in town. It took only minutes, but they were long, aching minutes, for Martin to return to his room, where he threw everything, bag, jacket, wallet, all his clothing, immediately on the bed, and stepped into the shower.

Every last corner of this hotel was spotlessly correct. So what was this smell? Far from relaxing Martin, the shower was disgusting. It seemed that any contact with soap or shampoo made the water smell like mushrooms. There must be some substance in the water supply, some feature of the complex geology of this region – would sulphur do that? He didn't linger, towelled himself down and lay back on the bed. When he closed his eyes, he saw red grit, the wink of minerals in complex patterns on tiny stones; or a flat, ungiving hard blue sky; or the lax green bushes in the mouth of the volcano, where nothing grew too big; or the little herbs that gripped the cinders on a mountainside where everything was moving, where every face was steep, except the floor inside the crater. And in his ears, high pitched voices, squealing: *Mr Slipman, Mr Slipman...*


WENDY HAD NO ILLUSIONS: they wouldn't in a million years have chosen each other for room-mates. So that period of time each night between going to their room and actually putting out the light was never going to be easy, was it? Ari was always busy with her various beauty regimes, and on her mobile, checking for new posts and listening to music, and Wendy wasn't sure whether it was out of a kind of politeness (it let them both off making conversation) or just to rub it in, because Wendy's own phone still hadn't turned up. She watched her now, reflected in the mirror: Ari held the phone as if it might have germs, in two fingers of her left hand, and as the index finger of the other hand scrolled down, it was held ridiculously straight so only the very tip made contact, and the little finger stuck out, in a particularly stupid way. Wendy had borrowed Whisper's mobile two days ago at Pompeii, and Jack had never replied. Or so she claimed. Whisper was too interested in Jack, though. Too interested in Jack by half. She gave you sympathy you didn't want. That was her speciality. Whereas Ari Clay just never offered any help to anybody. There went that perfect bubble noise again: a message. Now Ari was texting back. Then came another bubble answer, and she smirked.

Whisper came in without knocking, which was typical of her, and sat on the end of Ari's bed.

'So how was dinner with Mumsy? Was it really special? Any gorgeous waiters?'

''S OK. I've found something out. About Harper.'

'Go on,' said Ari.

'My mum told me. About his hippy bag, or to be more precise, that little make-up purse that fell out in the bus? I know what he's got in it, what he's carrying around everywhere. Which explains why he was so horrible to you. You're not going to believe this. It's human ashes. Bits of his dead wife.'

'Gross!'

'Obsessive. He needs to move on.'

'How did you find out?'

'Mom asked Hammer why he got stopped at the airport.' Wendy smarted at the thought that Whisper Blake, who didn't care one bit about Mr Harper, should be privileged to know something so private and so personal. And how could she sound so matter-of-fact, so cold? 'Mom says he's got a syndrome.'

Wendy broke in: 'That's ridiculous.' She had to say something, and now they had both turned and were looking at her.

'Might have known you'd defend him,' said Whisper, while Ari stood there flicking her hair back, like she was ten years old and playing horses in the playground. 'Why is it so ridiculous? Look at the way he behaved today. I said at the time, either he's on drugs, or he's mentally ill.'

'Why would anybody do something so… gruesome, though?' asked Ari, and did her silly all-purpose look of shock and horror, the one that told you she was an idiot. Wendy had long understood that Whisper Blake didn't need to raise her voice so long as Ariadne Clay was there to dramatise.

Wendy put her right. 'Some people do.'

'What, did you?'

'No. No, I didn't. But for some people, it's a memento. Like wearing a locket.'

Ari said, 'You're right, he could easily be on drugs. The way he behaves,' and you could see her eyes widening at the thought.

'That man has seriously lost it.'

'He has *so* lost it.'

'It's an *issue,* though. We ought to tell someone. We ought to raise a concern.'

Ari agreed. 'But Mrs Hammer already knows, doesn't she, and she doesn't care.' She added a horsey nod, and let the hair fall back in her eyes.

Whisper shook her head and pushed out her lower lip. 'She's another one of his BFFs.' She looked in Wendy's direction, as if to say, *like you.* 'She wouldn't want to take it seriously.'

Wendy told her straight. 'It's not a crime. What's he done wrong?'

'You're as sick as him. He shouldn't be in charge of us. It isn't right. He isn't fit. That's the point.'

'That's the whole point,' said Ari. 'You can't feel safe with him around.'

'Is that what your mum thinks?'

Whisper answered, 'No. She says he's grieving and we should be understanding.'

'Understanding? It's gross,' said Ari.

'Yeah,' said Whisper, 'I don't understand it.' She stared blankly at her friend for a minute, then said, 'I know what to do.' She sounded neutral, unbothered, almost helpful. The same voice she'd use to say, *I know how to make the safe work*. 'Tim said, if ever there was anything we needed, to get in touch. And he's here, somewhere, we saw him, didn't we? Hammer would have to take him seriously. She won't listen to us.'

'What harm is he doing you?' asked Wendy. She knew the red patches would be rising on her neck and chest.

Ari was quick to tell her. 'He's doing none of us any good, is he? My mum made an official complaint to the school but he's still there. The man's a freak.'

'How does it help, if he gets into trouble with the school? We lose our Classics teacher, a month before the exam.'

Whisper answered, 'It's a shame it's only a month. Tim should come and teach us. He'd be better.'

'Yeah, he'd be better.' They said it the way you'd say, that's not your colour, try the blue.

It was a long time before Whisper left and they could get to sleep. Wendy had been forced to listen to a lot of crap about how weird Harper was, from the way he talked using all those long words, right down to the colour of his shoes; then the topic turned to, who should know? Because they were obviously dying to tell everyone; but Whisper went all mature and said they had a responsibility not to upset the others, not to spoil their holiday, so maybe to keep it to themselves for now. Wendy wasn't holding her breath. She reckoned Whisper just wanted to pick her time. That was how a drama queen like her operated. Lying in the dark, Wendy thought about her own mother. Mrs Mundy was the opposite of Mrs Blake, modest, quiet, a background sort of person, who used to run the office for a plumbers' merchant; she was more like Jack really, better with numbers than with people; everyone said she looked like him too. Jack had picked up the ashes from the undertakers. They chose a Monday afternoon when it would be quiet because the kids would be at school. They went to the Country Park, up the hill where you could see right down the river to Canary Wharf. There were little cotton wool clouds on a poster-paint sky, and real wild roses out, and it was just Wendy and her brother, and Jack had been nice that day, somehow


MARTIN HAD NOT INTENDED to sleep after his shower, but was woken by a rapping at the door, and a girl's urgent voice calling, 'Mr Harper!' It took a moment to remember where he was; he was naked and cold, and the dark shape on the bed beside him was made up of his clothes, cast off awkwardly and creased now by his weight. He fumbled his way back into them. Shannon Matthews was standing in the doorway, in a long blue Mickey Mouse tee shirt – obviously serving as a nightdress – and unlaced trainers. 'Mr Harper. Can you come? There's something weird in our room and the hairspray fell off the wardrobe and hit Sam in the eye and she's in a right state.'

Damn, he thought, all I need. The clock showed 12.15. How could he have slept that long? He felt guilty for leaving Amy to sort out whatever problems they might have brought back with them. He had been dutifully carrying a small first aid kit everywhere, somewhat scornfully since, as he told Amy, you would never do that in real life, only in the distorted parallel universe of the school trip. He grabbed it, together with his key card, and heard the door slam behind him. Shannon led the way up to the next floor, along a corridor and into the twin bedded room she shared with Sam, who had been joined by George the Token Male and Emma. Were those two an item now, he wondered? Emma was in demure pyjamas, he wore long shorts and a tee shirt inside-out. There was hardly room to move, now there were five of them in there. It was all typical school trip chaos: towels, plastic coke bottles, and the faint spitting of music leaking from someone's discarded earphones. Yet they looked more worried than the situation seemed to warrant. Sam was sitting upright on the bed, not in it, with no sign of blood. Shannon plonked herself heavily at her feet; the other two, perched on the edge of the bed opposite, budged up to make room for Martin, and George took the opportunity to slip a protective arm behind Emma.

'Have you hurt yourself, Sam?' asked Martin.

'I'm OK,' she said, and tilted her face to point to one side of the bridge of her nose. 'It hit me here, there's a cut, see?' She opened her eyes wide and looked to the far corner of the room, as if this helped.

He stepped forward to look. There was a tiny red mark. 'I don't think you need a plaster,' he said. 'It's not very deep. It would be hard to put one there anyway. You might have a bit of a bruise, though.'

'It's not that. It's the way it happened. Everything moved. Didn't you feel it, sir?'

'What do you mean, everything moved?'

'It didn't,' said Shannon, 'it was just the wardrobe that moved, and we don't know what moved it.' They all stared at it. A low wardrobe, more of a tallboy really, whose doors you'd hardly have room to open, it was so close to the bed.

'Everything moved,' Sam insisted. 'It wasn't just the wardrobe.'

'The wardrobe definitely,' said Shannon. 'I saw it Something made the wardrobe move, and the hairspray wobbled a bit, then it toppled over. I thought maybe it was something on the other side of the wall, so I was going to knock and see if Emma and Jess were awake, only…'

'I went to the door,' said George. 'I think Sam's right, everything moved, I felt the whole building shake. Only Emma didn't feel anything at all.'

Shannon's lip curled into sarcasm. 'Yeah right, the whole earth moved for you, George…'

George looked embarrassed and closed his eyes tight for a minute. Martin reckoned it a safe bet that Jess would be with Hal right now. Simple room switch, oldest trick in the book. Emma was rattled and wouldn't be put down; she sneered right back.

'Look, what are you saying, you think the hotel's got a poltergeist? If you ask me, it was already hanging over the edge.'

'I still say it must have been an earth tremor,' said George. 'Because it lasted a few seconds.' Shannon shook her head, and Emma pointed out, 'An earth tremor is still a thousand times more likely than your single random isolated psychic phenomena.'

This was a good point logically made, thought Martin, who decided he would no more correct Emma's grammar than bawl George out for being in her room. Perhaps that was why they'd woken him instead of Amy – they had him down for a soft touch. 'An earth tremor's quite possible in this region,' he said. 'It'll probably make the local news, and that'll be that. Nothing to worry about, no harm done.'

'There was a massive earthquake before the eruption of 79AD, wasn't there?' offered George.

'Correct... Although that was fifteen years before the eruption, not fifteen minutes.' Martin tried not to come across as sarcastic, they hated that; and it seemed he'd hit the right tone, because George waggled his head and smacked his lips in good-natured disappointment.

'Oh my God,' said Sam, 'even so, what if it was, like, the real thing? A real earthquake? What would we do?' She looked round all of them, and drew every set of eyes to hers, before staring at Martin for an answer.

He remained deadpan. 'You'd have to keep your hairspray in a drawer.' Sam and Emma had to crack.

'Oh, sir,' they tutted and sucked their teeth. 'You never take anything seriously.'

George snorted a smile and shook his curly head. 'I still think it was, though.'

'Well, all I can say,' said Martin, 'was that if it was a tremor, it wasn't strong enough to wake me. And listen. The hotel's pretty quiet. People haven't got up. Except you. You were all awake already.'

'Sir,' said Shannon, 'what are we doing tomorrow?'

'You haven't been reading Mrs Hammer's booklet, have you?' Martin had picked up that *read your booklet* was getting to be a standing joke amongst the kids. He was disloyally happy to play along with that for the moment. Amy criticised them for behaving like passengers, when after all, passengers was what they were. He told them, 'Paestum.'

'Paestum. That's the one that's Greek,' said Sam.

'A Greek settlement, yes, and three fabulous temples. Including a textbook example of the Doric order.'

'And the pictures of the fit blokes,' said Shannon. 'Can't wait.'

'The funerary tablets. And the diving youth. Yes, that's the place.'

'The diver's on your wall.' Emma had noticed it, then. It was a simple, two-dimensional painting of a young man plunging into the water. Tomorrow they would see others, showing more young men chariot racing, drinking, and generally having fun.

'Only they were all gay, right?'

Kids. They had a way of taking an exquisite thing, and chopping off the corners to make it fit inside whatever plastic box they had to hand. It was salutary, really, stopped you taking yourself too seriously.

He stayed and chatted. They needed to calm down, and anyway, he liked their company, and felt so much better for it; they were frank and they were funny. Shannon the shop steward, quiet George, slack jawed and snuffly, who was falling simply, easily in love with Emma the brunette. Razor sharp, that girl. Eventually Sam resumed her cross-eyed quest for split ends, and he knew she was OK. They talked comfortable nonsense. Martin teased them about the awful music they listened to, and they teased him about being a hippy, and when he told them he wasn't even born in the sixties, they said, ooh sorry, how rubbish they were at Maths. So, there was the proof: if you took Whisper Blake and Ariadne Clay out of the equation, the atmosphere was fine. A pity Wendy wasn't there to join in. The class never included her, unless you shamed them into it.

In the end he said what any teacher ought to say in the circumstances. 'It's been a lovely party, but now can we all go back to our own beds and get some sleep?'

He returned calmer himself, and surprised to be feeling much better than he had all day. Typical teenagers, they'd panicked for a minute, total hysteria, then it had all subsided. Just as he'd panicked on the mountain. Time to let it all blow over. He picked up his guide to the Paestum site to refresh his memory for tomorrow's visit, until his eyes grew tired and he could easily fall back to sleep.

Outside, the street was wet from silent rain, and the traffic sparse enough to be annoying; his sleep was elbowed by the hiss of cars, each passing scooter punching him awake. In time the noises all became the fabric of a dream where he sped down many intersecting roads, all of them surfaced with flat, misshapen hexagons of basalt; they had been constructed specially for him, especially black, because basalt was his rock, formed by red-hot lava, tempered by tears to darkness, dark returning to the depths of lightless earth, pure, smooth, fine textured, wholly flawless black. Gradually, as he drove, he lost control; his foot grew numb, and somehow would not reach the brake.

WENDY WOKE EARLY, maybe five thirty, as the flat hotel furniture was beginning to cut its way out of the gloom. Last night's conversation with Whisper and Ari was re-assembling itself in her memory. By the time the soft dull grey about her had sharpened into lines and almost colour, she had decided she must tell Mr Harper that they'd found out about the contents of his bag. Which meant she'd have to get him on his own.

## Day 5 Paestum

MAYBE BECAUSE NAPLES and Sorrento were so cramped and busy, Paestum always felt to Martin like a balm. The road became a kind of promenade, abutted on one side by little shops and the museum, and now, in April, the site itself, spreading away on the right hand side, was a wash of green, exactly as in his hopeful memory. Open and lovely. Three Greek temples stood against a frank blue sky, crisply golden in the sun, with beyond them flatland. That rogue bamboo you saw everywhere about the plain had muscled its way through, but he knew it hid the reeds of ancient times, of Syrinx and of Pan. Beyond them, over the generous horizon, he sensed the nearness of the Tyrrhenian Sea.

This much he had expected. But not the scent of hay, which was what made his heart leap now; the long grass around the excavations had been cut, as on the day he had first brought Julia here; he distinctly heard her gasp again, now, at the sheer beauty of the place, and felt her hand clasp his forearm in delight.

There were several groups of Italian primary school children about the site, with smart haircuts and straight fringes, and uniforms which managed to look like normal clothes; these little ones were so innocently obedient and eager to be shown things. In contrast, the Hanningford party didn't do straight lines. They began their tour at the temple of Athena, where Martin delivered his lecture on the Doric order. Here, the students could now judge properly for themselves the aesthetic effect of *entasis,* the swelling half way up the fluted columns, so pronounced in this famous example. *Some say it mimics the tension of a flexed muscle, what do you think of that?* George looked as though he was ready to be persuaded, and so did Emma, but Shannon scrunched up her face and said she couldn't see it, sir. Then Ari Clay reminded them that this was on the syllabus. In the end, it all came down to naming things. *Frieze, pediment, entablature.* Some of them were barely looking at all. Once he had said his piece, the group walked on. The Judas trees that stood casually about the site were flowering now, their rosy pink so easy on the eye; but the Catsea girls, Shannon and Sam, pronounced them weird and spooky. It was strange the way the bloom burst straight from the trunk, with no stem for intermediary. Julia loved them, and wanted to grow one back in Essex, but they never did. Nearer the ground, tiny, bright, spring flowers, red, orange, yellow, purple, blue, had escaped the mower by sheltering amongst the stones. They bore a message, for sure. The ancients read signs in everything; each herb or shrub was named for something, some nymph translated. Some message was recorded here which he might now recover, if only he could be alone to see it, hear it, pick it up. The vastness and the openness of the site made it an easy matter to stray from the group; Martin had the excuse of a whole razed city here, whose low walls needed to be scrutinised. If any of the kids were to see him stooping over ruins, they'd have the sense to leave him to it. He'd only have to watch out for the adults, and that was hardly difficult, because their main focus was on mithering the students. They were annoying him today: they didn't care enough, they didn't appreciate Paestum for its beauty, only its strangeness, and the chance to uncover in the sun.

See? Another strappy top, and shoulders that ghastly English April white.

Amy had led them in the direction of the *bouleuterion*, the council building. So after that she would likely continue to the amphitheatre. Martin headed slowly to the opposite, western edge of the site, down the *via sacra*, as he had with Julia before. Half-consciously, he felt for her presence now; of course, he wouldn't see her, he never did, but she might slip from the green curtain of reeds beyond the honeycomb of ruined habitations to link her arm in his. Or he might feel her cheek against his own. He loved this place because of the way the natural world caressed it. Here his wife was immanent. He breathed the sweet hay and made himself as open to Julia as he could; her name repeated in his head. *Nurse the thought, think only of this...* Today was gone. He walked as in a former time, and he had only turned away; she must be there behind him, right now, surely, ready to exclaim, or sigh, or say his name. Even after twelve years together, he always quickened to hear his name upon her lips.

That was a woman's footfall close behind, light, rapid and assured.

'Mr Harper...'

It was Wendy, just a few feet away, and she was panting from the effort to catch up with him. 'Mr Harper...' Her unnaturally dark red eyebrows performed an extraordinary dance, from an arch to a frown, as she read his face, which could only express disappointment. And annoyance. *Not now. Don't pester me. Don't distract me now.* She was on her own, and that most likely meant that she was carrying some irksome message from Amy and the rest.

'Mr Harper... D'you mind if I...' She stopped walking, and stood, feet planted apart, like a sailor, with one hand on her hip, whilst the other pushed the hair out of her eyes, not with her fingers, but with the back of her wrist; an odd gesture, and inefficient, as repeatedly the henna-tinted hair just fell straight back in her face. 'Well, the thing is, I think I ought to tell you something.'

'Tell me.'

'About you. Well, what they're saying about you. Whisper is. And Ari Clay.'

'I know. It doesn't matter, though.'

'You don't know.'

'Try me.'

She stared at him, and her mouth hung open for a moment, a little mouth for such big flat unmatched front teeth. She frowned her pantomime frown, and the bright pencilled eyebrows pressed down again over the watery grey glass-marble eyes. 'You're not laughing,' she remarked.

'Is it a laughing matter?'

'Only, you usually do.' She wasn't laughing either. 'The thing is,' she went on, 'they know what it is. That you're carrying round everywhere.' She stared straight at the deep canvas bag which hung from his shoulder, and which he was gripping to his side.

'Mrs Hammer told Mrs Blake and Mrs Blake told Whisper. It's Mrs Harper, isn't it?' She smiled at him as you might smile at a child. He was utterly disarmed. He sat down on a low wall, the remnant of a home, and she placed herself on an equally low wall opposite him, across the ancient street. The bag now sat comfortably in his lap. The stone rasped against his palm and the fingers of his steadying hand rearranged themselves to find a comfortable hold. He felt sick to his stomach. Wendy said, 'They think it's weird that you're carrying her around. I think they're going to complain to the Head when they get back. I don't think they have yet.' Hastily, she added, 'I haven't said anything. Apart from telling Whisper you've done nothing wrong, but it *is* wrong to go poking your nose into other people's private lives.'

'I haven't done anything wrong,' he said, but he was starting to worry: it made sense to him, but it would make no sense to others, it made no sense to a bunch of teenagers, of course they were shocked, of course, it would make no sense to Amy or to Gareth Whittaker; or the bus driver, or the woman who sold their tickets, or that guy over there, or that woman there... Oh, but nothing would surprise Barbara Blake, she'd wring some twisted sense out of it. Probably already had. This was anguish: something which had seemed so natural was starting to seem out of place. In minutes, seconds, he saw everything with public eyes, and none of it would do. Back in October, it had mattered to him so much to be allowed to do this trip, not just to be officially back in the saddle, but to make sure that Julia was there in spirit with the kids, borrowing her itinerary, seeing to all the little things she used to care about. Now, his weight had shifted, and those weren't the things that filled his head.

In front of him, Wendy sat motionless. They remained like this for some time. She wouldn't take her eyes from him, and the steadiness of that gaze was like the holding of a hand. This girl knew things.

He asked, 'Where did you bury your mum?'

'We took her ashes to the country park. She sort of asked.' A smile of deep satisfaction settled on Wendy's face, the unmistakable smile of a job well done.

'We used to walk there too.' His left hand noticed how rough the lichen felt, and as they talked, he had to finger the uneven masonry. 'You can see so far. Right up the Thames to London. Past Catsea. Past the river crossing. We used to go there sometimes on Sunday afternoons. Or Hanningford woods. Or up to Burnham. That was our favourite place for a walk.' He saw them all at once, all those golden afternoons torn from a working week, sunlight through yellow leaves, chestnuts underfoot, clouds over Kent, shimmer of tall grass, the mudflats and the estuaries great and small. As vivid and as precious as the memory of walking here.

'Oh no, we never went,' said Wendy. 'Well, I did, with the school. But Mum didn't. It was somewhere she wanted to go, right? Because I'd told her about it, how it was really great up there away from all the houses. One time, when we still thought she'd get better, her physio said, "What's your goal, Mrs Mundy?" Because they always make you have a goal. And she said, "To walk up the country park." Only she never. So that's where I took her. Where she wanted to go?' Her voice ended every phrase on an uplift, and the triumphal smile winded him with its simplicity. No whiff of tragedy here, no regret, no might have beens. She'd bring the same smile to any tangible thing, a hand-decorated birthday cake or a nice cup of tea. Up to now, he had always seen this as an academic limitation – Wendy's lack of time for stuff that only *might* have happened. But now it began to look more like a spiritual accomplishment. She had hold of life. See how she hung on… It was an instinct with her.

'That was a good thing you did, Wendy, for your mum.'

'Why *do* you never let her from your sight?' she asked, and he listened for an answer. He was surprised that there was none. He couldn't remember. Meeting his silence, she put another question: 'What are you going to do? Only, you can't carry Mrs Harper round for ever.'

'I wasn't going to. I'm not going to.' His eyes were filming over, and she must surely be able to see this. Her look was grave now, and her thin lips had settled almost to a flat line. She still wouldn't look away. He wondered what were the things these glassy eyes had seen, which allowed her to be comfortable with him now?

'Maybe they won't tell, because they shouldn't know. Mrs Blake was well out of order.'

She had run up here and sought him out to warn him. She was worried for him. But what was to be done? His brain was somersaulting. Did it matter? Did it not? Should he be angry, or ashamed? Should he treat it like just another one of those annoying things kids can get up to, that you'd best ignore, don't be drawn in... Or was this the big one, the fatal wound that would bring him down... Because nobody would understand, and how could you expect them to? The Safeguarding mantra was, children had a right to feel safe. Did they not feel safe with him? They were standing maybe a hundred and fifty yards away, being lectured by Amy in an enclosed space; all in a safe circle. If the whisper went round... he couldn't imagine what words he might summon to explain – if he tried, they would say, see, he's lost it, we told you so, what kind of weirdo brings his dead wife on a school trip? And that was maybe the worst thought of all, that something which made sense to him six months ago, that made sense to him yesterday, was wrong – their word would be, *inappropriate* – now. He hadn't considered that. At least, not long enough to take it seriously.

'You've done a better job than me, Wendy.'

He was sickened. It would be something for everyone to talk about, over dinner, on the way home, back at school, endlessly... Speculation would smear along behind him now like dog shit on a shoe. He looked across the reed bed and wondered how far it was to the horizon. There was nothing worthwhile here on all this plain, and he was so weary now. Jump, from the steep dark side of the crater. Jump. Not fair on other people, she'd suggested. But other people were not being fair on him. He had let Julia down a second time, at the moment of her death, and now with this fiasco.

He looked across at the teenager who hadn't moved and hadn't answered. She seemed to be waiting for him to tell her more. He lifted the bag slightly and explained, with what he felt to be a broken smile: 'I promised I would never go back to Vesuvius without her.' He skim read the faint small type which stated that this was not a conversation he should be having with a pupil. Too late, he'd done it now. He was damned. He might as well ask Wendy one thing straight. 'Look... what was that guy Slipman doing there? Do you know much about him?'

Wendy grimaced. 'No. I only know one thing about him really. Ariadne Clay thinks he walks on water. So he's probably a wanker. Sorry sir but you asked.' Out came a stupid noise halfway between a chuckle and a snort, which his pupil returned in kind; it was nervous on both their parts, a release of tension. A pause, and he could see her thoughts gathering; she wanted to tell him something.

'Mr Harper,' said Wendy, 'about Mrs Harper... Only, I really think you need to let her go.'

He laughed. 'What do you mean, let her go? You make it sound as though I'm giving her the sack.'

The girl was unperturbed, the upward intonation back: 'I don't mean her remains. Some people keep that sort of thing, don't they? On the mantelpiece. No, I mean... just let her be dead.'

He hadn't seen it this way before: as a permission only he could grant.

'How do you do that, Wendy? How did you? If you have?'

'Look,' she said – her wide eyes focused on an empty middle distance, her face was upturned with her chin pushed slightly to one side, and she seemed so sure of herself – 'they say *rest in peace*, right? Well peace means, leave them alone, stop hassling them. Perhaps it was easier for me, because mum was so ill for so long, and I knew she wanted me to have everything I needed and be happy, and she couldn't really make that happen, could she? I mean with your mum, right, everyone's always on at their mum for something, every kid wants stuff from their parents. You don't stop wanting stuff but you learn to stop hassling. So the more I learned to sort myself out, the better it was for both of us. That way, she got to see me grow up. And I don't wonder now about how things might have been. I just leave her in peace.'

With a movement of his head to the left, he gestured towards the two great temples they had yet to visit, one set behind the other to the south side of the site, buildings which he knew to be massive but which from this distance appeared breathtakingly delicate, their chiselled columns fine and clear against the sky, in shades of ochre that were almost orange.

'What do you think of this place, Wendy?'
'Well, it's beautiful, isn't it.'
'It was once thick with people, a big town.'
'So it's prob'ly more beautiful now than it was then.'

PERCHED ON THE TOP TIER of rough stone seats, Ari and her best friend were far enough away from the rest of the party to carry on a muttered conversation unchecked. Whisper had got Tim's mobile number from her mother, weeks ago, but she claimed it was always on voicemail. She'd texted several times, and held out the phone to show it: *Hi. We're here in Italy, on the trip. Something's happened and we need to talk it over its very sesnstive. x wspa*

Did they really need to 'talk it over'? Ari had a bad feeling about this. There were times she didn't understand Whisper. Once she got hooked on an idea, it was like she was in her own world, and Ari couldn't follow it, any more than she could follow Harper when he was on one of his weird rants about the Tragedy.

A lot of the time these days, Ari felt there was something that she didn't understand, something that was obvious to other people but made no sense to her. As if she were stupid. She'd felt like that all year. Now a voice was telling her not to rock the boat. Her life needed to be as calm and as straightforward as possible at this time, she needed attention and quiet and lots of little rewards like hot chocolate at night and photos from the trip and proper notes and regular breaks from revision. Not to be distracted. 'If your mum was really worried about Harper,' she pointed out, 'she'd want the school to know. She's clever. She'd know what to do.'

Her friend seemed to hover over the idea. She didn't look sure. 'It's confidentiality, isn't it?' said Whisper, with a shrug. 'Hammer told her in confidence. With my mom's line of work, confidentiality is, like, a *big* thing. If she broke a confidence, that would be *professional suicide*.'

But she told you, thought Ari. 'Maybe she could be, you know, subtle?'

'D'you know what I think?' said Whisper. 'I think my mom believes she can help him. Which she probably can. She wants to. She says, some day, he's gotta come round and someone should be there for him.'

'Who's been there for us, in the meantime?' said Ari.

'Exactly. My mom just doesn't ever ask that question.'

'She could get the school to get Tim to come in and teach us, and everything. For Harper's own good. They'd listen to her.'

Whisper murmured without conviction, which meant she'd pretty well frustrated that conversation. Amy Hammer was droning on in the green semicircle below them. It was covered in low, blunt-leaved weeds. They hadn't even tried to make a lawn of it, and this was meant to be a World Heritage Site, for godssake. This whole place was a toilet, really.

Whisper nudged Ari and nodded in the direction of two figures some distance away, sitting opposite each other. Harper, with Wendy Mundy: just the two of them. 'Oh my god, oh my *god*,' said Ari. 'Gross!'

'Well that's one for the album,' said Whisper. 'Or how about a video this time?'

She held it in their direction for a minute or two, and started to pan around, maybe for some sort of effect.

'I'm out of water,' said Ari. 'Can I have some of yours?'

'Sure, help yourself.' She nodded to the shoulder bag at her feet, and Ari put her hand inside. It was a big, pouch shaped thing, with no proper compartments, so everything was in a muddle at the bottom, and she had to fish about. But before she came to the water bottle, she found a mobile phone.

'That's not yours.' Whisper's white phone was in her hand. This one was sludgy grey.

'My number two phone,' said Whisper. 'Just borrowing it.'

'It's Wendy Mundy's, isn't it?' Ari laughed, in a *what-are-you-like* sort of way, but it made her uneasy. How had Whisper got hold of it? And why?'

'Where d'you find it? Aren't you going to give it back?'

'Yes. I just found it lying around. I have no intention permanently to deprive,' she said, rather oddly, looking serious. 'That's the legal definition.'

'Definition?'

'Of theft. I found it, but I'm going to give it back. Of course I am. You're my witness.'


FOR THE REST of the visit, Wendy kept her distance from all the adults, as well as Whisper and Ari. Hal and Jessica were still joined at the hip, and now George and Emma seemed to have paired off, and she didn't really know Katy or Tiff, which just left Sam and Shannon to talk to. Wendy liked Shannon, you knew where you stood with her. She was careful not to pester them or interrupt, and in any case, she was trying her hardest now to concentrate on the purpose of the visit. The other two temples were enormous, farther away than you realised, and like with the temple of Athena, a little rail made sure you didn't get too near them. What Wendy most wanted to do was to walk up those steps, and to stand inside; although there wasn't an obvious inside, only parallel rows of columns you could see right through, for most of the length of the building. It was like looking through enormous railings that stopped you from seeing anything properly. If she hadn't felt so awkward now about Mrs Hammer – because let's face it, she'd dobbed her in well and proper with Mr Harper, telling him Mrs Hammer was the one who'd leaked his secret – she'd have liked to talk about this inside / outside thing, and tell the teachers how she wanted to find out what it felt like to stand where only the priests were allowed, and to know what they could see. Until you could stand up there, and look down, the temples could only make you feel insignificant.

Mr Harper was avoiding the adults, too. He hung near the lovers. He looked awful, his shoulders bent as if there was a load of house bricks in that bag of his, not a tiny precious purse, and the lines on his forehead made a black V in the strong sunlight, but the real giveaway was those little muscles round his mouth that couldn't lie and that made him look wrong. And old. It was well into the afternoon before they sat to eat their packed lunch outside the museum. He caught nobody's eye and had this little fake smile that you knew he'd just put on for show. At last they went inside, to see the diving boy and the funerary tablets, which he had on posters in his office at school and which were so much *his thing*, which you could tell from the way he'd gone on about them in the lesson, but he just disappeared. He saw all the students through the turnstile, but he didn't go round the museum with them. Wendy thought maybe he had overtaken them, so as to get straight to the thing he most wanted to see, which would be the paintings of the boys, obviously. There were so many pots on display, and even Wendy was starting to have had enough of looking at stuff, so you couldn't blame the rest of the group if there was a lot of shuffling and sighing and playing with phones going on. It was hard on Hal, because he didn't even do Class Civ, and museums weren't his thing. He and Jessica hurried on ahead, and everybody walked through from one room to the next; even Mrs Hammer wasn't exactly lingering. It was a funny place, not old, but not really modern either, with lots of different shaped rooms and more than one way round, so the group quickly broke up. When you finally came to the paintings, though, you had to stop because the colours were amazing, which meant they all met up there and took loads of photos, especially of the diver. You could see why it was famous. It wasn't a great drawing, but at least you could tell what it was. Not a myth. Just a great thing to do. Being alive.

Paintings or no paintings, they were all ready to leave a good half hour before the meeting time. They sat in the little garden outside the entrance; time went on, drinks were finished, there was time to buy ice creams from the kiosk down the way and eat them too. Everyone was getting restless. Hal and Jessica, arms tightly linked, started pushing each other sideways, playing a game where one of them would draw something in the dust with their feet, and the other had to wipe it out and scuffle it over. Jessica shrieked and laughed, until Hal bumped her with such force she almost knocked an Italian woman over, and Mrs Hammer told them to simmer down because it was a public place. Emma asked, who were they still waiting for, and Ari said, Mr Harper, and Whisper said, of course. Somebody groaned. Mrs Hammer zipped her rucksack up and asked Barbara Blake to look after it while she went back inside, to fetch him, obviously. When they finally appeared at the shiny glass doors, Wendy's stomach churned. They weren't just talking, they were arguing, and she knew it was her fault because of what she'd told him. He was the angry one; he kept cutting the air with his hand, and his head was bobbing up and down, having a real go at her, while Mrs Hammer was saying *no, no,* and her face was red and serious, but she wouldn't look him in the eye, just kept looking straight ahead at the party who were waiting for them, and who started to notice they were back. Mrs Hammer stopped in her tracks for a moment and turned to say something to him, and she was very quiet, as well as very definite, standing up very straight to face him; but he was in a temper, and Wendy was sure she heard him say, *only telling the truth? So that makes it alright, does it?* She hoped the others hadn't heard. For all Wendy knew, Mrs Hammer might have been the only friend he had, and now that would be the end of that friendship, and it was all her fault. She had been wrong to tell him, and wrong to get involved.

They all marched down to where the bus driver said he would be parked and found that not only was he there already, but the other schools were seated, and peering down at them from behind dark tinted windows.

Whisper said, 'Look, Mr Harper, see what you've done, you've made everybody wait.' She made it sound like an innocent comment, half teasing; it was the sort of thing Shannon might have come out with, and everyone would have laughed, teachers included. Nobody laughed at Whisper. And Mr Harper was beside himself. He spoke sharply to her – *Just get on the bus! Now!* – which only made her stare. Wendy cringed on his account, he had made such a mess of it; it came out all wrong, the way you might talk to a small child, your own child, not someone else's, and specially not a girl in the Sixth Form whose mum was standing right behind you. Whisper unfroze, brought her shoulders to her ears, and held her open hands up as if to meet the blast:

'Whoa, whoa, OK, OK,' then headed up the steps, her body language telling the whole world that he was the aggressor.

On the coach, everybody felt awkward. Like Wendy, Mrs Hammer wasn't at all sure where to sit.

MARTIN KNEW he had over-reacted, but turned his mind away from that, the better to arm himself with indignation. Throughout the journey back, as they drove past ploughed fields and through growing traffic, he raked over the bad behaviour of these two women. Starting with Amy's feeble defence, that she had only told the truth about why they'd stopped him at the airport. Let's look at all the things that we know to be true, shall we? Let's make the whole truth open to everyone. Every truth, mind. Let's all disclose how often we change the bed and what kind of porn we watch online. Let's hear why nobody at school has ever seen Mr Blake, and how Barb calculates her fees. Let's proclaim abroad that antibiotics can make you sick, that we don't live in a meritocracy, that whole nations exist without school uniform, that death is always closer to you than a rat on a London street, and the ability to talk complete and utter fluent bollocks is not the sole prerogative of the male of the species. Let's tell the children all that and see if it cheers them up. It wasn't just that Amy had always seemed so very much more professional than him, he'd thought she had more common sense than just about anyone he knew. Worse, he'd assumed some sort of loyalty from her, and this misreading was radical. She looked thoroughly miserable right now, behind her quirky spectacles, and well she bloody might.

Then there was Barbara Blake and her fucking psychobabble, and *Complicated Grief.* Ye gods, the idiocy of it.

So what about a *diagnosis* for her loopy daughter? Let's find a name for that, shall we... A syndrome. Something Greek. Whisper, who found her way to the foreground of every picture, who suffered every random misfortune from travel sickness to wilful underestimation of her academic potential; Whisper, who was so fiercely, indignantly blameless. Nothing stuck. Call it Iphigenia syndrome. Except that Iphigenia was a true sacrificial victim, whereas this little blonde was calculating, malevolent, manipulative. You couldn't blame a teenager, she was still only half-made. At her mother's knee, he speculated, she'd learnt that nothing she did carried moral responsibility, because the main thing in life was to *deal with it and move on*; she'd picked up a language which allowed her to banish every criticism into thin air. Iphigenia was a pawn, but Whisper was a protagonist, a mover, or at least a catalyst. In his mind's eye, Julia raised a warning hand: *don't hate a child. Where are you going with this, Martin? Listen to yourself.*

Julia's voice – so longed for, now so troubling – brought back another doubt. Was it possible that Whisper knew something more than she let on? Something about Timothy Slipman's relationship with his wife? In all those private tutorials, might he have mentioned Julia to her? Or to Ariadne Clay? There was that post card in Julia's file. He asked her now: *Did you ever visit the House of the Faun with him? I feel you did...* But there was no reason to think that, none at all. *All the same, I rattle from one question to the next and back again. I can't address a single one. I thought this jealousy was over, but I can't stop asking.* Eventually, a tiredness overtook him which was leaden, plutonic, the pull of gravity towards a molten core, and all his thoughts, which had been so sharp and energetic, now disintegrated in one ill-defined wretchedness, neither dreamed nor waking.

It was a long time before the mountain showed on the horizon, and when it did, they noticed a tiny lick of pale smoke rising from it, flattening slightly like an airline vapour trail or a little cloud, but the only cloud in an otherwise empty sky. In the full three hours it took them to get back, the cloud persisted without ever getting any bigger, and of course, everyone wanted a photograph, but through the bus windows, and so far away, a photograph could only disappoint; it just looked like a smudge; so they tutted and were keen to get into the open air. Hanningford was the last school group to be dropped off, and they'd had to stop at four separate hotels on the way, crawling through the traffic from the approach to Sorrento. Martin hung back and waited for everybody else to enter the building, on the pretext he would sweep the coach for lost property, although in fact they all swarmed across the road to the little square on the cliff edge, to get that shot of the smoking volcano. They sped away, whilst he had lead in his veins. Slowly, he picked up litter, plastic bottles, wrappers, rolled-up handouts. Arriving at the door of his room, he couldn't find the key card which ought to have been in his wallet. He returned downstairs, where Paolo the concierge and his colleague in the bar were watching the television news. Paolo listened, shook his head respectfully and suggested, with an easy, good-natured amusement, that perhaps Martin had the key card in his pocket? It was an easy mistake to make. Martin indulged him, turned all his pockets out, but they didn't find it. He didn't distinctly remember putting it away that morning, but that was an age ago, and he had travelled so far since then. Perhaps in your bag, said Paolo; this happens when we are tired, we lose things. Martin didn't want to disappoint this sweet-natured, soft-eyed man who eyed him in a kindly way, as if he were a child, and a child was what he wanted now to be, innocent and cared for and cradled, and with adults there to lift the questions off him like a sweater, arms up, so… Julia's bright Bolivian shoulder bag was sitting on Paolo's counter now, and as if in obedience to some sage parental request, Martin began to lift things out. Meekly, he emptied all its contents: first aid kit, phone, camera, pocket dictionary, guidebook, notebook, handouts, a couple of receipts, and of course, the glistening red brocade purse. 'Oh, oh, la bella… she's beautiful!' said Paolo, and Martin replied, 'She was.' 'Ragazzi!' said Paolo, perhaps realising his own indiscretion, and shaking his head in sympathy, 'Kids! They make you carry the lost property of all the world. And the girls are the worst. Who knows, the contents of a teacher's bag?' There was no key card. Paolo nodded to one side, serious, consoling, and said, 'Don't worry, sir, please wait. We can make another.' While Martin packed everything back, he did just that.

At dinner, Martin was so weary that sitting in a straight-backed chair almost hurt. The youngsters were scratchy and pronounced their seafood pasta disgusting, pushing their plates aside and ostentatiously filling up on bread rolls. It was Martin's turn to stand duty downstairs, which meant another couple of hours before he'd be allowed to stretch out and lie down. Not that it should involve much, other than being available and maybe following his coffee with a beer. He didn't expect company.

SO, MR HARPER was on duty, was he. Well he could damn well deal with it, thought Barbara Blake. There he was, the klutz, with his back to the TV, staring into space unaware, as if nothing was happening, while all around him people were on their phones, texting, or checking the net; the hotel staff weren't even trying to conceal that they had half an eye on the screen. Unhealthy introspection, that was his problem. Well, here was his wake-up call. She moved fluently and decisively to place herself on the low square leather armchair in front of him. She crossed her legs, one hand brushing down her cream Capri pants, then took the sunglasses off her head – it was evening now – and set them carefully on the shiny glass surface of the coffee table between them. Their slick black arms remained outstretched, marking a territory. She asked him what he was going to do about it, and of course, he had no idea what she was talking about.

'The alert? You haven't heard? The volcano. It's gone from green to yellow.'

'Has it?'

'I can't believe you haven't noticed. Nobody's talking about anything else. It's been on BBC and CNN. Look right behind you. It's trending' – she waved her mobile in case he didn't get it – 'and it's already gone round the kids like wildfire. So what are you going to do?'

At last, he quickened, and said, 'I could put in a word with the gods.' She scrutinised the little lines about his eyes; there was a softness, and although the words could be taken as facetious, the tone of their delivery was not; this might be genuine humour. An olive branch, held out from him to her. She was momentarily disarmed, and in spite of herself gave a little indulgent chuckle. This was one complex individual.

With the most extraordinarily expressive eyes, that every now and then lent their own spice to what he said.

'OK.' He was quite serious now, and his long fingers – musician's fingers – massaged both cheeks. 'OK. What does yellow mean?'

She tapped speedily at the phone and passed him the open tab, watching as he scrolled down, and adding her gloss. 'So, yellow is the second of four levels. *The Phase of Attention*. But look, the fourth level, the red level, *Alarm*, basically means it's already too late, you should have got the hell out of here by yesterday.' Nothing seemed to impress Martin Harper, however. When he'd finished reading, he looked up at her and said, 'So it's hardly panic stations, is it?'

That was patronising. She wasn't panicking. She was reacting. No, she was pre-empting. 'Martin, we have young people here who are likely to become very distressed. We need to be ready for that. Keep them calm. Give them some sort of reassurance that they're safe. We need a strategy for them.' He dipped his head in agreement, there, that was just like him, conciliatory again. But she shouldn't need to be telling him this. 'You guys are in charge. And you need to be ready. In case it escalates.'

'It's just a bit of smoke,' he said. 'Besides, we're at a safe distance.'

'Well, tell that to the parents.' Relaxed was one thing, but this man was downright complacent. 'They don't know whether to worry or not. So by default, they will, that's what a parent does.'

He seemed to accept it, from the way he dipped his head again. Of course, Barbara reflected, he wasn't a parent himself. But she could see that there was more to it than that.

Martin Harper's inability to empathise was general, she reckoned, not specific. Part and parcel of the way that he presented right now. She was ready to bet that it had not always been this way.

She breathed in, and out, digging deep to find her latent, native generosity; then gave him the help she could by saying, calmly, clearly, 'You've got to tell them the score. You've got to contact your parents and tell them what to think.'

'She's right, Martin. We've got to get round that contact list.' Well hallelujah, thought Barb, there was Amy Hammer right on cue, hovering over them, mobile in hand. She plonked her funny floral-printed knapsack bag thing on the sofa next to Martin, and for herself, drew up a chair at a third side of the low table. Amy's appearance turned this into a meeting. She smoothed a few stray wisps of hair back, and pinched her cute little nose, ready for action.

'I was looking for you earlier. I wondered where you were,' said Barbara.

'I've been on the phone non-stop. Feels like. So: I'll tell you what I've found out. We'll have to get the kids together pdq for a meeting, but before we do, let's work out what we're saying and how we're going to say it.'

As she spoke, she fixed her gaze on the table top. Amy had a lot to impart and wasn't going to be interrupted. She had already spoken to Gareth Whittaker, and the Head, who'd called her. But first, Amy had contacted the rep from their travel company, and as she explained, that had not been easy – getting them to answer was the first problem, getting sense out of them was harder. The rep had said it was probably nothing and would all blow over – unfortunate choice of phrase; they weren't anywhere near the evacuation zone so not to worry. As far as the company was concerned, it was business as usual and they would be picked up in two days' time from their hotel as planned; in the meantime they could enjoy their last day. But they planned to take the Circumvesuviana to Herculaneum next day; and that, surely, must be inside the danger zone? Oh, yes. She supposed so. Well in that case, the rep had said, it's up to you, it's only yellow, not orange. So the first decision was, could they chance going to Herculaneum the next day? Amy was thinking no.

Amy had talked the whole situation over with Gareth back in England. He'd been great, she said. He'd said, if the authorities called off the alert in the morning, which could happen, and if she judged it was safe to make the trip as planned, he'd back her up. If they called off the alert but she didn't feel comfortable, fine, miss out Herculaneum, it would still be there next year. Martin Harper sniggered at this point in her account. *If you wake up tomorrow morning and everything's the same,* Gareth had told her in no uncertain terms, *don't move. Don't go anywhere. Sit tight.* At that point in her narration Amy raised her eyes from the glassy surface of the coffee table and turned to Martin: 'That's a clear direction.' And again, Martin was in agreement. All through this exposition, Barbara's opinion of Amy Hammer was shifting, improving. She'd thought this funny little doll-faced woman, with her mania for lists and numbers and zipped compartments, must have pink fluff for brains. But here she was, taking control, a woman after her own heart. Amy guided their discussion with a pretty steady hand.

Barb and Amy pooled what they had learned about the yellow, second level alert, going back to the text on the phone. It simply meant that the authorities were preparing for escalation. The public weren't involved, and nothing much would be happening. It was the next level, the orange alert, that would mean they'd call a State of Emergency. Even that didn't entail out and out evacuation, other than for hospitals. It meant that the inhabitants who wished to leave would be helped, with civil defence posted to prevent looting. Looting! As far as they could understand, people would travel under their own steam but there would be some road diversions to help keep the flow moving in the right direction. That all sounded serious enough. You'd want to keep the youngsters as far away from that as possible.

So, asked Barbara, was there another place for them to visit tomorrow, locally, or ideally heading south? The Amalfi Drive was the obvious excursion. But they'd need to book a minibus or join a coach trip, and even if they could, at this short notice, would there be enough money in their contingency fund? Amy said that there might very well be other contingencies, if things got worse, and if they found themselves stranded. Not, she said – and she was actually wagging her finger at them both – that any of them should say that to the kids. 'With the students,' she said, 'we stick to what we know, we don't dramatise, we don't hypothesise either. We tell them that tomorrow's trip to Herculaneum is unlikely to take place, but we'll take a rain check in the morning; and they are completely safe here. Then, if we have to spend tomorrow here, here's what we do. We give them the run of the hotel, the piazzetta, the beach. We let them go up to the main road to shop, provided they hang out in twos and threes. There's plenty to keep them amused. They'll be fine with that. We tell them, contact your parents, if you haven't already, and let them know you're OK, although Mr Whittaker will probably have called them already by now.'

Martin had nodded, listened, and said very little. Barbara's mind began to race, and she snatched her turn to take the floor. Her point was this. If they didn't feel safe to travel to Herculaneum tomorrow, how would they be getting home on Friday? How did that idiot from the travel company imagine they would get from their position here, far to the south of Vesuvius, to the airport, which was north-west of Naples, and with the volcano right in their path? You'd think they'd have some basic grasp of Geography, in their line of business. In her opinion, they needed to be back on the telephone, not just to the rep, but to the rep's line manager, to the Head Office back in England if need be, to confirm an alternative flight.

But Amy, who had sounded so feisty a moment ago, seemed to have no stomach for that. She kept repeating, 'One thing at a time.' One thing at a time! At this point, Barbara put her straight: 'You're cooking a roast dinner. You can boil your peas five minutes before you sit down to eat. Your broccoli, your bread sauce, three minutes in the microwave, and that's just fine. But if you didn't de-frost that chicken in the first place, you have, no, dinner.' It was no surprise to Barbara that Martin Harper smirked. But Amy, well... Amy disappointed her. 'Your flight home is the chicken,' she added, just in case she hadn't understood.

*MRS HAMMER got us together for a meeting in the bar that night. We knew what it was about. Everyone had already started messaging, because some of the parents had seen it on the news and that was why I said, can anybody lend me a phone, to text Jack just in case he's worried. Mrs Hammer said the school was contacting the parents individually with a statement, then she remembered it was me and she said oh, sorry. So I said will they contact Jack and she said yes he's your contact isn't he but Mrs Hammer texted Jack anyway just to let him know I was OK. It had been a long enough day already and the teachers were stressed out. We got back quite late, it had been a slow drive and there was a really bad atmosphere. Whisper wouldn't stop slagging off Mr Harper because he'd shouted at her, and for keeping everyone waiting, and Mrs Hammer overheard her say he was probably stoned most of the time anyway, so she had to react didn't she, she couldn't let that go.*

*She told us she'd been on the phone to the school and the travel company and explained about the yellow alert and what it meant. And how we would probably need to change our plans for the next day, to be on the safe side. Also how we weren't in the evacuation zone because we were on the other side of the bay. Which was the truth. But Shannon kind of screeched, 'Oh my god, we were standing on it yesterday!' And there was a lot of, 'I can't believe they let us do that,' and 'didn't they know?' and for a minute, everyone went mental. Emma asked would it affect the journey home, and Mrs Blake piped up and said perhaps we would be flying back from another airport. Then some random guy who was just sitting in the bar (he was one of the northern lot, he'd been listening to everything), this random guy said if it looked bad, they'd close the motorway northwards to ordinary traffic. Ari Clay said, everybody's going to be leaving at once, she said it was going to be one big snarl-up out there. She said why couldn't we leave now while it was still possible, and the teachers tried to calm everybody down, because the travel company knew and they were getting the best advice. People were starting to panic, especially Ari, only she was really winding everybody up, until in the end Mrs Hammer shouted at her to shut up and get a grip. Personally I think that was an appropriate reaction.*

*The trouble was, when everyone went to bed, they all started working through the TV channels, trying to find out more. The ones in English gave you scary headlines (will this be the big one, sort of thing) but the languages we didn't understand were maybe worse, because all you had to go on was the pictures, and it was all explosions and molten lava and humungous clouds of ash, billowing away. When all we'd seen was a dainty little cloud that looked like it was just your neighbour having a bonfire.*

## Day 6 Herculaneum – cancelled

PROPPED IN BED WATCHING the news the next morning, Martin had enough Italian to work out they were talking about increased seismic activity in the region. Small tremors were a regular occurrence, and of themselves they might not mean anything much. More sinister, sensors had picked up changes in the composition of gases about the mountain. He zapped across to CNN, to check his version was correct. When he got down to the lobby bar, the TV offered old footage of eruptions, minus sound, starting with Vesuvius in 1944, glamorous in black and white; but he also recognised Mount St Helens, in colour, in his own living memory, albeit on another continent. It was intercut with graphics, and aerial shots of *Vesuvio* showing a lava stream. You couldn't tell if that was today, or last week, or last year. Amy was standing opposite the screen, on the edge of an untidy group of tourists, people whose posture told you they were strangers to each other. God, she looked awful, her little heart-shaped face blank with exhaustion. Now a message moved across the banner, something about the Circumvesuviana; Paolo, watching from the reception desk, confirmed to anybody listening, 'It's closed from Torre del Greco, we don't know why.' Some of the guests turned and nodded to acknowledge the information, 'Ah.' Martin took up his place alongside Amy and stood by her until the adverts started. Then he went with her to the breakfast room, and nudged his tray alongside hers.

'Well, that's that, they've done my risk assessment for me,' she said. 'So much for Herculaneum. We're not going anywhere today. Better sit tight.'

'Herculaneum. No, I suppose not. Still on yellow alert, and no train.'

Amy was asking him something. Did he hear that racket late last night? Some bloke had been mouthing off about the *Prefettura*, she couldn't work out what. Obligingly, a guest in the queue answered her. Martin stared at the man's plate, which was piled high with ham, cheese, tomatoes, slices of fruit and bread, all mixed in together. Its owner had weathered, blond-haired arms, in a short sleeved shirt, and spoke with a definite Mancunian accent. 'They can't win. If they evacuate too soon, it could be a false alarm. A very expensive one, an' all. If they leave it too late, they could have thousands dead. Millions. Chances are, though, it's nothing. Just run of the mill.'

'They would know, though, wouldn't they? If it were an eruption? I mean, all that equipment. All those scientists.'

The man shrugged. 'You'd think so.' Now she turned to Martin.

'We'll have to call school again, give them an update. I've got Gareth's mobile. How are we going to occupy the kids, Martin? They're going to run out of things to do here.' She must have read distraction on his face, because she dropped her head to look over the leaf-shaped lenses and said, 'Mart, I'm sorry, I know it's a pain, but the longer this goes on... Barbara's probably right, we ought to be thinking about how we'll get back. We need to start hassling the company. I'm thinking we should get Gareth on the case? We've got our work cut out right here.' She was right, Gareth liked a crisis, he would sit on the phone if need be, or get one of the support staff to, more likely. The authorities could declare a state of emergency in an hour's time, or tomorrow, or never. Martin judged the odds to be somewhere between tomorrow and never. It made no difference to him.

*SO LIKE I SAID, it had been a bad night. Nobody could sleep, everyone had stayed awake, scaring each other, talking about a real Plinian eruption, which is what they call it when it goes nuclear. Mrs Hammer and Mrs Blake had taken it in turns to walk round the corridors and if they heard a noise they knocked on the door and told us to shut up. Also there were guests coming in late and shouting all over the hotel, so even though Ari and I didn't have a lot to say to each other, we never got to sleep. We were scared there'd be a big explosion any minute. But there wasn't. Then on the Friday morning Ari was getting dressed and she opened one of her drawers and I caught sight of my phone in amongst her stuff. Can you believe it, she had the nerve to pretend she was surprised, and she accused me of putting it there, and when I said why would I do that, she said that was what she'd like to know. Only she looked guilty as hell. At breakfast Whisper said I'd probably made it all up about losing my phone in the first place, and I was just attention seeking all the time. That wasn't true and it made me really angry. Mrs Hammer weighed in to break up the argument, she said the main thing was I had found it. Ari was pissed off with Whisper about something, I caught them both squabbling a couple of times when they thought I wasn't looking. Anyway, the phone was dead, so as soon as I got back to my room I put it on charge.*

THE WEATHER HAD CHANGED, grown dull and humid, yet still warm. There had been no downgrading of the yellow alert, and by mid-morning everybody was getting bored. Martin knew that Amy was frustrated with him, and more specifically, by his failure to rise to the occasion and amuse them all, to tease them and jolly them along. That had always been his forte, of course. But he didn't want to think about them now. He was still troubled by all that had happened the day before. Wendy had opened his eyes to his own madness. Julia remained silent. There was something he needed to do, to put things right, but he had no idea what that was. Throughout the morning, the adults had camped in the lounge bar, where the students came and went, asking their pointless questions, *can't we, why can't we,* drifting off, disappointed. He and Amy occupied a sofa directly opposite the reception desk, which she favoured as offering the best vantage of their comings and goings. Martin held a novel in his hands, by way of defence from them all. His eyes read but the mind did not follow. From time to time he stared out of the picture window on his left towards the tops of the lime trees which were coming into downy pastel leaf now just below them on the piazzetta. They were more real than anything. Lit by a gap in the clouds, they sang out against the dark grey-blue bay; the sky had grown sullen and pummelled the waters to the colour and texture of air force flannel. Against the bruised sea and sky, these stubborn light-claiming buds were exquisite, dainty, but swelling, filling, changing shape by the minute; one more day, and the branches would be stretching fingers outwards, another day or so and they would hold hands, and finally obliterate the ugly pollarded stumps that were so indecently exposed right now. Across the bay, in contrast, Vesuvius was utterly two-dimensional, and it was hard enough to reconcile this flat slate with the dips and curves and deep-scooped shadows of the place he'd visited two days ago, let alone the monster that now dominated the TV screen.

At some point, Amy quit her post and walked off with Barbara Blake. He didn't take in their explanation, although he was aware of the women speaking to him. Small things happened around him. He smelt coffee brought to a table nearby. Conversations rose and fell, laughter, a squabble, a yawn. With each opening of the hotel's plate glass doors, an unwelcome draught of cool air caught the side of his neck. He noticed Paolo, at reception, raising his head and beckoning to attract the attention of his colleague over at the bar. It was discreet, but urgent, the sort of look a head waiter might give to say, *attend to this immediately*. As the older man walked over, Martin heard Paolo say, '*Si parte, Giorgio.*' Paolo held a slim mobile phone. The two men huddled over it; their heads moved from side to side, their lips were thrust out in some sort of judgement or debate, but their conversation was far too rapid for Martin to follow. The barman's swift movement across the room had attracted the curiosity of other people too; with so many guests stranded, and eager for news, this was an event. When Giorgio returned to his post, Paolo turned his attention back to his clients. He explained to the six or seven people who had unashamedly been watching him, 'Please excuse me, this can be important,' then shared with them what he had learned. People were asking why the prefecture had not taken the decision to evacuate, because the signs were bad, there was a small lava flow up on the mountain which was spreading down the *Valle del Gigante*. Some were saying it was time for the population to leave. Not here, of course. Here they were safe, on the opposite side of the bay.

Shortly after this, some of the Hanningford girls brushed past Martin; they ran down the marble steps, their cameras and phones in hand, excited about something. The concierge looked through the plate glass and pointed: sure enough, Vesuvius was smoking much more obviously now. It wasn't the massive billow of the 1944 eruption they'd shown on the TV, just a slightly twisting skein such as he'd seen on footage of great ocean-going steamships, a skein that swelled at first but which the wind soon spun out to a horizontal.line. It was darker than the cloud cover. Whisper, Ari, Shannon, then Hal and Jessica, and finally George loping along after; then Emma, Sam, Wendy, Katy, Tiff – that must be the whole lot of them – charged across the narrow road and onto the piazzetta, where they disappeared past the lime trees and behind the little café. They were hoping for a good photograph again, and they'd get one this time, leaning on the stone wall and looking across the bay.

Vesuvius dominated the lunchtime news. The broadcast flitted between the volcano itself and the rumblings on social media, where there was speculation over the likelihood of an evacuation. Martin tried to follow as best he could. *72 hours are what is planned to empty both the red zone, most at risk from the sort of pyroclastic flow that ended Pompeii, and the blue zone, where mud flow is the danger.* The largest, yellow zone – where they expected falling ash and lapilli – had been modelled on an assumption of prevailing winds, and now the meteorologists were taking centre stage, because it seemed the wind might be behaving in contrary fashion and blowing – albeit very gently – from the north east, something more typical of winter months. Computer graphics plotted the areas out, superimposing what was required on what had been planned. A north easterly wind would blow most of the ash cloud away to sea, but the yellow zone would need to be re-drawn, creeping further south, maybe as close to them as Meta. More shots of the lava flow, *in tempo reale*. A small, bright, pulsating stream. Then a man in spectacles was being interviewed, but his lips barely moved and Martin caught nothing of what he said. Then someone in uniform. It was impossible to remember what all these different uniforms meant. The *Twitter Italia* logo, green-white-red with white bird superimposed, filled the screen for a moment. Then came an argument in the studio, a volcanologist and, maybe, a minor politician, he didn't catch. More satellite images of the lava flow whilst they talked. You didn't really know when to evacuate, or where. If you waited to predict the wind direction, insisted the scientist, it would be too late, because the ash would blot out the sunlight and driving would become impossible. The seismographic evidence would be enough to trigger an evacuation in advance of the main eruption. One simple word shuttled back and forth: *Sappiamo – Non sappiamo – Non sappiamo per certo.* We know, we don't know, we don't know for sure. Back to the anchor man and woman, more serious-faced than ever: they had closed the airport, *come precauzione*, not because its location was in danger, being to the north west of Naples, but because of the threat to incoming aviation from the ash cloud. And hard on that, another explanation: *stato di emergenza* on the screen, but this was not, he thought, the present tense; they were explaining that once a state of emergency had been declared, everything would move from a regional to a national level of alert. Those who wished to go would be invited to leave. On the streets, a *vox pop* with locals who had already decided to stay put come what may. Shots of a primary school making its preparations to become a reception centre. Or was this a drill? All bus services would be suspended in order to facilitate evacuation. Then a rumour (unconfirmed – another tweet) that plans were under way to move a million priceless artefacts away from the museum in Naples. This was no surprise, said the woman in the studio, it was all part of the *Metodo Augustus*. The Augustus method. Of course, thought Martin, it was named after the first Roman emperor, the man who knocked a troubled world into some sort of shape. The journalist explained: the Augustus method was based on clear chains of communication between local and central government, and decreed that every group of professionals, from firemen to train drivers to museum curators, should know what to do in the event of this sort of crisis. Detailed plans – right down to which streets would become one-way – were in place, published well in advance of any misfortune.

Martin, however, had no plan, beyond that of coming on this trip and bringing the last of Julia with him. Here she was, tucked in the bag at his feet, which he pulled now onto his lap. He lacked all sense of future. This thought grew as hard as an object. It sliced across the noisy fidgeting of the TV coverage, a glistening idea, clean, sharp, with its own white sound that absorbed his whole attention. Here he was. What next? If only the mountain were moving on its way to meet him, and to eat him up. Perhaps he should sail from this beach on the Sorrentine peninsula, as Pliny had from his base at Misenum, out to embrace the forces of nature. But Pliny was driven by humanity, as well as the pursuit of knowledge, whereas he, Martin, cared nothing for his fellow man, but simply wondered, idly, whether death might be worth entertaining now.

In front of the hotel, the grey diagonal of the ash cloud, widening then flattening, gradually assumed the shape of an over-sized wafer sitting on a mound of ice-cream. Barbara Blake walked briskly up and stood in front of him, clearly in no mood to sit. Her smile took the shape of a curtsey, in the way it gathered the flesh around her mouth in swags, but also in its polite, perfunctory nature.

'Oh, Mr Harper. Good, I might as well tell you, now that I've got you. I'm going to get us out of here. Whisper and me. There's an airport at Salerno. There are trains. There's no point hanging around here, and if we don't go now we may never get away. I have clients to attend to. We're due home tomorrow and home's where I intend to be. Your travel company are just washing their hands. Washing their hands.' Martin noticed for the first time that she had a good voice, low, nicely focused, purposeful but soft. The music intrigued him, and claimed his full attention; he felt no need to make an answer. She took a few paces over to the concierge. 'Can you advise me please? How can we get home?'

The man smiled, 'Madam, you are quite safe here.'

'I know I'm safe. Safe, yes. Prison would be *safe*. I have to get back and there seem to be no plans to re-schedule our flight.'

Now Paolo's eyes softened to look serious and calm. 'Madam, they only just closed the airspace today. It will take a little time, but they will make arrangements. And they can open it again tomorrow, we don't know. We have no group coming in now, so you are welcome to stay here as long as you like.' A sympathetic smile, a widening gesture of the arms; coaxing her, professionally, because he knew this wasn't what the client wanted.

'The trains are still running, yes? If we can just get a train to Salerno.'

'There is some disruption, because the track's damaged at Torre del Greco.'

'That's in the other direction.'

'It's a problem.' He nodded respectfully.

'Well if we have to, we'll take a taxi. Look, can you make the arrangements? I'm going to get us packed. We should be ready any time after... three, say? It's room 34, Blake.' She walked away. That was Barbara Blake, the workaholic, keen to be back at her desk or her couch or whatever it was. She had a reason to go home. Martin didn't care. On one level, it made no difference to him whether he stayed or left. His time was there to be endured, so did the place matter? Yes, he acknowledged, he wanted to be in Julia's old haunts. But whilst she'd often admired Vesuvius, she'd never once in life set foot in this particular hotel. His fingers closed tenderly over her.

A few minutes later, Amy was back. 'Lunch, Martin?'

'Well, yes... I was watching the news...'

'No, Mart, that wasn't an invitation. It was a question. What happened? I sorted the kids' lunch, you were meant to tell them, remember? But you didn't. So I've been dashing round like an idiot trying to round them up.' So that was what she'd told him earlier. 'I don't suppose you've come up with any activities for them either?'

'Activities...'

'I thought maybe a treasure hunt. I've been looking for ideas, just here, round the hotel, the square, the beach... but I can't do it all by myself.'

'Isn't that a bit young for them, a treasure hunt?'

She pursed her lips and nodded in exasperation, because she knew that he was right. 'But they can't just do nothing.'

'What would they like to do? Have you asked them?'

'Well, have you?' Her tone had been unusually tart and she apologised immediately. 'Sorry Mart, it's just that, you know, I could do with some support here.' Did she look flushed? 'They're all over the place. Once they go down that tunnel – have you seen it, Mart, the tunnel to the beach? That ramp by the square goes into a tunnel, inside the cliff, then it sort of zigzags down to the shore. It's a warren, you'd never find them, if you wanted to. In the end I texted them, about lunch. But half of them don't confirm they've read it.' They both knew Martin hadn't responded either. It occurred to him his phone was likely dead, he didn't remember when he last charged it. 'And they don't answer a call. Not from me, anyway. And once they've gone down that tunnel you'd never find them.'

'You worry too much, Amy.'

'Yeah, probably.' She'd found her little rosy smile again, which was a sweet smile. Something he'd always liked about her. 'We've done Paestum, we can't travel north so that's knocked out Herculaneum, Oplontis, Baia... What if we let them go into Sorrento this afternoon, if they want to, if the buses are running. If they stay in twos and threes. It's not too far to walk back, either, if the need arose. That would be fine, wouldn't it? They'd be happy with that, and they know the lie of the land now.'

That was Amy back on form, posing problems, then solving them herself. Martin acknowledged he'd been pretty useless. The least he could do now would be to back her judgment. 'Why not. We can't do what we planned, but they're not in danger here. Let's tell them they must be back in time for dinner, seven say?'

'Let's,' she answered, plonking herself next to him, and taking out her phone. 'I'll go into town with them.'

IT WAS TYPICAL, thought Ariadne, that Whisper and Barbara got a sea view, and a nicer room than the one she shared with Wendy. The Blakes had extra furniture, a chair and a table and a little balcony looking onto the piazzetta. They'd probably got it because they were the only ones in the whole group who could share a double bed. Right now, as far as Ariadne was concerned, Whisper had one hell of a lot of making up to do, for planting stolen goods in the middle of her best friend's personal belongings. The two girls had been stretched out on the creamy counterpane, propped on extra pillows that Whisper had fetched from the wardrobe. They were multitasking, watching MTV, checking Facebook on their phones, and glancing from time to time at the window, where the ash cloud had nudged its way into view, when Barbara walked in. Ariadne didn't even get to say 'Hi,' because Barbara totally ignored her, behaved as if she wasn't in the room in fact, and announced to Whisper that, *come hell or high water*, she was going to get *us two* out of here. Ari was disappointed at the thought of being left behind by the Blakes. But if Barbara was blanking her, Whisper was getting weird. Anyone else would be grateful for a chance to go home, but she didn't want to leave.

'Wouldn't you like to see it, though? Oh, mom. I mean, a real eruption. Who ever gets to see that? It would just be awesome. Besides, all the others are going to get to stay.'

To Ariadne's surprise, they started to bicker. *It might never happen, so what's the rush? – It's the transport situation. – What's the transport situation? – OK fine so how would anyone get out anyway?* All the while the two of them were arguing, Barbara was making as if to pack yet not quite managing it, folding and unfolding cashmere jumpers that she'd taken from a drawer, and a pair of pale grey satin pyjamas that kept sliding out of shape. At one point she walked into the bathroom, still arguing, and returned with a selection of jars and bottles which she spread on the bed, perfume, shampoo, some very nice makeup, her whole skin regime spread out at Ari's feet. Whisper lay rigid and wouldn't take her eyes from the little screen. The sound was muted. They both knew most of these videos by heart anyway. The dispute was interrupted by a scattering of electronic notification tones: one by one, they each received a text. Ari took one glance and said, 'It's only from Hammer.' Whisper opened hers and howled, 'She says we can go into town this afternoon.' 'You're going nowhere, young lady, you've got to pack that case.' Ari's disappointment grew at the prospect of going into town alone. Mother and daughter argued for ages about the travel options and yet neither of them seemed to have the faintest idea what they were talking about, so far as Ari could see. There were no facts, no times, no departures, nothing definite.

In the end she spoke up. 'You know what, Barbara? Tim would know what to do. You could ask him for advice. He's not far away, after all.' Barabara, who was now sitting at the side of the bed zipping and unzipping a leather toilet bag, leaned over and rubbed the centre of her daughter's forehead with a thumb, which meant, don't frown, it spoils your looks. Her thumbnail was huge, oval, manicured in the old-fashioned way, and lacquered a pearly peach which matched her lipstick. Ari wasn't sure whether Barbara was listening. She felt defeat and conceded, 'But he's probably busy.'

On the contrary, it turned out Barbara was impressed. 'You know, Ariadne, that's not a bad idea. He would have local knowledge... I'll call him. I do hope he's OK.'

'I'd love to see his house,' said Whisper, and glanced across at her mother for the first time since she'd walked in. 'Wouldn't you?'

'Yes, honey, but that's not going to happen. We don't need to impose. We're going home *soon as*. The only question is how.'

'Google it.'

'What do you think I've been doing all morning? Whenever this Mickey Mouse broadband has let me. That and checking Twitter. If this mountain's gonna explode, I don't want to be at the back of the queue waiting for Loser Travel to beg a passage home. Look, don't tell the others, OK? They'll only panic. But if it blows, this could be quite a show.'

'That's my whole point,' said Whisper, who hadn't moved an inch.

Ari needed to know: 'It isn't going to hurt anybody, is it?'

'Not here. And not us, especially if we go south.'

'I'll call Tim,' said Whisper's mother, positioning herself at the table. Her big leather bag jingled as she lifted out the mobile. To Ari's astonishment, Tim picked up straight away. Now she had to bear the frustration of a one-sided phone call. It wasn't Barbara's normal voice. It was a special voice she obviously kept for people she needed, anyone she was schmoozing. She started by asking how he was, which was the rule when you want something from somebody, and how he was affected by it all; from the sound of her 'uh-huh, uh-huh, good, I'm so glad to hear that,' his holiday home was out of harm's way. But it didn't take her long to get to the point. She asked about transport options, *uh-huh, uh-huh...* then looked up to make excited eye contact with her daughter: it sounded as though he'd made some sort of offer, and now she was giving their hotel name, describing its precise location, even telling him how to access the car park. 'That is *so* kind of you, Tim. We'll be ready. How long? OK, if you're sure, safe journey. See you soon.' She tapped the phone and sat back with a big smile. 'I think I've fixed it. He'll take us to Salerno. Flights might be cancelled, but we can pick up a train there.'

'Mom, it's gonna cost so much...'

'Why do we have insurance? I have clients to get back to. What sort of a mother would leave you behind?'

'But what about the luggage? It won't fit on the moped. And we won't, either.'

'Moped? Why would he come over on a moped? Come on crazy girl, get yourself packed.'

And she never even thanked Ari, although it had all been her idea.

*SO I WANT TO TEXT JACK. I've noticed all these notifications from Klappa, but I don't look at them straight away. What I do notice is, all our chat, mine and Jack's, has disappeared. The whole thread, going back weeks, months maybe. Which makes no sense. Anyway, I message to say Hi, I'm good, but our day is cancelled. When he gets back to me, which is a bit later, he says Hi, seen the photos, good you're good, but is he bothering you? Which I don't understand so I text him to say, what photos, who. He texts back, the ones on Klappa. And he says, do you still think he fancies you then? So then I look at the notifications and it's a picture and videos of me and Mr Harper, and it turns out Whisper Blake has been stalking us, well, stalking one of us. She's taken all these pictures, and videos too. They're not close up. There's one in the ruins at Paestum. We were just talking. So I message, why do you think that, and he gets back, you said. You texted me, Tuesday. So I figure, someone stole my phone, and used it to contact Jack, pretending to be me*

*First I thought it was Ari, because we shared a room, but then I figured she isn't bright enough to hide anything from anyone so I blamed Whisper and I still do.*

*Then I realise, Jack's been on Klappa, that means he's in breach of his restraining order, and I'm just hoping he keeps that to himself so nobody finds out.*

## State of Emergency

AMY WAS BACK from the bus stop within the hour. It was hopeless, she told Martin. They had waited so long for a bus that the kids had given up and headed back, some of them to the hotel, some down to the beach, some to the cafe at the end of the piazzetta. She figured the best thing she could do now, if he didn't mind, would be to have a shower and close her eyes for a few minutes.

As the afternoon dragged on, the lounge bar showed no sign of emptying; there were more guests about the hotel than usual. With traffic disruption to the north, it wasn't only the Hanningford group who found their planned excursion cancelled; everyone suddenly wanted to do the Amalfi coast drive, and the rumour was that seats were booked up three days hence. The hotel's clientele was mostly middle-aged. There was a tour party from Germany, as well as the Mancunians who made up the other group from the UK. Bit by bit, their numbers grew until the bar was full, with everyone keeping half an eye on the TV. The Brits were constantly busy with their phones, and competitive about getting information; Martin watched them lavishly constructing their own crisis. Someone said the ground was heating up. A couple of the younger guys stood out as the best sleuths, giving their elders regular bulletins. One of them had the website of the Vesuvius Observatory on his tablet, and kept checking for updates; you could view the seismograph live online, it was buzzing, it was rumbling; people craned around the little screen, looking at the busy coloured charts, saying, 'What does it mean?' and 'I don't like the look of that.' 'Well it's like when you have your ECG isn't it. Same principle.' 'I don't rate the patient's chances, then.'

The hotel's broadband was faltering under the weight of usage, and from time to time one of them would look up and raise a hand in frustration. Just before 6.30, like corn in the wind, the Mancunians stirred and turned towards the door; their tour rep had arrived for a meeting. She resembled Mary Parry, Head of Key Stage 4: drip-dry, permanent creases, blue for authority, eyebrows plucked and painted to the default setting *no nonsense here while I'm in charge*. Before she could speak, though, a groan from the Germans made them all whirl around again. The television screen confirmed *fase di preallarmi – stato di emergenza*. A state of emergency. Orange. Evacuation was beginning, for those residents who wished to leave. The whole room, maybe forty people now, was watching the screen. One of the Englishmen persuaded the staff to switch to CNN, and they all watched some minutes of breaking news, a Swiss scientist explaining that the long term events embedded in the seismographic patterns indicated that a full-scale explosion could be expected within the next four days. In the end, the switch to an upcoming climate change conference allowed the heads to turn away and the tour rep's meeting to be called to order. The whole room listened, and the Germans were attentive, straining to hear and understand. There would be no flights from either Naples or Salerno, which in any case was mainly a domestic airport, for the foreseeable future, she said. She was authoritative, sympathetic, but firm. The operator was looking to get coaches to take the party south, to a place called Bari, which none of them had heard of. 'But …' All the muttering ceased at this. 'But…' She slowed down to enunciate each word. 'But all the local transport companies are on standby for the evacuation of Naples. So every coach for miles around is tied up. The tour groups here on the Sorrentine peninsula are not, repeat not, in any danger. Which means, although everyone is doing their best, we are not, officially, a priority.' 'Well, fair dos, we're not,' said a woman. A mutter went round the British group. 'You can't argue with that. We ahn't got hot rocks dropping on our homes.' They murmured, reasonable, compliant. The rep was doing well, conducting the band, until a shout changed the music. It was the man who'd been showing everyone the charts from the Observatory: 'The site's down!' Voices rose in pitch and volume. 'Oh my God.' 'Well that's it then, they're going to go up with it.' 'They're right on the side of the volcano.' 'We saw it, didn't we? The Observatory?' 'Poor sods.' 'Oh my God.' If the site was down, they reasoned, the observatory had been hit, or at least abandoned. 'It's kickin' off now alright.' 'You don't *know* that,' whined a young lad, maybe sixteen or seventeen, white-armed in a black Metallica tee shirt. 'The whole world's hitting their site right now, it's bound to go down.' 'Well *you* don't know *that,*' said his dad. 'It's prob'ly all automated, Dad. They prob'ly evacuated ages ago. Ah bet there's nuwwon there.' In the midst of a natural disaster the like of which they'd never seen, a family stuck to what it had rehearsed.

The sky had been overcast all day. To add to that, throughout the afternoon, the cloud from the mountain had been spreading across the picture windows, and conspired with the weather to weaken the sun and dull the sea still further. It churned and fascinated. Martin watched the ash plume obliterate the higher clouds and wondered what it was going to mean. Every citizen and every visitor had known that an eruption was possible, but no-one had expected it, and nobody had thought things could escalate so quickly. The piazzetta opposite, with its clipped limes and straight lined benches, was grown dull and untidy; shadowless, it had lost its crispness and its elegance. The stone balustrades were obscured now by a crowd of onlookers, of all ages, and they too were smudged by the gloom and made to harmonise, as if the cinder grey they gazed upon had entered them.

As Martin watched the watchers, in dimming light, he felt that something in him was receding. He had no desire. On the far shore, in all the conurbation of Naples and throughout the towns and villages about the volcano, there were thousands upon thousands of people who had to decide, this very moment, what to do, whether, and how, to make their escape. What to take with them. Whom to contact. Yet from here, they were all invisible. The sight of Vesuvius, a flat triangle of charcoal grey, was hypnotic, magnetic. Flames spat and lava flowed only in his mind's eye – but that was no matter, they were no less compelling, no less strident, no less glorious for being hidden. Here was energy, here were life and anger tearing through cold stone, come from the bottom of the world to rip it open and re-make. He moved to join the crowd outside.

Martin was overtaken on the steps by Barbara Blake. There was a big smile on her heavy oval face. She was tripping down the grey-white marble, virtually hand in hand with a pigtailed man. 'Timothy,' she was saying, 'once again you have proved *our saviour*, did you have an *awful* time getting here?' When she realised it was Martin they had just jostled aside, she stopped on the pavement to explain.

'Martin, hi! Tim here is going to take Whisper and me south, so there you are, we'll be out of your hair in a jiffy.' She paused and eyed him up and down, with a theatrical grin. 'Well, you're allowed to be pleased.'

Sprung from nowhere, this was Timothy Slipman, standing next to him. Was this by his own doing? By dint of thinking so hard about this man, had he conjured him up? All Martin's fears, and all his anguish, reified. And it was an affront that this man should stand before him, that he should live whilst Julia did not. Slipman's face was made of clefts and bosses, but now they were shadowless; Martin tried hard to see him with Julia's eyes, and tried to decide whether these features might be strong in another light, or were just plain ugly, as they seemed to him. He was wearing a leather jacket. He was muscular, shorter than Martin remembered from the pub at Christmas, but probably much stronger than Martin. It was odd the way he fawned over the woman. Behind the smart, dark spectacles, his smirking eyes were two thin downturned crescents whose exact colour could not be discerned. So pleased with himself. Close enough to hit.

'Our bags are down,' the woman trilled in Martin's direction, 'so all we need to do is find my daughter. She's down here, with her friends, on the piazzetta. It's quite a show, isn't it ? And here we all are, front row of the dress circle, just where I like to be. Close enough to see the actors, without them actually spitting on you, you know what I mean?' Her voice dropped. 'You two have already met, right?' Clearly, Martin had not concealed his hatred of this man. Slipman, however, avoided looking him in the eye, and instead made great play of apologising that it had taken him so long to get here. He told Barbara Blake that the traffic had built up, and so the sooner they were on the road the better.

This was the same voice Martin had heard on the telephone. Then all those nights, in his dreams of Julia. Unlocked now, let loose. It wasn't an unpleasant voice, it was deep, deeper than his own, well-modulated; it had a weight which made it carry easily against the murmur of the crowd across the street, even on this felted air.

'You sent my wife a card. A postcard.' Martin had cut through their conversation and yes, Barb, that was very rude, but he didn't care. Slipman tried to turn towards her and away from him, but Martin was not having that; he pushed himself between them and looked him squarely in the face. He took in every pore, every bristle, noticed the places where the black hair had turned to grey, a smear of grease and dust on the left lens of his glasses. He saw the parts and could not grasp the whole, perhaps he was going to be sick, there was something wrong with his vision, perhaps this was a migraine coming on, or worse. The details were too real, the long straight hairs scraped back on his forehead were too distinct against the skin. Slipman. He hadn't answered. Martin repeated: 'You sent her a post card. You wrote *here I am again, hoping you are feeling better.*' Slipman made a feeble movement, and looked away. 'What did you mean?' His lips moved oddly. Maybe it was a tic, or an affectation; a moue; there was something effeminate about it. Martin understood at once that Slipman wouldn't fight, and wouldn't answer; he remained tight-lipped, shook his head, protested that he had no idea what Martin could be talking about. '*Here I am again*, you wrote – did you go there together? Just to Pompeii, or to the House of the Faun?' The man looked away, down towards the gutter, which Martin took as a yes. 'You followed her, that's what I think, you stalked her all those years like some sick person. I think – *I know* – you hurt her. So what happened here, in Italy?' These questions had torn through the air, in the full-throated pleasure of a shout. Martin registered with satisfaction that people on the piazzetta had turned around, and looked away from the volcano for a minute. Until this man appeared, Martin had been tremulous and small, a tiny particle in the thrall of black gravity. But Slipman was smaller. In every sense, smaller than him. The man was embarrassed. He was ashamed, he would not meet Martin's eye.

'And look, the thing I don't understand, how would you know, if she was ill? Who told you?'

At this, Slipman looked to the side and back and finally faced him, and shrugged as if trying to be reasonable: 'Look, everyone knew,' he said. 'Everyone knew. It was in the *Echo.* About the accident.'

He was right, it was. 'But it wasn't just the accident, was it?' Martin saw again that night in the bathroom, the slash of hard light, Julia blaming herself for terminating the pregnancy that must have been Slipman's child; she believed that both the pain, and the childlessness, were caused by that; and for a second Martin felt the cold of that moment, even here in this increasingly close, sticky atmosphere. He told the man straight: 'You did her so much damage. You should have let her be.'

'She was special,' he replied. That phrase again. But this time they were not speaking on the telephone, and Martin could see the owner of that voice. His expression was strangely hang-dog, at once anxious and pathetic. Standing at the bar of the Flitch on Boxing Day, he had been robust, erect; Martin had thought he worked out, and had taken him for a skier. But now that they talked of Julia, now that he was challenged, he was cowed, his shoulders hunched, his back quite bent. He was according Martin the higher status. As befitted the husband. The widower. He was grovelling. Martin saw him differently. Roused from its sluggishness, his mind began to race. What kind of man did Timothy Slipman turn out to be? It took only seconds to work it out. *A coward. A man who lives alone. Who needs to be important. He starts, as a teenager, by having it off with younger kids, then teaches, because that lends a spurious significance, makes you someone's teacher... and he carves his niche by making people believe they need him, people who lack something, knowledge, wit, experience, confidence, control... the Ariadne Clays, the Barbara Blakes... 'Our saviour,' she called him. He's no worse than me, in that. We all want to believe we make a difference. We only know we are alive by changing things around us. We act on people, if we can. In fact, we all lack something. We set out to meet each other's neediness; and we aim to leave a hollow where we've been, in the hard rock.*

Barbara Blake was hovering almost in the road, and Martin knew that she was trying to fathom just what their shared backstory was, his and Slipman's. She couldn't have gathered much from these few scraps. At least he had succeeded in shutting the woman up. She had been in such a hurry, and Martin could see that Slipman wanted to be away from him. So now Slipman turned towards the woman, and he sounded hapless, almost desperate, when he pointed vaguely to the crowd and said, 'I think I can see Whisper over there.' This time, when Slipman tried to cross the road, Martin didn't attempt to stop him. Barb stared for a moment, then told Slipman, 'You go, I'll wait here in case she comes this way. There's such a crowd.' Martin stepped back to the hotel terrace, dropped to a chair, and watched the pigtailed man dodge the cars. Barbara Blake also turned back towards the hotel, and for a moment a slight curve of her shoulder made it look as though she was going to sit down beside him; then she must have thought better of it, and went inside. Maybe she read something on his face. He felt a pulse inside his head that hurt, and told himself – rational, detached – it was just the awfulness of seeing all these catastrophes at once, small and large, in section, each stratum exposed – this one more recent, that one buried deep down in a past he had never shared and couldn't interpret.

ARI HAD PUT her new white top on, to make her skin look browner, and played with the charms on her bracelet as she eyed the crowd. On the square, it was almost like a festival, so many people had come here to hang out and watch, locals as well as tourists from all the hotels around. She posted a few pictures; it would look cool to anyone at home. All the same, it annoyed her that they were basically stuck here in a suburb, away from the centre of Sorrento. The square jutted out into the sea almost like a platform, and you didn't realise from the road that you were actually on a cliff top. But it was dull today and not so nice as when they'd been here before. The light was fading. The sea was grey like home. Also there wasn't a lot happening, volcano-wise, just a load of smoke which was boring really once you'd got used to it. A short woman in black, maybe in her early thirties, pushed her way through the crowd with a box of bread. Ari recognised her from behind the counter at the cafe bar: they were starting to run out of stuff. She and Whisper had managed to get themselves an Orangina but it wasn't properly chilled, which showed you they couldn't keep up with the sudden rush of trade. The woman was smiling, but only because they had to be nice to the customers; she looked well stressed out. Whisper's moaning and whining about having to go home was beginning to get on Ari's nerves. In the end she snapped, 'Well why don't you stay here then and I'll go back with your mum?' and Whisper said, 'Y'know what, that's a really good idea. You are welcome. Go ahead.' So it was brilliant timing that Tim should appear, before they had time to get into a serious argument.

When he said 'I'm glad I've found you,' he looked at Whisper first, but only for a moment. Tim always looked at Ari more than he did at Whisper, even though Whisper did more of the talking. Ari had noticed that a long time ago, and that was right because he was her tutor first, and she was older. Also she was nicer looking, and taller. And maybe he didn't like the way Whisper spoke to him, which was a bit too familiar. Like now.

'Hi Tim, oh, Tim, well this is amazing. Don't you think it's amazing, being right here, at this moment?' He nodded and said it was all pretty spectacular. What bad luck, he said, for this to happen in the middle of their trip, creating all these problems. He wasn't in his motorcycle gear but he did have a sort of leather jacket on, and Ari couldn't decide whether it was smart and Italian-looking or a bit naff.

Whisper argued. 'It isn't logical for my mom to want us to go home, when this is the closest I've ever come to witnessing a historic event. Nothing like this is ever going to happen to me again. You know what I think?' she said. She held her palms flat out with fingers outstretched, and made a little pressing movement, down on the air, which meant, she wasn't the one who was panicking; and then she touched him! She put her right hand flat on his arm, a bit down from the elbow, just like her mum would do, and moved her face till it was almost in his. Or at least it would have been if she'd been normal height. And Whisper's thought, that was so significant, turned out to be this: 'I think she's actually afraid. My mom's scared.' She moved back and turned round to acknowledge her friend and get her reaction. So her mum was scared. Ari was scared herself, not only of an eruption, but of bigger tremors, that might break mirrors and close the roads, and of missing their flights, and the journey back being a nightmare, and the ATMs not working, and running out of clean clothes while they were stranded there. Because whatever happened next, it couldn't possibly be good.

She knew how her friend operated. The more blank Whisper looked, the more she wanted something; she had to make it look like she didn't care. Sure enough, she asked Tim, 'Can't you persuade my mom to let me stay?'

Tim said, 'I don't think your mum's scared, Whisper. She just has business to get back to, you know?'

'I know. That's what she says. For them, she has all the time in the world. I just have to get by. I don't even try now, to tell her what I feel. I know it's all going to be discounted, you know what I mean?'

'That's not fair,' said Ari. 'She came here to be with you, after all. She so cares, about everything you do. I think your mum's great, and she's so cool.'

'On the surface, yes,' said Whisper, 'but she's making excuses for that man. You know... she's turning a blind eye.'

'To what?' asked Tim. That was so like him, to pick up on things; he had a sixth sense, thought Ari, about the things you're scared of and stuff that makes you panic in exams, which was why he was just the best tutor you could ever have. He made you tell him what you couldn't do, and then he showed you how to do it.

'Oh,' said Whisper calmly, 'Just Harper again. He's... getting worse. More irrational. Mood swings, OK, I get that, but an obsession with a pupil... Well, that's inappropriate.'

'Inappropriate,' said Ari, nodding, and realising what was going to happen. Sure enough, Whisper held out the little white phone, and Ari knew just where she'd start the camera roll: it would be the House of the Faun, and the pair of them, Harper and Wendy, by the horrible little statue; and walking along an empty Pompeii backstreet side by side; the brothel; loads of shots of them having this long conversation in the distance, taken at Paestum; and so on. 'But you have to understand,' said Whisper, 'He isn't really in his right mind. You wouldn't believe what he's carrying around with him. No, Ari,' she said – as if Ari had tried to stop her, which she hadn't – 'We can tell Tim. Harper's got this bag, this kind of hippy shoulder bag thing he carries round just everywhere – '

'He got stopped at the airport and everything.'

'– Yeah, he carries it with him all the time, and do you know what's inside it? A woman's silk make-up bag, with his dead wife's ashes inside. I mean it's gross. And creepy. And that means it's upsetting for us, and inappropriate, and makes us feel unsafe. Because he's mentally ill and we shouldn't be in his care.'

'His wife?' said Tim, twice. Then he went quiet. Ari waited for him to reassure them, and to say, leave it with me, like when she'd told him about the gaps in the syllabus last year, and he'd given her the notes and phoned the school to complain, as one professional to another, on her behalf.

Nothing. Instead, he frowned, and his eyes sort of went inside his head, and he looked strange.

He handed back the device – he had stopped looking at it – and stared at Whisper. Ari took this as a sign that he was really shocked. The whole thing must be every bit as bad as they said, for Tim to be as shocked as this, when he was so much older than them and so experienced. It was a kind of proof.

She watched him, waiting to hear what he would say, when something just over his shoulder caught her eye. 'Oh my god,' she said, 'oh my god. There they are again, look, together, right now.' And she pointed across the road to where Harper and Wendy sat, as brazen as anything, sharing a little table on the terrace. Then Wendy seemed to recognise her, and got up, and started crossing the road. Tim turned round to see, and suddenly, he set off as well. Ari assumed that he was walking over to meet Wendy, and help her, since obviously Wendy was, as Whisper always said, a vulnerable young person in all this. But he shot right past her, past the orange muppet, over the road, and up the hotel steps towards the terrace straight for Harper.

'He's going to hit him. He's that disgusted,' said Whisper.

'I hope he does,' said Ari. 'Serve him right.'

To their astonishment, he took a seat and sat down next to Harper, and they started chatting like they were old mates. Wendy, meanwhile, was heading towards them, shouting and looking angrier than Ari had ever seen her. Which was saying something.

*I HAD TO FIND THEM and have it out with the pair of them there and then. I was that mad. When I came out of the hotel, there were loads of people outside watching the volcano, and I saw Mr Harper was sitting at a table on the front, near the steps. He said, you OK Wendy and I said no I'm not OK I'm well pissed off if you want to know. I told him, good news, got my mobile back, bad news, someone stole it, and pretended to be me, then posted loads of stuff on Klappa and I'm that mad. So he says who and I say Whisper Blake. So he says, what has she posted? So I had to tell him. Only I didn't know how to tell him, so I showed him the pictures. I said, it's like I've got a stalker. Or you've got a stalker. Or she's trying to set us up. I told him all the messages with Jack had disappeared, and how she must have written bad stuff, that now I couldn't see, because she'd deleted them to cover her tracks. And how she'd made Jack go on to Klappa, and that's the internet, so if anyone found out, he'll be in trouble, so maybe she was out to get him. Only I didn't know why. And it was all rushing round in my head and yes it's true, I was upset. And I said to Mr Harper how I never would write a bad thing about him because let's face it he was the only person who'd been nice to me, and it was only because of him that I was there now. And I sort of blurted out, how he was the only one who cared about me, and I stand by that, because he was. Which is what some busybody overheard. I was upset, I was tired and maybe I was crying a bit, it was all so horrible, like they say, just because you're paranoid doesn't mean they're not out to get you. If you ask me what he was like, he was looking kind of shocked and he just looked at me, kind of blank, and I said I was sure now it was Whisper, because she had a thing about Jack didn't she.*

*And he said did she? As if he didn't know. Only you could see he was thinking. I told him I was on my way to tell the pair of them what I thought of them right now. Then he smiled properly and he looked me straight in the eye and he said, 'what you must never forget, Wendy, is, you're bigger than them.' That's what he said. He told me I was bigger than them, and I thought, you know what Wendy, he's right.*


SO NOW WENDY WAS on the warpath for Whisper Blake and Ariadne Clay, *a right pair of sad bitches from hell*, as she had put it to Martin. It struck him as an awkward phrase; unpeel it, and you found anger, a belief in evil, and that grain of self-respect that was pure gold and that would see this young woman through life. *Sad* bitches. Deficient, you see, not as lucky as Wendy. Who had nothing, but was bigger than them. She had sped off to challenge them, she didn't sit on anger. Whereas in all these months, Martin had never thought for a minute of tracking Slipman down, and confronting him. He hadn't wanted Slipman to be real. Yet that was precisely how he had ended up giving him power. Now that Martin had seen the man with his own eyes, he was grown ludicrous. Pathetic.

He watched the girl as she crossed the road, stopped and looked at her mobile again before hurrying on. The waiter came to clear the tables, and he ordered an espresso; it might help dull this headache, which was making him feel absent and slightly nauseous. When he leant his head back, he could hear the tendons crackle and strain. He sat for a while with eyes half closed, wishing it were possible to sleep, rerunning their chance meeting, searching for reasons why Slipman looked the way he did. That expression looked like guilt. He knew he was in the wrong. And he was a coward. And here he came now, walking back towards the hotel alone. He couldn't have found his pupil. Martin nodded in recognition as he reached the steps – he wasn't going to do that English thing of pretending not to see – and Slipman approached, clearly wanting to talk. The terrace was busy, and the seats opposite had been turned around in order to accommodate a big group of the Mancunians on the table in front. He slipped awkwardly behind Martin, and moved a chair to his left, scraping it carelessly against the stone, and setting it as close to Martin's table as he could; but the terrace was busy and he couldn't quite set the chair at a decent angle. Not quite alongside each other, and not quite opposite, they both faced out towards the bay and the churning sky.

'Martin,' he said, 'I know what you're carrying there. I know what's in your bag. What are you going to do with her?'

This was the very thing he'd wanted to know back in October, when he had telephoned: to ask where Julia was. Where to go in order to pay what he called his respects. It was that telephone call that had sent Martin on a downward path.

'Surely you've got to let her rest?' said the voice in Martin's left ear.

'I have. That's what I'm trying to do. But you will understand why she couldn't lie in her father's churchyard.'

'No,' he said, 'I don't.' He looked genuinely puzzled, this man sitting on the slant. Instinctively, Martin had never liked him. He had no reason to trust him, after all the deliberate harm that he'd done at work, and the worse harm he did to the woman that he most loved and would love in all the time in all the world. But he realised that it could all be wrong, this story Julia told him, because she never told it living. Was it a story Martin had told himself? Some of it must be true, but which elements, he couldn't discern.

'Where will you take her?' he insisted, but would get no answer. 'You should leave her here, in Italy.'

'In this mayhem?' On the piazzetta in front of them, the cliff-edge balustrades were all but hidden now by swarming people. This was the strangest sort of tourism, all these idlers watching the column of ash rise from the mountain, only half-horrified, aware of the potential for a more spectacular show, and half wanting it. Smartphones at the ready, every one. Keen to have a view, glad to be safely at a distance.

'Come back to Italy another time. Come back and stay with me. I'll take you, wherever you want to leave her.'

'No.' This was beyond grotesque. Martin stood up, conscious that the slight weight of his precious Julia was in the bag at his side, once again wanting to stride a thousand miles away but lacking any destination. It was a simple, easy, physical expediency that took him straight in the direction he was facing: down the marble steps again, but so much quicker this time, across the road, onto the piazza; and all the time Slipman was at his elbow, hanging on to him and trying to make him stop. There was something so feeble about his voice; he was almost whining. Pleading.

'Look, you must understand, I only wish her well. It's just, I never said goodbye. I never said goodbye.'

It rang around Martin's head, but he wasn't going to confess: nor did I; and straightaway, Martin saw himself back on the hospital ward, bludgeoned by fluorescent light; he had left her for a moment, he went to get the help he thought she needed, and when he came back, she'd gone. Here on the piazzetta, there were people in his way, but he needed to move. He found space at a ramp that seemed to go down below the level of the square, so he followed it, past a fountain in the wall to his right, a public notice to his left; then they were underground. There was something municipally sanctioned about this place, a proper thoroughfare; they would likely meet somebody soon; still Slipman was at his side, but it was possible to stride out here more comfortably, and as he paced downwards, the word *allegro* came to mind. There was logic in the music of his steps, as if something was moving to a resolution. Here it came, here was the thing: maybe they both wanted her, and maybe in their different ways they both felt bad because they never said goodbye, but Martin didn't need to know the whys and wherefores of this man's pathetic obsession with his wife, because at that awful moment when she quit this world, Martin's was the hand she wanted to hold.

They were in a sort of tunnel in the cliff side now, broad and paved with black basalt and studded with little white cat's eyes, just like the roads at Pompeii, and sloping away. Another path half way down the gallery led down to the left, while some thirty yards in front of them there was an opening made in the rock at waist height, where you could see daylight and the cliff side opposite, beyond maybe a metre thickness of stone. That was a dead end, so he turned left to descend, and as he did, Slipman stumbled on the uneven paving and fell against him. As he pushed his weight away, Martin shouted with all his might: 'She loved *me*. *Me*. She loved *me*!' It echoed so positively round the tunnel walls, he had to shout again, this time for joy. Because every atom of his body knew, that this man didn't matter. He signified nothing. *She loved me*. He heard someone cheer, and heard people joining in and clapping, without knowing where they were or why they clapped. But he was happy enough to take the applause as his own.

It felt so good to be moving, as if he were pacing back into health and sanity. And he seemed to apprehend so very many things at once; he knew he had possession of his wife, not just because he held her remains here in the little purse, but because Julia belonged to him in a region beyond place and time. He felt that he could walk for miles, simply for joy. What curious, contrapuntal surroundings he now found himself in; a tunnel carved inside the cliff face, its walls rough-hewn and hence impossible to date, the paving classic Roman. He didn't know if it was real or imitation, but there was no sign of electric lighting and the apertures offered glimpses of the cliff opposite, no more than fifty yards away. This tunnel, which was cool and smelt of dust, must lead down to the private beach, so maybe it had been the fantasy of the original hotel owner, cashing in on the taste for all things Roman.

Cutting through all these notions, he heard the shrieking voices of girls, voices he recognised. A fierce argument was going on. Where the tunnel ended, now just in front of him, there was shadowless dusk and a level mezzanine, and there stood Whisper, Ari Clay, and Wendy, who was shouting at them. Whisper hissed, 'Well he is weird, it's fair comment isn't it?' and Ari shouted 'Fair comment.' So Wendy had found them, then. They must be arguing about the photographs that she had shown him only minutes ago. It was touching that Wendy had felt she needed to apologise, when she was the victim here, not Martin. On his own account, he barely cared what anybody thought of him. In this meagre light, Wendy seemed to shine; her hair, eyebrows, clothing, all burnt orange, bronze and brass. She told them they were slime, and worse than Jack because at least he cared about somebody besides himself. Martin realised that somehow he still hadn't told Slipman he was slime. *Perhaps I pity him.*

The three girls were standing against a masonry wall which was balustraded just like the piazza above, and curled downward on either side, after the baroque manner; as he approached he saw that at this place, two steeply curving outdoor paths, one coming up the cliff from the left, one from the right, meet in daylight for the last time, on a long flat platform, before entering the tunnel in the rock where he now stood.

'Well it's evidence, isn't it,' said Whisper, tapping her pocket, "and we've got more today, just five minutes ago. So you still don't get it, do you? Can't you see he's grooming you? Unless you're after him. And come to think of it, that's how it looks. You're always after him. You and him, and no-one else around, time after time. How do you think that looks, to anybody normal? '

'Sick,' said Ari.

'And you're too late. It's already out there. It's all been posted. Anyone can see it. Jack, school, anyone. All the evidence is out there, for anyone to figure it out.'

'There's nothing *to* figure out.' Wendy's face looked more sallow than ever against the pewter sky, and she was immobile. But only for a minute; she flew at Whisper, pushed Ari Clay aside, and suddenly her hands had gripped the fabric of Whisper's thin pale top at each shoulder, and she was shaking her; it was almost comical the way her little fists were twisted inside the cotton fabric, as if aiming punches that couldn't quite be thrown. Martin ran up to them. He had to stop this. Wendy was trying to push Whisper hard against the balustrade – it was barely three feet high, so her body arched backwards – and her left hand grasped for Whisper's pocket. She was wrestling for her phone. Whisper tried to push her away with one hand, while the other hand clamped nails into Wendy's face. He tried to prise them apart and was bitten on the arm. Ari was shouting something, and he felt blows against his back which distracted more than they hurt. Wendy had the mobile now, but that left her only one free hand with which to hold Whisper back, and that was not enough; the smaller girl wriggled and wrested her body round, so that now it was Wendy whose feet were pinned against the wall and whose body bent. Their arms were working, and he was hit by both of them. Wendy shouted, 'I'm going to throw – this – thing – in the sea,' and kicked out at Whisper, pushing her so hard that she was sent sprawling on the path. The force of that last push had left Wendy lying on the flat of the balustrade, leaning backwards over the edge, still waving the phone in the air. It was clear that she intended to throw it over her shoulder. She wouldn't just drop it; you could see from the swing she was trying to take, she wanted it far away. Martin glimpsed the sea some fifty metres down below. From here, the girl could overbalance and fall backwards. Instinctively, he threw himself forward to cover her, pulling her arms down to her sides. The little object had dropped from her hand; he heard it fall against the stone and to the ground. Was she OK? She nodded. Martin held her by her shoulders at arm's length. Her hair fell over her forehead, quivering like wire in time to panting breath. She became still, then she bent down, picked up the phone, and handed it over to him. She sobbed and slumped forward, and her shaking head burrowed into his chest. Whisper shouted, 'Oh for fuckssake,' then, to Ari, 'waddaya waiting for? You get the shot. Take it! Take their photograph.'

It was only afterwards that he realised – and then only because he saw it lying on its side just inside the tunnel – that he had put it down. The bag which held the last of his Julia's ashes. He'd forgotten all about it.

# CODA

*DOWN THE PIER*

*MY MUM ALWAYS SAID, trouble with you, Wendy, you always have to have the last word. And I used to say, only because I'm always the one who's right. Jack might be older than me but he never had an ounce of common sense. Anyway, here's my last word on Mr Harper and the Italian trip.*

*After our last A2 exam, me and Shannon and Sam went up to Southend. Shannon had this crazy idea that she was going to throw her Geography notes off the pier, and besides, we wanted to do the rides and everything, then go out and hit the town, because now we really had left school. We took the train up the pier like a bunch of little kids on a birthday outing, only instead of carrying a balloon saying* I am 5, *she had a big yellow lever arch file on her lap. When we got off, she started to take all the pages out and handed them to us in little piles. The idea was that we'd all let them drop on a count of 3 and watch them float down. Only it was too windy. A lot of the papers flew back onto the deck and we ended up running round like idiots trying to catch them, and getting funny looks from the people in the caff. So we only did the first batch, then she just tipped the whole file over the rail and we cheered.*

*It was funny to think she had chucked away all this stuff about volcanos. She said it had been a really hard topic and she'd never got into it, until she saw the real thing. The Classics trip turned out to be the best Geography lesson she'd ever had, because it got her interested. Not interested enough to want to hang on to her notes, though. It's over a year now and that trip is not something any of us will ever forget. Specially not me, because of the crap about me on social media. I know it's all over but it still bugs me.*

*When I remember that time now, and all the hell that broke loose after me and Whisper had that fight, there's one thing that really gets me, and it's this. We were getting worked up over nothing, weren't we? It was nothing really when you consider that on the other side of the water, two days later, people were going to die. From our hotel, you could watch everything without really seeing anything happen to human beings at all. Before the big eruption, time really dragged, through the Friday into Saturday, so Facebook and Twitter and Klappa was something for people to do, wasn't it, and the last photo Ariadne had taken, of Mr Harper holding me, had gone round everyone and got loads of comments. Including from Whisper, who had gone back home with her mum before the volcano really kicked off. Mrs Hammer tried to stop it, all the posts, and said there would be consequences when we got back to school but she couldn't say what, and besides, it was everybody. I had to get round them all to put them straight and I told a few people what I thought of them, which meant then I got ignored for the rest of the trip which was fine by me. I kept away from Mr Harper, too, in fairness to him, and I told Mrs Hammer why, and to tell him thank you, but that I wasn't going to give anyone the opportunity to video the two of us together ever again.*

*At first the eruption was like watching something on a screen, it seemed so far away, when it was just smoking. But then we saw part of the evacuation, on the shopping street which was a main road, busloads full of real people who'd actually left their homes, and you knew it was serious. Later you could hear the traffic all through the night. The staff in the hotel were just fantastic with us, they fed us and everything because we had nowhere to go and no-one else was moving, and you wouldn't have known, except their usual suppliers weren't available and they ran out of bread and stuff. Also they stopped smiling, even Paolo. Because once it really started, on Saturday afternoon, the eruption was horrible. It was so loud, even from miles away, and the noise just wouldn't stop, and you couldn't help wanting to look but it was so frightening you didn't want to see it. The ash cloud was thick and incredibly solid looking, not like any smoke I've ever seen, and so tall, it split the whole sky. At one point it was as if someone had jabbed a wide brush loaded with black paint up high at the side of it, and let it drip down in one long dark grey stripe. It almost looked still, hanging there, although you could just see it was moving. It looked like rain, but they told us it was ash, and rocks, thousands and thousands of them. Even the sea got noisier. It had been calm until the real eruption, but in the end the waves were wild, like they were all pushing each other out of the way. Then at night, you could see the lava flow glowing and sometimes bits of bright orange spitting out.*

*In the end it was Monday before we left for home. We had to take a coach, then the train, then a plane, but we made a massive detour further south, the way the Blakes had gone, because there was so much disruption nearer Naples. There were no flights because of the ash cloud. And after all that, it wasn't exactly a warm welcome home.*

*I'll tell you what should have happened. They should have listened to me, instead of just talking about me. Instead of sending my photo round the world, all those photos of Mr Harper with his arms round me, they should've asked, did I mind Mr Harper saving my life like that? Because I'm really*

*really grateful. But it's as if that moment on the photos – which is something I hardly remember, because all I could think was that I'd nearly fallen into the sea and I could even of died just like that – that moment, right, has been turned into something it wasn't and every bad thing has followed from that. First thing, that cow Whisper Blake made sure Jack saw them, to add to all the stuff she'd already posted, because she had his contact, didn't she. In fact she had it twice over, from when she stole my mobile, and from when she lent me hers that same day at Pompeii. So obviously Jack, who like I say has no more sense than he was born with, gets on the internet, and he's breached his order, and all for nothing, and he can't keep it quiet, can he? He's on to the school, so then the police are on to him. Then the minute we get back Mr Harper gets suspended, and that wasn't fair, because he was a hero if you ask me.*

*Some woman came to talk to me, and she didn't get it at first, and for a minute I thought it was all going to turn the wrong way. Because it was all, oh so Mr Harper is someone you look up to then, and next thing it was, oh, so you and Martin Harper had a special understanding, a particularly close relationship, and I had to tell her it was Mr Harper actually and yes but only because he understood stuff other people didn't see. Then I read on Facebook that he's a charismatic teacher who has some kind of hold on me. Exerts, was the word they used. And they were all breaking the law anyway, spreading it about like that. They'd already made my life hell, with all the photos then all the discussion on social media, and this hero or paedo debate – I mean it got well out of order. And people started asking Shannon and Jessica and everyone, did I have a boyfriend and why not. So next thing I'm reading complete strangers saying how I'm a loner and a vulnerable young woman so people should be sorry for me. Also, they said Mr Harper was a widower who hadn't got over the death of his wife, like this made him some sort of creep.*

*There was only one person who came out of it better than I would have thought, and that was Mr Slipman. I had* him *down for a creep. I thought he looked a real slime ball with his shiny jacket and his smarmy hair. But fair's fair, he told the truth about what happened. He was the adult witness. He'd seen the fight, so they had to listen to him and that was the end of that. It was a lot of fuss about nothing. Mr Harper stayed at school, and this year he's been great and helped me a lot. They went for Jack, because he was easy pickings, breaching his order like that, although he did have what they call mitigating circumstances. The whole thing could've messed up my A levels but I wouldn't let it and my mum can be proud of me because I've got a place at Anglia to do Classical Studies. That's what she would've wanted.*

*I do rabbit on. So, back to Southend Pier.*

*After Shannon's little ceremony we got the train back to Adventure Island, and it was when we were slowing down to pull in to the station that I saw Mr Harper and his new girlfriend, walking along arm in arm. Although what I saw first was the woman's red hair, because it stood out from a long way away like a little round blob, especially from behind. Then I clocked him by his walk and his good old crumply jacket flapping out to one side in the breeze. It looked like they'd done the same journey as us only on foot, because they were facing the same direction. This woman's hair was amazing, what they call proper auburn, and as you got up closer you could see it was a really smart haircut. Quite short. I'd love to have hair like that. Mine's really unruly and hers was so thick, it just sat there and it was like the wind hadn't touched it. Like nothing could touch it. The train overtook them and we all waved like mad but they didn't see us at first. Shannon said she looked just his type, and we agreed they made quite an arty couple. She wasn't too tall and she wasn't too short and I thought, good on you Mr Harper. When we got off we ran up to them and said hi that was our last exam today, and Shannon asked if they were going on the Dragon's Claw then, which was a bit cheeky really, but they didn't mind, and the woman said, no thanks but what about the Big Wheel, Martin? Obviously we weren't going to intrude. She looked nice. She wasn't too old for him and she wasn't too young either and she looked kind of smiley. So I think he made a good pick. Then he said, see you on the dodgems, and we said yeah.*

## About the Author

GILL OLIVER grew up in Liverpool, a place where self-expression is the norm – whether through music, art, writing or just having a good shout. She grew up with the belief that you could laugh at just about anything. Her first attempts at fiction were improvised bedtime stories for her brothers and sister, which carried on long after they'd fallen asleep.

She read Modern Languages as a way of accessing French and Russian Literature, and after taking a PhD in Surrealist Poetry, finally started earning a living as a teacher and became, officially, a linguist. She has worked in the Midlands, Essex and Dorset in a variety of roles, publishing teaching materials along the way, but now devotes her time to writing.

Coming soon:   *Art My Eye and other stories*

> www.gilloliver.info
> www.facebook.com/gilloliverbooks
> Twitter: @gillsbooks
> Email:   gill@gilloliver.info